NOT A DREA[...]
AN ENTIRELY NEW
AND ORIGINAL ADVENTURE
IN THE BESTSELLING WORLD OF

WISHBRINGER®

"Allow me to introduce myself," the voice said. "I am a Grue."

"Very pleased to meet you. My name is Simon, and I'm the postman."

"I see," the Grue replied. "I take it that you're not from around here?"

"I'm afraid not," Simon answered. "How could you tell?"

"Well, for one thing, you didn't shriek and cower, or try to run blindly away from me when I introduced myself. You see, no human being has ever seen a Grue and lived. We in Gruedom are quite proud of that tradition."

"Does that mean," Simon said, forcing the words out, "that you are going to have to kill me?"

Other Avon Books in the
INFOCOM™ Series

PLANETFALL® *by Arthur Byron Cover*

WISHBRINGER®

Craig Shaw Gardner

A Byron Preiss Book

AN **INFOCOM**™ BOOK

AVON BOOKS  NEW YORK

WISHBRINGER: THE NOVEL is an original publication of Avon Books. This work has never before appeared in book form. This work is a novel. Any similarity to actual persons or events is purely coincidental.

Special thanks to Joel Berez, Mike Dornbrook, Brian Moriarity, John Douglas, Michael Kazan, Jill Bauman, Merrilee Heifetz, John Henry Cox, and Gwendolyn Smith.

AVON BOOKS
A division of
The Hearst Corporation
105 Madison Avenue
New York, New York 10016

Cover and book design by Alex Jay/Studio J.
Cover painting by Walter Velez
Edited by David M. Harris

First Avon Books Printing: August 1988

AVON TRADEMARK REG. U.S. PAT. OFF. AND IN OTHER COUNTRIES, MARCA REGISTRADA, HECHO EN U.S.A.

Printed in the U.S.A.

K-R 10 9 8 7 6 5 4 3 2 1

This one's for Victoria, Mary, and Jeffrey,
for their help with the Boot Patrol;
and to Richard,
who's sensitive about his poetry

....

PART ONE

"The Beginning"

....

CHAPTER
ONE

 IMON POCKETED THE
sucker's coin with a smile.

"Too bad," he said encouragingly. "Try your luck
again?"

The sucker smiled back uncertainly. "I don't know."
He glanced at his girlfriend. "That stone just seems to
disappear!"

Simon frowned slightly. "Now are you sure you were
paying attention?" He looked at the sucker's girl, a good-
looking kid with a full head of blonde curls, maybe fifteen
or sixteen; a couple of years younger than Simon, anyway.
The girl smiled back. It made her look even prettier.

"What do you think?" he asked her. "Was your boyfriend paying attention?"

The girl laughed. "Oh, Brad's terrible at paying attention." She giggled, then squeezed the boy's arm. "At least
about *some* things."

Yes, she certainly was cute. Too bad she was all
wrapped up with this guy. Oh, well, Simon thought, he
shouldn't let his feelings get in the way of a perfectly good
scam.

"Well, then," Simon asked her, "why don't you try to
find it? See, I put the stone under this cup here." He put

3

the pebble under the farthest right of the three upside-down styrofoam cups he had set up on the tray table in front of him. "Now all you have to do is watch how I move the cups." Simon placed his hands on two of the styrofoam containers, pushing each of them gently so that their open tops stayed flush against the tray below. He maneuvered the cups around so that the one containing the pebble was now in the middle.

"Do you know where the stone is now?"

The girl pointed to the cup in the middle. She clapped her hands when Simon lifted the cup to show her the pebble.

"That was too easy!" Brad protested.

"Okay. We'll make it harder then." Simon glanced at the girl. "Are you ready?" She nodded happily. At her side, Brad bit his lip as he tried to concentrate on Simon's moves.

"Fine," Simon replied. "The stone goes in here." This time he turned the right-hand cup right side up and dropped the pebble in. He swished the cup around so that Brad and his girl could hear the stone inside, then flipped the cup over quickly, pushing it against the table before the pebble inside could fall out. Simon smiled to himself. He always liked those dramatic touches.

He grabbed two of the cups and switched their positions, then moved his right hand to the cup he hadn't yet touched. He switched the cups again, and then a third time much faster than before, but not so fast as he did when there was money on the line. He asked the girl which cup she thought the stone was under. She pointed, and he lifted the cup. She screamed with glee when she saw the pebble. Brad looked up from the cups with a scowl. He was getting annoyed. This, Simon thought, was almost too easy.

"Well, sorry, Brad," he remarked casually. "I guess some of us can do this, and some of us can't."

Brad glowered at Simon. "I want to do it again."

"Brad?" his girlfriend began.

"Are you sure?" Simon asked hurriedly, before Brad's girl had time to object. "Since I've sort of explained how I do it, I'm gonna have to be tough this time."

"Yeah." Brad pushed his girlfriend away. "If she can do it, I can too."

"Well, okay." Simon grinned warily. "Care to put a little wager on this?"

"You got it." Brad dug deep into the pocket of his jeans, finally fishing out a large gold coin. He plunked it on the table.

"Brad!"

"Be quiet, Shirley," Brad replied firmly. "I know I can beat this thing now."

"But it's so much!"

"That's the whole point." Brad shook his head. "If I bet this, I can win back everything I lost."

"Okay, then," Simon replied. "Watch real careful, now." He grabbed the pebble and placed his hand under one of the cups. "Here we go."

He placed his hands on top of the cups and began to move them back and forth, changing their positions a dozen times in rapid succession.

"Okay," he said at last. "Where's the stone?"

Brad pointed triumphantly at the cup on the left.

"Think so?" Simon placed his hand on top of the cup. "You absolutely sure?"

Doubt made Brad's smile falter for only one instant. He nodded.

Simon lifted the cup. There was nothing there. Brad groaned.

"Oh, come on, now," Simon chided gently. "Don't be so glum. It was a really good try." Better, actually, than Simon had thought Brad capable of. The sucker actually had picked out the cup that the stone should have been under. If Simon hadn't taken the extra precaution of palming the stone before he started moving the cups around,

5

Brad would have won. But then, Simon was always cautious. In his line of work he had to be.

Simon jumped when he heard the foghorn noise.

"Oh, Brad!" Shirley exclaimed. Her boyfriend told her to be quiet, and they both turned to face the large green and purple flag that flew above the Fun Pier.

What was going on? Simon looked around, and noticed that everyone on the pier had stopped playing their video games and was looking up at the flag as well, standing at attention, their hands over their hearts. Must be some sort of a local ritual. Simon decided that perhaps it was for the best that he was already standing.

Music blared from loudspeakers overhead, the same loudspeakers that had emitted the foghorn noise a moment before. Everyone around Simon began to sing. He strained to make out the words. It started out "Oh, Festeron, my Festeron", but he couldn't catch the rest. Simon guessed it was some sort of anthem. That was one thing about his occupation; it kept him on the move, relocating often, traveling from one of these little countries to the next. And every place has its own, odd native customs.

The singing stopped. The people around him smiled happily at each other and went back to their games.

"Oh, Brad!" Shirley exclaimed again. "You were supposed to buy us lunch two hours ago. How could you!"

Her boyfriend shrugged helplessly and pointed at the three cups. "But, honey, I could have sworn—"

"Bad luck," Simon interjected. He didn't want an argument in front of his table. It could be bad for business. "Believe me, this is tougher than you think."

"I don't care what you could have done, Brad MacGuffin!" Shirley stamped her foot loudly on the wooden pier. "It's time to take us to lunch, this minute!"

"Um—" Brad chewed on his lip. "That's gonna be tough, honey." He nodded at the gold coin, still on the table. "That was the end of my money."

"Oh, Brad!" Shirley looked like she was going to cry.

6

"Hey," Brad offered lamely. "Maybe Gloria has got a little something left over—"

"Leave my sister out of this!" Shirley wailed. "Oh, I should never have let you talk us into coming here!"

"Let me talk *you* into coming!" Brad exploded. "Who kept going on—" his voice slid up to a high falsetto, "—'Oh, Brad, we never go to the Fun Pier anymore?' 'Oh, Brad, let's take Sis out somewhere. She's so depressed since she broke up with whatshisname. Oh! Why don't we go to the Fun Pier?' "

"And I suppose I forced you to bet all your money, too?" Shirley retorted, hands on hips.

Simon had to put a stop to this now.

"Hey, folks," he began. "Listen—"

"Well, you didn't stop me from betting, did you?" Brad yelled.

Shirley laughed derisively. "Hey, I found where the pebble was right away. How did I know you'd be so stupid—"

"Is something wrong, kids?" Another woman's voice cut between the shouts of the arguing couple. They both turned to look at the newcomer. Simon looked up, too.

He liked what he saw. He knew at once that this must be the sister; the resemblance was striking. She was the older sister, too. Her smile had a knowing humor to it that her younger sibling lacked. Her coloring was a little darker than the very fair Shirley, too, but Simon decided that was all to the better. Her hair, the color of chestnuts in autumn, gleamed in the sun that streamed through the windows.

"Gloria, you wouldn't believe—" Shirley began.

"Gloria, don't listen to a—" Brad interjected.

"Brad!" Simon exclaimed in a voice honed by three years of competing with carnival barkers.

All three of them turned to look at Simon. He pointed at the coin.

"So, aren't you going to take that back?"

Brad looked confused. "What do you mean?"

"Well, I've been trying to explain this to you—if you hadn't been shouting so much—this is embarrassing enough as it is!" Simon sighed. "I guess I have to start all over again, huh? Well, as soon as we finished the last round of the game, I happened to look down at the pier. Here," he reached a hand down by one of his shoes, "look what I found." He brought his closed fist above the table, then opened it under Brad's nose.

"The pebble!" Brad exclaimed.

"I'm afraid so," Simon admitted. "I was so intent on beating you that I must have moved the cups around a bit too fast. It looks like the stone flew out of the cup and off the table altogether." He shrugged. "Well, when something like that happens, there's no way either one of us can win."

"Really?" Brad swallowed, then smiled. "Hey, maybe I figured out where the stone should have been after all!"

"There's no way we can know," Simon lied earnestly. Why couldn't this guy just take his coin and leave? Simon hoped his generous impulse wasn't going to backfire on him.

"Well, big guy," Brad sneered, "why don't we try it again?"

"Brad!" Shirley squealed.

"Sorry," Simon replied curtly. "I never take anybody's last coin. It's a superstition, I guess."

Brad leaned down over Simon. "You don't want to play me because you know I'll win!"

Simon turned away. "Sorry. The game is closed. Time for my coffee break."

Shirley grabbed Brad's arm and dragged him away. Gloria stopped to look at Simon across the table.

"That was nice," she said. "You didn't have to do it."

Simon grinned. "Hey, you should never let them leave empty-handed. That's something I learned from my father."

8

"Oh?" Gloria's beautiful eyebrows rose in surprise. "Was your father in the same line of work?"

"Well, not exactly," Simon confessed. "Maybe it was my uncle. Or my second cousin." He didn't know exactly what he was saying. He didn't care what he was saying, as long as he was saying it to her.

Gloria glanced at her retreating sister, still dragging Brad away. She smiled again at Simon. "We'll have to talk about your family some other time. Thanks again. I'll see you around the pier, won't I?"

Simon nodded dumbly as she waved and ran after her companions. She even ran wonderfully. Simon watched her until she passed through the doorway and turned out of sight, walking up the trail that led to the village.

Before this afternoon, he had thought of the tiny country of Festeron as a pretty dull place. He had even considered moving on someplace else. Now, though, it looked like he would be staying around for a while.

Simon sighed and looked around him. Gloria. What a wonderful name. He watched the kids playing the electronic games along the far wall. He had never seen boys and girls so well-scrubbed and polite, at least not in a place like this. If two of them reached a machine at the same time, they would have an argument, each child insisting that the other one play the game first. Of course, it was a very polite argument, and then the two boys and/or girls would end up playing the game together. It was the same story at the row of pinball machines on the other side of the Fun Pier's shed. If Simon hadn't seen the fight between Brad and Shirley, he would have thought something was really wrong with Festeron.

But then he had met Gloria. Simon sighed.

"That was a very noble thing," someone said by his right ear.

Simon jumped for the second time this afternoon.

"Who?" he began. He sat back down when he saw

9

the small man in the rumpled raincoat. "Oh." Simon took a deep breath. "Sorry. I didn't notice you."

The little man nodded a bit sadly. "That's all right. People usually don't."

"What?" Simon asked. He was feeling a bit disoriented. "Don't what?"

"Don't notice," the small man replied with a sad smile. "It seems to be a part of my nature." He stuck a small hand in Simon's direction. "But I haven't introduced myself. Sneed is the name."

"Sneed?" Simon shook the proffered hand.

The little man nodded again. "Mr. Sneed."

"Mr. Sneed? Don't you have a first name?"

Mr. Sneed sighed distractedly. "Is it all that important? I just wanted you to know that what you did about the pebble, it was a noble thing."

Simon stared at the small man in astonishment.

"You watched the whole thing?"

Sneed nodded. "You're very good at palming the stone. A real professional."

"You were here the whole time?" Simon demanded. "But I didn't—"

"Notice me?" Sneed's shrug contained a bit of melancholy. "What did I tell you? I'm hardly ever noticed."

Simon looked away from the small man and stared at the row of pinball machines. This was crazy. He was always very careful just where people stood when he played the pebble game, especially if he planned to palm the stone. Now Sneed was intimating that he stood by Simon's shoulder through the whole scam. How could Simon have missed him?

Simon looked back to the small man. Oddly, it took him a moment to get Sneed in focus. Simon wondered, if he didn't know where to look, he might have missed Sneed altogether.

"People don't notice you." Simon said it as a statement rather than a question. "That must be terrible."

"Not really," Snead replied, attempting a smile. "Some might look on it as a curse, but I see it as a gift. Well, rather a small gift, I grant you, but a gift nonetheless. Still, I wanted to congratulate you on your generosity, especially with someone like Brad MacGuffin. It's not often we get new faces around here, especially interesting new faces like yours."

"So it's always this quiet around here?" Simon asked.

"Oh, no." Snead shook his head emphatically. "Sometimes it becomes, well, much less quiet."

There was a banging noise somewhere nearby, like the sound of something heavy crashing across the planks outside. Sneed nodded his head pleasantly. "Nice meeting you. If you ever have any more questions, feel free to look me up."

Simon looked past Sneed and saw half a dozen large uniformed men walk in through the Fun Pier entranceway. Their uniforms sported shiny badges.

Uh-oh, Simon thought. Police officers. It was time to retire the game for the day.

The burliest of the uniformed men pointed right at Simon.

"There he is. Arrest him, men!"

Apparently, it was already too late. It was time to leave, any way he could. Simon looked around. The police stood in the only exit.

It looked like things were going to get much less quiet right now.

CHAPTER
TWO

"DON'T EVEN THINK of escape," the largest cop said as all six advanced on Simon. They had formed a semicircle that reached from the video games all the way over to the pinball machines. All the other people on the Fun Pier had stopped playing their games and were standing politely against the walls, as far out of the way as they could manage. The six took another step forward.

Simon couldn't believe it. He never let himself get into a corner like this in a place that he couldn't escape from. It was one of the basic rules of his trade. But Festeron was so calm, so pleasant, almost as if it had come from an earlier, more trusting time. Simon had let the mood around here get to him. He had let his guard down as well, and gone as soft as the town around him. And this, he thought, is what happens when you let yourself get soft.

The six policemen had joined hands as they took another step forward. A human chain, Simon thought. Or a human jail cell, ready to close him in for good.

There was no way out of here, unless he smashed through the plate glass window behind him. But what was on the other side? As he recalled, this part of the Fun Pier hung out over the water. But was that water deep enough for a dive? What if there was something hiding under that rolling blue surface—jagged rocks or something worse?

The cops had taken a couple more steps while he was thinking the situation over. He wondered for an instant at the extreme newness of their bright blue uniforms, the brilliant shine of their badges, the sameness of all their pleasant smiles. Simon glanced over his shoulder a final time. It looked like the window behind him or nothing. He took a quick step backward.

"Don't think of jumping, either," the big cop remarked casually, as if it was the simplest thing in the world to read Simon's mind.

Simon stopped. The window glass felt cold against his back.

"For one thing," the cop continued, "there's those sharpened wooden spikes just below the surface." He nodded to his fellows. They all took another step closer.

"Spikes?" Simon laughed. Who ever heard of a harbor filled with spikes, especially in a peaceful little town like Festeron? He glanced over at Mr. Sneed. In all the excitement, Simon had almost forgotten the little man was still here. Sneed looked sadly at Simon and nodded. Was the small guy telling him there were indeed spikes in the harbor?

"Of course," the policeman continued with his slight smile, "there's a slight chance you might fall into one of the spaces between the spikes. Then all you'd have to worry about is the sharks."

"Sharks?" Simon repeated. He tried to laugh again, but somehow this time the laugh died in his throat. He glanced at Sneed, who nodded again. So there were sharks in the harbor, too? What kind of place was this Festeron, anyway?

And then the cops were on him. A dozen hands grabbed him all at once. Simon felt his feet rise from the rough hewn planks of the pier.

"Excuse me—" Mr. Sneed began as the police passed, but the cops kept on moving as if they didn't even hear him.

"Don't worry!" Sneed called to Simon as the young man was carried away. "You did a noble thing! I'll gladly testify at your trial!"

Somehow, that didn't make Simon feel a great deal better.

The six policemen maneuvered themselves into a ragged line so that they could fit through the door.

"Hey!" Simon called. "Why don't you let me walk?"

The cops grunted as they pushed Simon through the door. His nose passed a fraction of an inch below the doorway's upper sill. Then he was out in the sunlight.

"Sorry," the lead cop stated politely, "but we of the Festeron Police Assembly believe that when we take someone into custody, we *really* take him into custody!"

"Don't worry, though," another of the policemen stated helpfully. "You'll be back on your feet soon enough."

"Surely," a third cop added cheerfully. "We'll put you down as soon as we reach our nice, secure jail."

"And we'll give you a clean, quiet cell of your very own!" a fourth uniformed officer exclaimed.

"With all the amenities, we assure you!" the fifth fellow cajoled.

"Of course!" the final cop remarked as if everything the others before him said should have been self-evident. "We of Festeron are *nothing* if we are not civilized!"

"So why not relax?" the first cop asked. "Struggling is, of course, completely useless. You're being taken to the police station whether you want to go or not. Just think how much more pleasant it will be if you just lie back and enjoy the ride? Plus, as a bonus, we'll be glad to indicate some of Festeron's main points of interest as we travel!"

The other policemen heartily agreed with their leader's offer.

Simon didn't know what to think. After some initial fidgeting, he hadn't struggled at all. It was the policemen's attitudes that had done it to him. Their overwhelming courtesy had totally disarmed him, made him feel more like he was buying a pair of shoes than getting arrested. It seemed like almost everyone in Festeron was like that. So maybe the police were right; he should stop worrying and relax. After all, what was the worst that could happen to him? These cops were so polite he'd probably only get some sort of little slap on the wrist, and they'd let him go.

The lead policeman pointed out a movie theater to their right. Simon craned his neck to see. According to the marquee, they were showing a double feature: *The Return of Rebecca of Sunnybrook Farm* and *The Cuddly Bears Save the World*. Simon looked back overhead. There were some parts of Festeron that were just *too* nice.

Unless, Simon thought, all this niceness was just an act. They *had* arrested him, after all, and that didn't seem nice at all, at least not to Simon.

"Over to our left," the tour guide cop continued, "you'll see the back door of the fabulously well-stocked Festeron Library."

"Every Thornton W. Burgess book ever written!" another cop added proudly.

Maybe, Simon thought with a chill, all this niceness was just a ploy to get him to come along quietly. Then, once they'd gotten him to the jail, and they were behind closed, locked, barred doors, the cops' true, violent selves would come out.

Maybe he should be looking around more, seeking a way to escape.

"And to our right, as we travel around the Festeron Central Rotary," the guide continued, "you'll see the showpiece of the city!"

The group of police bearers stopped. Simon guessed

that they really wanted him to see their showpiece. He turned his head. A uniformed statue stood above a gushing fountain.

"Yes, here he is," the guide gushed happily, "the founder of our fair country, Phineas T. Fester!"

The remaining cops cheered at the mention of the name.

"Here we go again," the guide called to Simon. "Let us know if we're jostling you too much."

His bearers started forward once more. Simon decided again that he was worrying about nothing. These cops were so nice that he didn't think they had it in them to have true, violent selves. If he escaped now, he'd have to spend all night hiding in the cold. Besides, the way things had gone so far, the jail cells would probably all be decorated with fresh flowers.

"And here, just ahead," the guide continued, his voice, if possible, filled with even more pride than before, "is the Festeron Police Station."

Simon lifted his head to see a gray stone edifice rising before him. It looked pretty ordinary, maybe even a little, sinister, full of heavily barred windows, just like a real jail. It was not at all as pleasant as he had hoped.

Still, he reminded himself, appearances could be deceiving. The cops took the steps leading to the entrance at a brisk trot.

"Watch your head!" one of them called. Simon marveled again at how pleasant theses fellows were. What could he possibly have to be afraid of?

The lead cop opened the front door. "Sergeant! Oh, Sergeant MacGuffin!" he called as they carried Simon inside. "We've brought the miscreant!"

MacGuffin? Hadn't Simon heard that name somewhere before?

The cops lowered Simon gently to the ground. He found himself standing in a large room, facing a raised desk of dark, polished wood. In fact, everything in this room was bright and shining. Somehow, though, it wasn't cheering him up.

"There," their leader murmured as he brushed Simon's shirt clean with a small whisk broom. "That wasn't so bad, now, was it? I tell you, there's nothing so relaxing as a good carry."

Simon nodded pleasantly to the police officer, and was about to assure him that he had never ever had such a pleasant time being arrested, when a door slammed open behind the desk, hitting the wall with such tremendous force that it sounded like a rifle going off. Simon jumped instead.

"So where is that scum?" a gruff voice echoed across the bright and cheery room.

"Oh, Sergeant MacGuffin!" the six cops shouted in unison. "We have him here for you, sir!"

"Where?" the sergeant demanded, his voice a mix of anger and barely controlled hysteria. Simon heard the sound of boots climbing hollow wooden stairs. A red-bearded head looked down from above the elevated desk. "THERE!"

"Yes, sir, Sergeant MacGuffin!" the six policemen chorused cheerfully.

The sergeant stared down at Simon, his face a livid pink, his eyes bulging beneath bushy brows, his quivering mouth temporarily silenced by a speechless rage. This, Simon thought, was not a positive sign.

"You . . ." he managed after a long moment. He tried to point an accusing finger at Simon, but his hand shook too violently. "YOU!" he repeated, somewhat more forcefully.

"What would you like us to do with him, Sergeant MacGuffin?" Simon's police escort asked.

The sergeant seemed distracted. He stared at his right hand, the fingers spread wide. With his left hand, he folded his fingers down, one after another. "Strangle?" he muttered to himself. "Whip? Garrote?" He shook himself and

17

looked down at his police officers. "No, even something as low as this vermin deserves a trial. Toss him in a cell!"

"Yes, sir, Sergeant MacGuffin!" The six policemen once again lifted Simon aloft.

But their chief was once again staring at his quivering hand. "Straitjacket? Cattle prod? Keelhauling?" MacGuffin shivered, and folded all his fingers into a fist. "After the trial," he murmured to himself. The words seemed to give him strength. He sneered at Simon. "And no special treatment. We'll show *his* kind that we of Festeron mean business. Put him on bread and water!"

"Aye, aye, Sergeant MacGuffin!" his fellows cried merrily as they began to move.

Simon felt himself being carried away. He no longer felt so positive about the nature of Festeron police treatment. Perhaps he should have tried to escape after all. What had he been thinking of, anyway? What could possibly be so bad about spending the night hiding in the cold and damp?

"Watch your head!" one of the cops remarked jovially as they passed through a thick iron doorway. A thick iron door clanged shut behind them.

"You shouldn't worry," another of the officers added.

"Exactly!" a third cop added. "After all, you're in jail now."

"A nice, safe, secure jail," someone else continued.

"The most secure place in the world," a fifth voice elucidated. "So why worry?"

Simon grunted weakly. They were all so polite he felt he really should answer them. Still, he didn't find them very convincing.

"Now, now, you have to think positively!" one of them chuckled. "Look at it this way. Even if Sergeant MacGuffin decided to have you drawn, quartered, and fed to the fishes, there's nothing you could do about it."

"Right!" another cop patted him on the back. "You're locked up in jail."

"Exactly!" three or four others rejoined as they passed through another set of iron bars. "So why worry about it?"

With that, the police squad put him down again. Simon looked glumly around. He was in a jail cell.

Oh, it was a nice jail cell, what with the thick shag rug on the floor, and the cushioned teakwood bunk. But he was in prison, at the mercy of that Sergeant MacGuffin, who seemed to be very upset with him about something. Simon wasn't even particularly sure he wanted to find out what that something was. He sighed moodily, staring at the framed Impressionist print over the home entertainment center. Even the fresh flowers in the corner didn't cheer him up.

"Anything else we can do for you?" one of the friendly cops asked hopefully.

Simon shook his head, and walked past them to stare out of the barred window of his new home. He couldn't stand their cheerfulness any longer. Right now, he wanted to be alone with his pain and suffering. He looked out at the blue sky and young, green trees; a beautiful spring day. He heard the police leave his cell, and the iron door clang shut behind them.

He blinked at the vision approaching the police station. No, he wasn't dreaming. It had to be real.

It was more than real. It was that girl from the arcade. Gloria.

Then again, who really needed to be alone with pain and suffering? Simon decided he could change his mind about almost anything.

CHAPTER
THREE

"Er—" SOMEONE cleared his throat behind Simon.

Simon spun around. One of the police officers stood outside the jail cell. He was holding a tray.

"Dinner," he murmured with a sheepish smile. "What little there is of it."

Simon smiled and nodded at the cop. "The old bread and water, huh?" Actually, he was surprisingly hungry. Simon decided it had been all that worrying. He walked over to the bars as the cop slid the tray through the gap that appeared to have been provided for just that purpose.

"Afraid it is," the policeman replied. "I apologize for this, but when our sergeant gets something in his cap, there's no talking to him."

Simon grunted sympathetically as he accepted the tray. He was about to say more when he looked down at his meal. This was bread and water? Well, after a fashion, he guessed it was, except that the bread was actually a pair of croissants, and the water appeared to have been bottled somewhere in France. Simon thought the small yellow rose in the off-white vase was a nice touch, too.

"Well, I won't ask you if everything's satisfactory," the cop continued apologetically. "If you want seconds, just yell. I'll be on the other side of the door." He waved at the large iron doorway at the end of the corridor.

"This is just fine," Simon replied. "Thanks for your consideration."

The policeman told him to think nothing of it and strolled back to his station. Simon marveled at the courtesy around here. It was even making him polite. He wondered if there was some way he could use that politeness to get himself sprung.

After a moment, he decided it would be easier thinking of escape plans on a full stomach. He took a large bite out of a croissant. It was still warm, as if it had just come out of the oven.

The large iron door at the end of the hall slammed shut. Simon removed the nicely chilled water bottle's twist-off cap. He noted with approval that the water was naturally carbonated. He took a hearty swig as he settled down on his cushioned bunk. He might be in jail, but there were worse ways to live. Maybe he could spend a pleasant evening fantasizing about the woman who had just passed by outside.

The iron door slammed open, causing Simon to swallow a bite suddenly. He looked up from his meal, a trifle annoyed. What was going on now? Didn't they realize that that sort of noise didn't fit in with this place's ambience?

"I hope we're not interrupting your dinner," a voice called down the hall, "but you have a visitor."

Simon's appetite vanished as he thought of the vision he had seen walking by the jail. Could she have actually come inside?

The large iron door opened, and Sneed stepped through.

"Oh," Simon said as he took another bite of his croissant. "Nice to see you again."

"It's nice to be seen," the small man replied. "It's like I said before. Some people can't see me at all."

"Here's your visitor!" one of the cops called from the

other side of the doorway. A uniformed officer stepped into the corridor, leading Gloria.

"Then that's—" Simon began. "But, if that's my visitor, how did you—"

"Like I said," Sneed replied with a look of forlorn resignation. "Some people can't see me at all."

Simon looked away from the little fellow, straight at the dark-haired beauty approaching him.

"Simon," she said with a delightful smile.

"Gloria," he replied with what he was sure was an idiotic grin.

"I'll leave you two alone," the policeman said. "I'm sure you want your privacy."

Simon heard the iron door slam a moment later. He walked to the edge of the cell and grabbed the bars. He couldn't take his eyes off of the girl.

She was glorious.

"I probably shouldn't have come here," she said softly. Her large brown eyes looked deeply into his. "But I had to!"

Simon nodded sympathetically. He knew that look in her eyes; he had seen it so many times before. Another woman had fallen victim to his fatal charm. It came from his being a traveling man, bringing with him stories and romance from far-distant countries. That always got them, especially in little provincial places like Festeron. And it didn't hurt that he knew how to talk fast, either.

For the first time since he had met this woman, Simon began to feel like his old confident self. From here on in, he could pretty much go on automatic, saying just the right things, leading her on, pausing just long enough before he made his move. And what a move he wanted to make with this one.

"Hey," he said, using one of the lines he knew by heart. "Nice to run into you again."

Simon swallowed. If this was so easy, why was his mouth so dry?

"Trying to keep your spirits up?" she answered with a little frown. "That's brave of you, using humor at a time like this."

The depth of her sincerity startled him. Just about everything about her startled him. Maybe he was completely wrong about her. Simon felt his confidence slipping away again.

"A time like what?" he asked.

Gloria sighed. "Where do I begin?" She reached out her long-fingered hand to brush lightly against where Simon held the bars. "I have trouble framing my thoughts when you are around."

So he wasn't wrong. She had fallen for him.

"Gloria," Simon whispered, all his clever lines forgotten. He wanted to take her hand, to kiss her, to find a place where they could be alone for a long, long time. He would show her things beyond her wildest dreams.

Gloria touched his hand again. "I find myself strangely attracted to you. And I suspect that you are as attracted to me." Just as quickly, she snatched her hand away. She bit her lip, then spoke again. "I am glad the bars are here. They shall keep our romance chaste. We will be an example for all of Festeron."

"What?" Simon demanded. This whole thing had finally gone too far. "What are you talking about?"

Gloria batted her eyes demurely. "Chastity is highly valued in our little country, as are purity, civil obedience, and proper hygienic habits. These are things you must understand, if you are to remain in Festeron."

Simon laughed, trying to comprehend just what was happening here. He rapped the bars with his knuckles. "I don't know how I'm going to get out. But is that what you came here to tell me about? That you wanted to have a romance at a distance?"

Gloria pursed her lips coquettishly. "No, of course not, my never-to-be-fulfilled dream lover." She paused, her beautiful face becoming grim and hard. "I came here to

23

warn you. The quaint little town of Festeron has a dark secret, an ugly blot upon its past—"

"I would have told him about that!" Sneed piped up.

"Who's that?" Gloria demanded. She turned around, and stared suspiciously at Sneed, who cowered against the jailhouse wall. Looking at him now, Simon was amazed how Sneed's gray raincoat blended in with the cinderblock wall. But maybe Sneed was right. Since Simon had started to talk to Gloria, he had forgotten all about the little man.

"After everything I said to you?" Gloria turned back to him. "Has he been here all along?" she asked angrily.

"I'm—afraid so," Simon began hesitantly. How could he possibly explain Mr. Sneed? "You see, he came to visit, but the cops didn't see—"

"It doesn't matter," Sneed sighed. "I've gotten used to fading into the background. It's a part of my personality, I'm afraid."

"It's all a little strange," Simon added a little lamely.

But Gloria nodded her head as if his remark made perfect sense. "Everything about Festeron is a little strange. You'll see, if you survive long enough."

"That's why I've come," Sneed confided softly to the pair. "While I was standing around the station, waiting for them to open the door, I overheard the police officers talking about your trial. You're to go before the judges first thing tomorrow morning. Rest assured, though, that I will be there for your defense."

"I will as well," Gloria whispered. "And we can only hope for the best."

The iron door at the end of the hall slammed open again.

"Sorry to bother you!" one of the cops called. "But we're getting close to curfew. We do like to give our prisoners a chance to become sufficiently rested. Especially with tomorrow being such a busy day!"

"Goodbye." Gloria impulsively squeezed Simon's hand. "And good luck."

"I'd better go too," Sneed added. "Otherwise, I'll be locked up here all night."

The two of them walked quickly up the hall and out of sight. One of the policemen stuck his head through the doorway after they had gone.

"Very good," the cop said cheerfully. "It's now time for our evening musical interlude. Thirty minutes of soothing music will be piped into your cell to help you relax and prepare for the coming day. After that, it's lights out!" He waved and disappeared. The iron door slammed shut.

Quiet piano music came from somewhere overhead. Simon sat down to finish what was left of his meal. He had a lot to think about, like a woman to whom he was very attracted, and who said she was attracted to him, but who for that very reason had to stay away from him. And then, of course, there was Sneed, a man you had a tendency to never notice. Not to mention this comfortable jail cell, and all the polite police. Except, of course, for Sergeant MacGuffin. And what about Sergeant MacGuffin?

Did anything in Festeron make any sense at all?

CHAPTER
FOUR

IMON OPENED HIS
eyes. Somewhere, someone (he thought it might be Petula
Clark) was singing a bright pop song.

"Good morning!" an all-too-affable voice called to
him. Simon looked around. Oh, yeah. That's right. He
was in a jail cell. He turned his head to the side so he
could look out through the bars.

One of the policemen stood smiling on the other side.

"Breakfast time!" he exclaimed brightly, adding, in a
softer voice: "I stretched the rules a little and brought you
cinnamon buns."

Simon thanked him, taking the tray. He noticed that
the water this morning contained a hint of orange flavor-
ing. At least that was what it said on the label. Simon sat
back on his designer bunk, determined to enjoy a final
meal before whatever might be in store for him this day.
(The hidden speakers continued to play bright pop songs.
Simon thought that this one was by the Archies.) After all,
with a jail cell this nice, how bad could the trial be?

"There you are!" a gruff voice demanded.

Simon swallowed the remains of his cinnamon bun
somewhat more rapidly than he had planned. Sergeant
MacGuffin was staring at him through the bars.

"Scum!" the sergeant barked, his face purple with rage. "Maggot! Slime mold! Today—" he paused, allowing a twisted grin to spread across his face, "—you will learn what it means to flaunt the laws of our fair community. You will find that there is justice in Festeron. No, more than that!" MacGuffin began to jump up and down, his voice rising with every word. "You will find there is retribution!"

"Uh, Sergeant?"

Simon looked past the livid MacGuffin to see a group of policemen standing meekly at the end of the corridor.

"In a minute!" the sergeant replied brusquely. He took out a handkerchief and wiped at the spots where spittle had stained his beard. "I have to finish my interrogation of the prisoner." He stared at Simon with his small, bloodshot eyes. "Leech! Degenerate! Hairball!"

The policemen crept quietly down the hall as the sergeant continued to fume. One of the cops gently put a hand on MacGuffin's shoulder.

"Now, now," he said soothingly.

"Worm!" MacGuffin yelled.

"You know what the doctor said about your blood pressure," the cop added.

"Sleazebag!" MacGuffin screamed.

"Besides," the cop continued, "it's time to take the prisoner to trial."

"Ingrown toenail!" MacGuffin paused, restraining himself with a massive effort of will. "Yes," he whispered. "The trial. *The trial!*"

MacGuffin smiled as his police officers pried his fingers loose from the bars of Simon's cell.

"Take him to the courtroom," the cop said to a pair of his fellows. They gently led the sergeant away.

"Now, I'm afraid it's time for you to come along with us as well," the cop said to Simon. "I'm sorry if this inconveniences you, but I assure you that it will be over quickly."

27

Simon took a final swig of his water and stood as they unlocked his cell door. He didn't see what choice he had. The cops were probably right. It was best to get it over with.

"That's a good prisoner," the cop said with a smile. "Now, if you'll just come with us."

The four remaining policemen encircled him as Simon emerged from the cell, so that two of the police were just before him to his left and right, and two more took up similar positions to his rear. The cops started to walk, and Simon found himself pushed along in their midst.

"See how painless this is?" the talking cop asked. Simon grunted. They were moving too quickly for him to answer in a coherent sentence. Simon felt himself swept quickly through the iron doorway, across the large central room he had seen before, and through another doorway, above which hung a sign that read: COURTROOM OF FESTERON.

Once inside the door, all four policemen stepped away. Simon stumbled, almost losing his balance. He glanced at his escort, but they were all staring, impassive, at the front of the room. He gazed beyond them at the rest of his surroundings.

The courtroom was nowhere near as festive as his jail cell. It looked pretty much like courtrooms did everywhere, except perhaps that it was a bit tidier than some he had been in. Besides that, it was pretty much standard courtroom issue, with long rows of dark wooden benches surrounding a raised dais. On the bench closest to the dais, Simon saw the two other policemen restraining Sergeant MacGuffin. The sergeant struggled under the grip of his men, his hair and beard wild, his eyes wilder as he stared at Simon.

Brad and his girlfriend Shirley sat behind the sergeant. Next to them was Shirley's sister Gloria.

Gloria! Simon had to take a deep breath before he could continue.

Simon thought he might have glimpsed Mr. Sneed,

too, cowering in a corner. He didn't have time to consider the implications of any of this, however, because seeing Brad had reminded Simon of something that had slipped his mind.

He remembered Brad's last name.

His girlfriend had used it when they had argued on the Festeron Fun Pier.

Brad's last name was MacGuffin.

Suddenly, a number of things that hadn't seemed to make any sense became all too logical. No wonder Sergeant MacGuffin was out to prosecute Simon to the full letter of the law. Heck, Simon knew the sergeant wanted to add a few letters of his own. This was far worse than he had thought. Still, a small, friendly country like Festeron should have small, friendly laws. Shouldn't it?

"Come forward, prisoner!"

Simon looked up to not one, but three judges standing behind the dais in their long, white robes.

"And now, before we begin," the center judge, a woman of middle years, intoned, "we will, of course, sing the national anthem."

Everyone in the courtroom stood. Simon recognized the tinny music coming from speakers overhead as the same tune he had heard in the arcade the previous afternoon. This time he managed to make out a few of the words as everyone else in the courtroom sang:

"Oh, Festeron, my Festeron,
We won't let you get messed around!"

There were sixteen other verses, more or less the same.

The anthem ended with a fanfare. People resumed their seats with a rustle of clothing and papers.

"Let the trial begin!" the central judge exclaimed with some satisfaction.

"Will the prisoner step forward?" asked the judge on the left, an elderly man whose hands shook as he spoke.

This was the second time they had asked him to come

to the dais. He supposed he should go. With some trepidation, Simon walked to the front of the courtroom.

"Toad! Miscreant! Fungus!" Sergeant MacGuffin exploded as Simon drew near.

"Now, now," chided the judge on the right, a man much younger than his fellows, who sported a blonde mustache that curled up at the ends. "There's a time and a place for that. Please wait your turn."

"Oh," the sergeant mumbled, obviously chastened. "Of course, Your Honor."

"Very good," the judge replied. "Now, shall we get down to cases?"

"Begging the other justices' pardon," the eldest of the three remarked, "but perhaps we should explain a bit of the Festeron legal system to our foreign visitor, here, seeing as he's the one on trial and all."

"An excellent suggestion," the central judge said warmly. "You may proceed!"

"Very well," the elder began. "Listen carefully, prisoner, so that you may realize how lucky you are to be put on trial in a country as forward-thinking as Festeron." The judge pointed to a flag above the podium, the same garish flag Simon had seen flying over the Festeron Fun Pier.

"For here," the elder continued, "we avoid many of the pitfalls legal systems fall prey to. For example, you will never see just one judge pass sentence in our fair country. For what if that single judge has had a bad day? What if he does not like the color of your hair, or the way you tie your shoes? If any of these things happen, would you expect to get a fair sentence? Of course not! But here in Festeron we use three judges!" The elder waved grandly at his fellows. "In this way, personal prejudice cannot enter into the picture. The judgment of three justices is three times as fair as that of one! And what could be more fair than that?"

Simon nodded his head, although he wasn't absolutely sure he followed the logic of the justice's argument.

Still, it wouldn't hurt to listen, and maybe, if he could figure out the way these three judges thought, he might be able to walk away from this trial a free man.

"For similar reasons," the judge continued, "you will never find a so-called 'jury of your peers' in Festeron, for juries, drawn as they are from unlearned masses from the countryside, are much more easily swayed than learned judges."

"Besides that, who would you call his peers?" the youngest judge sneered. "Perhaps we could find twelve more foreigners who make their living cheating the people of Festeron!"

"Chauncey, please." The eldest gave the youngest a withering glance. He then turned back to Simon, the benevolent smile once again upon his face. "Therefore, no more uninformed juries. What could be more fair than that?"

No juries? Simon didn't like that. He imagined he could fast-talk a jury into just about anything. It was going to be a little harder to fool a trio of judges.

"And we go farther than that!" the elder continued. "In Festeron we have no prosecutor to make everything look ten times as bad as what actually happened, and no defense attorney to make things look impossibly rosy. What could be more fair than that?"

There was no prosecutor, either? Well, who knew? Maybe this would work out for the best after all. Still, Simon didn't like the way the youngest judge (Chauncey?) had jumped on that "jury of his peers" thing. He didn't think Chauncey liked him very much. But then that's why there were two other judges, right? Maybe the Festeron system was as fair as the old guy was saying.

"Very well," the justice in the middle remarked. "Thank you, Horace. Now, shall we get down to business?"

"With pleasure, Grand Justice." Chauncey sneered in Simon's general direction. "The prisoner before us is accused of a great many crimes; to wit, that he did willfully and callously set up a game of chance in the middle of Festeron's famous Fun Pier."

"A serious charge," the Grand Justice replied solemnly. Was it? It hadn't sounded so bad to Simon.

"In addition," Chauncey continued, "he furthermore lured the innocents upon that Fun Pier to participate in this game of chance!"

"No!" Horace, the eldest justice, whispered, horrified. "I had no idea."

"And beyond this!" Chauncey's voice rose as he spoke, emotion pouring into his every word. "Beyond this, he actually caused these innocents to wager actual money upon his vile game!"

Horace and the Grand Justice gasped as one. Simon had to admit that this was not going as well as he had hoped.

"And even worse!" Chauncey's voice shook now with the weight of his words. "When the evening playing of the national anthem began, he didn't even sing!"

"Death!" Horace screamed, quite beside himself. He pounded a white wooden gavel on the desk before him. "Death to the prisoner!"

"Now, now," the Grand Justice cautioned. "Let us not jump to conclusions. We have not heard the whole story. Does anyone wish to speak for the prisoner?"

Uh-oh, Simon thought. Time for some fast talking. He cleared his throat.

The three judges stared frostily at the prisoner. The Grand Justice raised her hand peremptorily, as if Simon's speaking just now was entirely out of the question.

"I ask again," the Grand Justice repeated. "Is there anyone in this courtroom who will speak for the accused?"

Simon waited, listening for a long moment to the silence. Wait a minute! Didn't he hear something?

"I will!" called a voice so faint that Simon almost couldn't make out the words. "He did a noble thing!"

"Well?" Chauncey remarked cooly. "How long must

we wait? It is obvious that no one will speak up for someone like *him*."

"Here I come!" Mr. Sneed called as he hastened from his spot in the back corner. His voice seemed to grow louder with every passing step. "I will speak for the prisoner. He did a noble thing!"

The Grand Justice frowned at her younger colleague. "You know as well as I do the rules of Festeron justice. We will wait the traditional three minutes before we pass sentence."

"But I will speak for him!" Mr. Sneed cried as he rushed toward the bench; his wrinkled raincoat rustled horribly with every step. "I am speaking for him! He was noble!"

"Well," the Grand Justice said slowly, "if no one wishes to speak in the prisoner's—"

"Wait!" another woman's voice interrupted the Grand Justice's. Simon pulled his eyes away from Sneed's gray frame.

It was Gloria! Simon smiled to himself. The judges were sure to like testimony from someone as magnificent as she.

"I can keep silent no longer," she said as she stood, tall and straight, her long dark hair falling gracefully to her shoulders. Simon decided he really liked the way she moved. If she could help him get out of this fix, he'd show her just how thankful he could be.

"I wanted to keep out of this," she continued, "for the sake of my sister, and her—" she paused, glancing disdainfully at Brad, "—boyfriend."

"But what about me?" Sneed yelled, waving at the judges. "I want to talk about this fellow's nobility!"

"You see," Gloria went on as if Sneed hadn't even spoken, "I was there when Brad and my sister were involved in their game of chance—"

"That proves it!" Chauncey exclaimed.

"Death!" Horace shrieked. "Death is too good for him!"

"Fellow justices," the chief remarked softly. "Please."

The other two judges looked sheepishly at their leader, their tongues temporarily stilled.

The chief turned to Gloria. "Now, if you would continue with your testimony?"

Gloria nodded at the justice. "As I was saying, I saw their game of chance, and how Simon here—"

"If you please," the Grand Justice interrupted, "we'd prefer it if you referred to the prisoner as 'the prisoner'." She smiled at Gloria. "It makes everything so much tidier." Horace and Chauncey nodded their heads in agreement.

"Very well," Gloria replied. "I saw how the prisoner—" she looked at Simon, and the last word caught in her throat, "—how the prisoner tried to end the game, and how Brad MacGuffin kept insisting on playing again, even though it meant betting his last coin!"

Brad jumped up, spinning to face Gloria. "How dare you say that about me!"

"That proves it!" Chauncey added.

"Death!" Horace echoed. "Death is too good for him!"

"What about my testimony?" Mr. Sneed wailed, banging his fists against the front on the judge's bench. "He was noble, I tell you!"

"Will everybody quiet down!" the Grand Justice stated with remarkable force. She continued in a somewhat quieter tone. "Something has already come out of this testimony, I am afraid." She looked at Gloria. "I sense a budding romantic involvement."

"But—" Gloria began.

"I'm afraid your objections can no longer move the court," the Grand Justice replied curtly. "I am sorry, my dear, but your testimony appears to be biased. It must be disallowed."

"But what about my testimony?" Sneed was growing hoarse. "Noble! Noble!" His fists still pounded against the wood, but there was no force left behind his blows.

"Since there appears to be no further testimony in

the prisoner's defense," the Grand Justice remarked, "we can continue with the trial."

"Noble!" Sneed croaked a final time as he collapsed.

Gloria, looking somewhat confused, returned to her seat. Brad, a triumphant smile upon his face, sat as well. Simon looked back at the judges. He was getting confused. What did they mean "no further testimony"? Couldn't anybody hear Sneed except Simon?

And what about Gloria? What did they mean by "romantic involvement"? Simon turned back to look at Gloria, who stared angrily down the bench at Brad. He wished fervently that they could get this trial over with so he could find out.

In the row before Gloria, the police sergeant made little grumbling noises in his throat.

"Sergeant MacGuffin?" the youngish judge on the right politely inquired.

"Oh, yes," the Grand Justice remarked with a hint of surprise in her voice, as if she had forgotten, "the basic case has been presented. Now is the proper time for name-calling."

The sergeant smiled and took a deep breath as he pointed a shaking finger at Simon.

"Weasel! Arachnid! Cheat!"

Sergeant MacGuffin cleared his throat and spoke to the judges in a much more reasonable tone. "Thank you. That makes me feel so much better."

"Oh, no problem at all," the Grand Justice assured him. "That's why we make a space for it. It makes everything so much tidier."

The elder judge nodded his agreement. "What could be fairer than that?"

The chief smiled at her two compatriots. "And so, fellow justices, I believe it is time for us to issue our final summaries."

The three judges conferred with each other for a long moment, speaking in hushed tones. Simon strained to overhear, but aside from an occasional "ipso facto" or "quid pro quo", he could make out none of it. What was going to happen now? He had depended on his wits to see him through this trial. But how could you depend on your wits when you couldn't even understand what was going on? It sounded now as if the judges were planning to finish up the trial and pronounce the verdict before they had even given him a chance to speak! But that couldn't possibly be right, could it? Simon had to say something; he knew that his quick tongue was his only chance to save himself.

He raised his hand.

"Um," he began, doing his very best to sound humble. "Excuse me?"

The three justices looked up from their conference to stare at him.

"Yes?" the Grand Justice asked in a voice that was not at all pleased.

"Pardon," Simon replied, "but don't I get to say something?"

"That proves it!" Chauncey screamed, jumping up and down and waving his arms.

"Death!" Horace added as he began to jump as well. The dais quivered with their combined bouncing. "Death is too good for him!"

But the Grand Justice only laughed and shook her head. "Foreigners! Can't you see?" She made a *tsking* noise with her tongue. "With your closeness to the subject, you couldn't possibly have a clear view of the matter. No, no, I'm afraid that your testimony is quite out of the question."

What? Simon thought. He couldn't even defend himself? What kind of a court was this?

"But—" he began.

The Grand Justice seemed not to hear him. "Now, shall we get on with the summaries?"

"Gladly," the eldest judge replied. "And may I say that my eyes have been opened by the evidence brought before us this day? I believe that my esteemed colleague—" he nodded graciously at Chauncey, "—gave a fair description of the particulars of this case. Still, his reasoned argument can barely touch upon the true heinousness of this vermin's crime. When this sort of thing happens at a place as innocent as the Fun Pier, the very good name of Festeron is instantly at stake." He paused and stared at the accused.

This, Simon admitted, looked very bad.

"Therefore," Horace continued, "I can see no alternative but reinstitution of the death penalty."

This, Simon had to admit, looked even worse.

"The death penalty?" the Grand Justice mused. "Aren't we being a bit severe?"

"On the contrary!" the young judge piped up. "This scum before us has virtually confessed to his crimes, which may I remind the court includes cheating children out of whatever meager funds they can gather to have a good time. I ask the court: Is there anything more un-Festeronian?"

The Grand Justice was silent.

"Therefore, while I believe that my distinguished colleague—" the youngster nodded at Horace, "—is taking the right steps in reinstituting the death penalty, I feel that his years of service in our mild and fair country have still perhaps left him far too lenient in dealing with excrement like this!" He looked out at Simon and smiled. "For this reason, I recommend that we reinstitute some older, even less humane death penalty. Drawing and quartering would be nice." He glanced over at the Grand Justice. "Tell me, does anyone know if we still have the facilities to boil oil?"

Drawing and quartering? Boiling oil? Simon had to admit that he didn't want to hear another word. Why hadn't he tried to escape when he'd had the chance? After all, what were sharks and submerged stakes when compared with this?

Still, he comforted himself, he hadn't heard what the Grand Justice had to say. So far, she had seemed to be the voice of moderation among the three. Simon prayed that she might once again quiet the others down.

"Well?" Horace asked, looking to the Grand Justice.

"Will you not see justice done," Chauncey added, "for Festeron?"

"Now, now," their chief replied. "I want to see justice done as much as anyone in this courtroom. In fact I agree with everything you've said, except for one particular: the death penalty."

"What?" Simon and Horace cried as one.

Simon wiped the sweat from his forehead. Here at last was some compassion!

"Before you object," the justice told her companions, "hear me out. In a case like this, death is too mild a punishment. After an excruciatingly painful moment, or maybe two, the miscreant is forever beyond our grasp. I know of something much better."

She paused and looked around the room.

"It seems to me," she said at last, "that the Post Office has a vacancy."

"The Post Office?" Horace whispered.

"The Post Office?" Chauncey echoed.

Horace clapped. Chauncey laughed. Sergeant Mac-Guffin cheered.

"Very well," the Grand Justice said. "It is decided. Simon the thief, we sentence you to be a postal worker!" She pointed her gavel at Simon as she added these final words:

"And may Festeron have mercy on your soul."

Simon was surrounded once again by his police guard and led from the courtroom. Now that it was over, he was even more confused than he had been before. They hadn't sentenced him to the death penalty. Instead he had been reprieved. Hadn't he? What, after all, could be so bad about being a postman?

And why, when he was escorted from the room, had Gloria been crying?

CHAPTER
FIVE

SIMON HAD BEEN A
great many different things during his relatively short life.
His mother had run off with another man, but his father
had been too busy with another woman to notice. Simon
had been left with a strict uncle, but before long Simon
decided it was time for him to run away as well. After
that, he had done all sorts of things to stay alive. He had
worked on farms and in factories before he had gotten
good enough with his hands to go out and work for himself. He had spent some time in jail and even some in
school. But he had never been a postman.

His police escort put him down gently. They had
reached the post office. The officer in charge opened the
door for Simon. He walked inside, and the half-dozen cops
followed him.

The interior of the post office was quite dark. It took
Simon's eyes a moment to adjust to the dusty, diffuse illumination, most of it coming through multi-paned windows that looked like they hadn't been washed in twenty
years. The rest of the room was done in dark wood paneling, scratched and worn with age. There was plenty of
graffiti carved in the walls as well. Simon read a few ex-
amples from the paneling just inside the door: "George

39

sunk the Titanic by looking at it!", "Heather + Kenneth 1908", "Mary likes the Kaiser". Simon wondered just how old this place was. He walked further into the dim room, glancing at the mail slots and post office boxes. Just before the counter was a cluster of Wanted posters on a bulletin board, tacked on top of each other so that you could only read parts of names and see parts of faces. The poster on top was for some guy named David Harris, a.k.a. "The Editor".

Simon wondered if there was a poster of him somewhere in the pile.

A thin, balding man in a bright blue uniform stood behind the counter, engrossed in the fold-out center section of a magazine. His eyes grew wider as his gaze traveled down the page.

Simon's police escort coughed politely in unison.

"Eh?" the man looked up with a frown. "Who's that—" He stood, for a moment, blinking at the police officers. "Pardon me. You caught me inspecting the mail." He held the magazine aloft and shook it. "Smut! While I am postmaster, nothing like this will go through the mails of Festeron!"

"Oh, we are quite certain you will fulfill your duties to the utmost, Mr. Crisp," the police leader replied. "In fact, we have brought you a new worker so that you may better run your office."

"Ah." Mr. Crisp's face broke into a satisfied smile. "Yes. Your sergeant called to inform me that you were on your way. I understand, actually, that this fellow has been *sentenced* to work with me."

"That is absolutely correct," the cop responded. "He is here by the direct order of the High Court of Festeron."

"That means he can't leave?" Mr. Crisp asked eagerly.

"Indubitably," the police officer replied. "He has been ordered to stay."

"Then he can't quit, no matter what?" Mr. Crisp chuckled.

"Positively," the cop said. "He has been sentenced to be a postal worker for as long as the High Court sees fit."

Crisp laughed out loud, a sound Simon did not at all appreciate.

"At last!" the postmaster shouted. "Someone I can really work with!"

"Glad we could be of service, Mr. Crisp," the police said in unison. They all turned and left.

Mr. Crisp stood there, staring at Simon and wringing his hands. His smile had grown to Cheshire Cat proportions.

"Welcome aboard," he chortled. "I have a feeling we're going to be working together for a long, long time." He stepped forward and opened a mahogany gate at the far end of the counter. "Come in, come in. We must find you a uniform so you can get to work."

Simon looked back at the closed door that the police had just left through. What was to prevent him from running away right now? Well, the police were probably still in hailing distance of the post office; that was one reason. And he had no idea what would happen if he was caught trying to escape from his sentence. Well, actually, he had an inkling of what direction the punishment would take. Despite the fact that he couldn't even begin to figure out what had happened in the courtroom only an hour before, he still got the feeling that, if he should decide to leave before they told him it was all right, the consequences could be very dire indeed. What had they kept saying? "Death was too good for him?" Simon suppressed a shiver. What kind of place was this Festeron, anyway?

Well, if you wanted to find out about a place, working for the post office was a pretty good place to start. He imagined he would learn everything he needed to know about the tiny country of Festeron in just a few days. And without any policemen breathing down his neck, either.

He had been surprised, at first, that the police had simply left him here. He guessed that they expected him to work on the honor system. Well, he guessed he would honor their system, at least until he had a better idea.

Simon nodded to the waiting Mr. Crisp. He had another reason why he couldn't leave just yet. Escape was completely out of the question until he had a chance to see Gloria again.

Simon walked through the open gate into the rear of the post office.

"If you'll just follow me?" Mr. Crisp requested. He turned and walked down a pathway lined by bulging sacks of mail. He stopped at a door that Simon hadn't seen from the other side of the counter. Simon obediently followed.

"We lost our last postal worker under rather unfortunate circumstances," Crisp continued. "Well, I suppose I don't need to go into that just yet. We'll have plenty of time to talk about that, and so many other things as well. Yes, yes, so much time!"

The postmaster took a minute to chuckle softly as he stepped aside so that Simon could see the room beyond.

"This—Simon, is it not?" Crisp inquired. Simon nodded, dumbfounded. "Yes, Simon, this will be your room."

Simon nodded again. For the moment, his power of speech failed him. For one thing, "his room", as Crisp had put it, was little larger than a broom closet. But its size was nothing compared to the condition it was in.

It gave new meaning to the word "messy". Boxes, papers, letters, magazines—anything and everything was piled in mounds that reached halfway to the ceiling. It looked like someone had fought a war in here. Simon had never seen such disarray. Compared to this room, the rest of the cluttered post office was spotless.

"Now, if you'll follow me, we'll find you a uniform." Crisp entered the room on tiptoe. "Careful now! There might be something fragile underfoot!"

Simon cautiously stepped into the battle zone.

"The lockers are over here somewhere," the postmaster explained. He thrust his hands into a mound of letters, feeling for the wall behind. "Ah! I've located your cot! You'll have to clean up in here a bit, of course, before you go to sleep."

Mr. Crisp bit his lip as he surveyed the room. "That means the lockers have to be—over here!" He took three gingerly steps to his right, then pushed aside a box as tall as Simon. "Ah! Here we are. That wasn't so difficult, was it? How easy things are to find when you know where to look!"

He opened the locker and made a clicking sound with his tongue on the roof of his mouth. "Let's see. Let's see. Just what have we here?"

He reached into the locker and pulled out a blue uniform much like the one he wore.

"Ah!" he began, but he started to click his tongue again when he saw that the uniform shirt was practically ripped in two. "No, not that one." He smiled apologetically at Simon. "Some of our past postal workers have been hard on their uniforms."

He pulled another set of clothes free. His tongue-clicking continued as he examined a large brown stain.

"Dear, dear," he murmured. "I don't know if we can save this one. Blood stains are so difficult to remove once they've set."

He pulled a large brown parcel from the bottom of the locker. "I guess we'll have to use a new one. Expenses, always expenses." He turned to regard Simon. "Let's see. You're—say—a forty long, aren't you? Oh, don't be surprised. I get a lot of experience at this sort of thing." He untied the string and ripped off the brown paper, revealing a crisp, blue uniform. He tossed the clothes at Simon. "Here, try these on. Don't worry. I'll look the other way while you change."

Simon frowned and unfolded the clothes. Just what had happened to the other uniforms? Even worse, what had happened to the people who had been wearing them? Shirt in one hand, trousers in the other, he examined the outfit. It looked just like the one Mr. Crisp wore, dark blue pants and brighter shirt, except that the one Simon held lacked the postmaster's gold shoulder-braid.

"Well, come on, now," Mr. Crisp urged. He had turned completely around, and was now facing the locker. "Tell me when I can look."

"Just a minute," Simon called back, quickly stripping off his jeans and T-shirt and pulling on the uniform.

"Okay," he said as he finished buttoning up the shirt.

"Ah, much better!" Mr. Crisp clapped in approval. "Now you are a member of Festeron's finest. Oh, yes, the police call themselves that sometimes, but we know who has the best uniforms, don't we?"

The postmaster allowed himself the slightest of frowns. "Well, then, now that you have a uniform, don't you think it's time you got to work?" He marched back into the larger room. Simon followed, almost tripping. Not only were there papers everywhere, but his pants were too long. He stopped for a moment to roll up his cuffs.

"Now, now, a postal officer never dawdles!" Mr. Crisp called over his shoulder.

"But—" Simon began to protest, pointing at his pants-legs.

"Maybe you'd like to visit the High Court again!" the postmaster suggested. "I'm sure *they'd* be interested in your dawdling!"

So that was the way it was going to be? Simon stood up straight.

"Yes, Mr. Crisp."

"Much better," the postmaster remarked. "Much more like a postal officer. Yes, we're going to have such good times here." He unclasped his wringing hands long enough to wave at his surroundings. "Now, what is it that we see here?"

Simon held back the clever answer he thought of first.

"Mail sacks, Mr. Crisp," is what he said instead.

"Yes, how true." Crisp shook his head sadly. "They've just been piling up. For weeks and weeks, ever since the last postal worker—Well, that's neither here nor there. And still people complain!" He laughed derisively. "I mean, they can't expect me to deliver the mail, too. Not with all my other duties!"

He nodded at Simon. "Well, all that's going to change, now that you're here." He reached into his back pocket and pulled out a folded piece of paper. He handed it to Simon. It was a map of Festeron.

"This should let you get around," Crisp informed him. "If you have any trouble, ask directions. The folks of Festeron are friendly, especially towards postmen!"

Simon unfolded the map, quickly finding the route the police had taken carrying him from the Fun Pier to the jail. But there were plenty of places here that he hadn't been, most notably a graveyard, and a bridge that led to another island!

"You can study that map as you deliver mail," the postmaster remarked. "Now, let's see. Where to begin?" He looked at the mail sacks gathered about his feet. "Eenie, meenie, minie, mo; ah, I guess this one will do." He poked at a bag with his shoe. "Pick this one up, won't you?"

Simon reached over and hefted the gray sack. It was quite heavy. The postmaster opened the gate out to the public area so Simon could drag the sack through.

"Don't worry," Mr. Crisp added. "Your load will get lighter with every letter you deliver." He clapped his hands again. "So hurry up and learn your rounds, and when you get back you can start cleaning out the post office!"

The postmaster chortled merrily, as if he had just made the funniest joke in the world.

"Oh, and I do suggest you get back here before dark. Not that Festeron is dangerous after sunset, oh, my, no. It's simple a matter of—" Crisp paused and coughed. "Well, let's just say it's better to be on the safe side, and leave it at that. Happy delivering!"

Crisp opened the door for Simon. The lad hefted the mailbag over his shoulder and stepped out into the sunlight. The door slammed shut behind him, almost brushing his heels. As Simon glanced back at the heavy oak door, he heard the distinct sound of a heavy bolt being slid into place.

Simon shrugged and began to carry his sack down the hill to the village.

He still had no idea what was going on here.

But he did know one thing. As soon as he possibly could, he was getting out of here.

CHAPTER
SIX

IN THE MEANTIME, Simon supposed, he should deliver some mail.

He opened up the pack and pulled out a handful of envelopes. The paper was glaringly white in the bright noonday sun, and Simon had to squint to make out the addresses. He had pulled out twelve pieces of mail, no two of them going to the same place. He checked his map. About half the street names, places like Main Street, Broadway, and Festeron Blvd., seemed to be in the middle of town. The rest of the mail, however, was addressed to places all over the island, from the Fun Pier at one end to the office of the Festeron Cemetery at the other!

Simon sighed. He guessed he had no right to expect that the mail would be given to him in any order, especially after seeing the way Mr. Crisp kept the post office. Maybe this was why the three judges sentenced him to be a postal worker. Trying to make any sense out of this job would have to be defined as "hard labor".

Still, he would just have to make the best out of a bad situation. So far, Simon had only learned one thing from Festeron: The longer he stayed, the less he understood. Now, however, that he could go wherever he wanted on the two islands that made up this tiny country, and he had a map besides to show him precisely where he was going, Simon expected he would find some answers. Answers that he hoped would get him safely out of this strange place once and for all.

However, there were things to do before he could escape. Simon had to do something with all this mail on his hands. How to go about it, though? Simon had learned to survive these half-dozen years by using his wits, by somehow finding the simplest solutions to the most complex problems.

Simon stared glumly at the heavy bag by his feet, a bag so stuffed with mail that it had to be dragged rather than carried. The simplest solution here would probably be to dump the mail outright in some place—say, a secluded patch of forest or a deep well, where no one would think to look for it until this particular mailman was half a world away from Festeron.

Still, there were problems with that exact course of action. For one thing, Simon didn't know the islands well enough to be sure there was any spot he could successfully hide the mail, and he hated to think what the smiling authorities would do if they found him shirking his duty.

But he faced a deeper dilemma as well. Simon didn't like the thought of just dumping the mail. In all the time since he had run away from home, he had only had himself to depend on. Because of this, he had always thrown himself into whatever he did. If there were five people running the shell game in the same park, Simon would run it faster, with a better line of patter, and even let the marks win once in a while. Because of that the suckers would come back to him, again and again; they'd even have some fun while they lost their money.

It was like that with everything else he'd tried, from selling brushes door-to-door to singing on street corners. Anything he did, he did it to the fullest. What it came down to, he realized, was that he had a personal code he lived by—a code of honor, he supposed you might call it.

After all, that was the one thing that separated adventurers like Simon from common cutpurses and thieves.

Simon looked grimly at the letters in his hands. Maybe he was the sucker now for thinking this way, but there was really only one answer. Until he found a way to escape, he would have to be the best mailman that Festeron had ever had.

A slight breeze had sprung up as he stood there considering his options. It ruffled the envelopes he held in his hands, and threatened to blow his new postman's cap completely off his head. The post office had been built on a hill overlooking the village of Festeron (for he had also found from the map that "Festeron" somehow referred to both the entire country of two islands and the capital township as well). On a clear day like this, he could see the whole village spread before him, bulky brick buildings—churches, the library, the movie theater, the jail—all clustered at the center of town, surrounded by white clapboard houses lining the roads out of the village, each row of dwellings blossoming outward like petals on a bright spring flower.

Simon had to admit it. Festeron seemed like a nice town, filled with nice people. He was glad he was no longer in jail, and had a chance to stand outside instead. If he had to deliver mail, he couldn't think of a better day to do it.

But how could he drag this sack all over the countryside? And how could he do any sort of job at all if the mail always came to him in such a jumbled mess?

He tossed the dozen envelopes he had held in his hands back in the sack. He'd have to find someplace in the village to sort the mail—someplace away from this windy hill.

He was about to draw the mail sack's strings closed when he saw something down among the envelopes; something darker that didn't look at all like the rest of the mail. He frowned and stuck his hand deep into the mass of paper. There it was, a box of some sort. A rather large box, he realized as he felt along its edge; it seemed to take up fully half the sack. Well, Simon thought, this requires further investigation. Placing a leg to either side of the sack so that he might keep the mass of mail steady between his knees, he reached both hands deep inside, and, after a moment of struggle, pulled the box free and set it down on the ground.

A square of white flashed before his eyes. Apparently, he had pulled out another envelope along with the package. The hilltop breeze sent this new letter spinning to the ground. Cursing softly to himself, he bent over to pick it up. If he wasn't careful, he'd have mail flying around everywhere.

Simon's heart nearly stopped when he read the address:

Miss Gloria Magnifico
114 River Road
Festeron Township, Festeron H7P432W691-63H79

He looked quickly to his map, trying to determine just where 114 River Road might be. It seemed to be on the western side of the island, right by the ocean. Surely, it had to be *his* Gloria. Simon tried to stay calm, but after all, how many Glorias could a place as small as Festeron have? It had to be his Gloria, didn't it?

And then another thought rose unbidden to his mind. If this letter was addressed to his Gloria, what kind of a letter was it? What did he really know about Gloria, anyway? He had only just met her, and found her very attractive. Wouldn't other young men find her attractive as well?

What if the envelope he held in his hand contained a love letter?

He looked again at the white square in his hand. There was no return address. Surely a love letter would have a return address? Simon resisted the urge to hold the envelope up to the sun to see if he could read what was inside. A postman wouldn't read other people's mail. Besides, this letter gave him a chance to go see Gloria in person and, Simon was sure, once he'd had a chance to really speak with her—say perhaps this very evening when, with luck, there might be a little moonlight—whoever wrote this piece of mail in his hand, even if it was a love letter, wouldn't stand a chance.

He smiled to himself. Now he was thinking more like the Simon he remembered. There was something about this place, what with the way everything was happening to him, that seemed to have thrown him off his rhythm, made him feel definitely un-Simon. That was over now, though. He promised himself that. Even if he had to be a mailman for a little while, he'd still do whatever he wanted.

But first he had to look at the box.

It was a big, heavy thing, not quite square, that rose almost to his knees. It was an odd color too, a dark brown cardboard, so dark that it had appeared almost midnight-black against the sea of white envelopes in the bag. He flipped the box over until he found the address:

Miss V. Voss
Festeron Public Library
Festeron Village, Festeron WP3XC77LFD-XX663

The public library, huh? The would explain the box's weight. The carton must be filled with books. The return address said the box came from Midnight Publishers, back on the mainland. Books it was, then. Simon once again consulted his map. It looked like the library was just down at the bottom of this hill. Well, then that was where he would start his deliveries.

Actually, Simon realized, finding this package solved two of his problems. Once he delivered this box, he'd have half the weight of the sack off his hands. And what better place to sort the rest of the mail than a nice, cozy, quiet library?

Twisting the mail sack's rope around his right wrist, Simon lifted the carton with a grunt. He decided he would have to drag the mail sack to one side while he carried the box down the hill. It might not look very pretty, but it would get the job done. He didn't even know why he was worried about appearances, anyway. Since he'd stepped out of the post office, he had not seen another soul on this side of Festeron.

"Oh, there you are," a mild-mannered voice said by his side. "I've been looking for you."

Simon spun quickly, dropping the box in the process. How could he have missed someone who had gotten that close to him?

For an instant, Simon didn't think there was anyone there. Well, there did seem to be this gray smudge, like some sort of morning haze hanging over the hill. Simon blinked, and the haze took on definition. The lower portions seemed to solidify into a somewhat rumpled raincoat, while the top developed what could charitably be called facial features.

"Mr. Sneed," Simon remarked.

"I'm pleased you remember me," Sneed replied. "So few people do."

Simon didn't respond for a moment. How could someone walk around on a day as bright as this and be almost invisible? Simon almost asked Sneed, but thought better of it. The nondescript fellow seemed to have enough trouble with his identity without having others point it out to him.

"I've been looking for you," the mild-mannered man repeated. "I wanted to apologize for what happened this morning. You know, in court."

Simon frowned at Sneed. "In court? What do you have to apologize for?"

"They didn't hear me," Sneed whispered. "I tried to tell them about your noble act, but they wouldn't listen!"

"Sure," Simon nodded. "But was that your fault?"

Sneed looked miserable. "Sometimes I think everything is my fault."

Simon's frown deepened. He wondered if this fellow's attitude had something to do with his invisibility. He tried to give Sneed a comradely punch in the shoulder, but must have misjudged just where the gray man stood, for his fist only hit the empty air.

"Look," Simon said instead. "I don't feel that way about you. Why don't you come along with me while I deliver my mail? I could use somebody who knows the area to help show me around."

"Oh. Do you think I could?" Sneed's smile seemed to brighten up his whole face. Simon thought he saw wrinkles there he had never noticed before. And he had never realized that the little man's eyes were blue.

"I'll do whatever I can," the little man continued. "I so much want to make up for this morning, you know."

Simon decided to let that comment pass. If Sneed wanted to dwell on his own shortcomings, there wasn't much Simon could do about it. In fact, maybe he could get the little guy to help with his mailman duties.

"I tell you what." He smiled reassuringly at Sneed. "That Postmaster Crisp has given me too much to carry. Think you could manage a mailbag?"

"Oh, dear," Sneed replied.

"It's just down to the library," Simon coaxed.

The little man nodded doubtfully. "Normally, I would be more than happy to comply. It's simply that—" he paused, his face reddening slightly, "—well, I'm afraid that I'm feeling particularly insubstantial today. I'm sure you know how that is."

Simon nodded, not having the faintest idea what Sneed was talking about. He once again twisted the rope around his wrist and hefted the box.

"Well, let's get going," he added. "We have to deliver this package to Miss Voss."

"Miss Voss?" What little color there was in Sneed's face drained away. "Oh, dear. Well, if we must."

The little man turned and started down the hill. Simon had to jog to catch up.

"Is there something wrong with Miss Voss?" he called after the rapidly descending man in the raincoat.

But Sneed just shook his head.

"Dear, dear," was his only answer.

CHAPTER
SEVEN

SIMON TRIED THE main door of the library. It was an impressive-looking double door, maybe ten feet high, made of polished maple, with a lion's head carved in the center of each great panel. The doors also appeared to be locked; neither pushing nor pulling had any effect, and the knobs seemed frozen in place. After a moment's consideration, he found a bell, half hidden within the ivy-covered brick that surrounded the huge door frame. He rang it.

The door swung open almost immediately. A woman scowled out at him. "Who dares disturb the busy librari—" Her eyes fell on the package in Simon's hands.

"Oh. All deliveries to the rear door!" she declared as she slammed the door.

Rear door? Simon sighed. This postman stuff was going to take some getting used to. Now where was the rear door?

"This way," Sneed murmured without being asked. He walked to the side of the building. Simon followed, and found the small man standing by a second entranceway. There, framed by crumbling brick, was a weather-beaten door, badly in need of paint, which bore a hand-lettered sign: DELIVERIES—KNOCK LOUD!

Simon made a fist and pounded on the gray wood.

The door swung open even faster this time. The same disapproving woman glared out at them.

"Not so loud!" she demanded. "This is a library, you know!"

"Oh." Simon took half a step back at the force of the woman's exclamation. "But the sign said—"

The woman placed an emphatic finger across her lips. "Ssshhh!"

Simon was amazed anyone could make a shushing noise that loudly.

"Very well." The woman's thin lips curled up in the slightest of smiles when she realized she had silenced Simon. "Follow me."

Simon untwisted the rope that bound him to his mail sack. Still carrying the box, he walked inside. Sneed followed a pace or two behind.

The woman led them down a long, ill-lit corridor, and through a second doorway into a large room dominated by a large counter made of the same dark maple as the front doorway. Simon blinked. It was much brighter in here. A professionally lettered sign in a frame stood on the counter top. It read "Check out books here".

The woman pointed to the counter. "You may put the package there." She glanced at the label as Simon placed the box on the counter. "It is for me, of course."

"Oh?" Simon said, attempting to be friendly. "Then you must be Miss Voss?"

"What did I tell you about being quiet?" the woman almost screamed. She took a deep breath, struggling to control herself. After a moment, she answered in a more reasonable tone of voice: "Yes, I am Miss Voss."

Simon looked quickly around the room. Everything here, from the linoleum floor to the dark maple counter-top to the glass covering the framed pastoral prints, was shined to a high gloss. The early-afternoon sun poured in through a skylight in the ceiling, making the whole room gleam. From Miss Voss's attitude, he guessed no one was allowed to talk in this building. It looked as if no one was allowed to walk here, either. Simon glanced again at Miss Voss, who glared back with her usual frown. Actually, Simon doubted if anyone was even allowed to breathe in here.

The librarian walked quickly past him, getting her hands on the box. Simon backed away from her single-minded enthusiasm. He bumped into a door. Simon glanced behind him, and saw a sign that read: "Thornton W. Burgess Room".

"Thornton W. Burgess?" Simon mused.

"Possibly the finest collection in this part of the world," Miss Voss replied proudly as she tore open the box.

"Do you mind if I look around?" he asked. There must be a quiet spot around here somewhere where he could sort his mail.

Miss Voss looked up from where she had been opening the cardboard top. "The library is closed!"

"Oh," Simon replied, still taken aback by her vehemence. The library was closed in the middle of a weekday? Perhaps, Simon thought, it was lunchtime or something. "Well, maybe I could come back sometime when it was open."

The librarian grunted and went back to her ripping.

"Pardon me," Simon interrupted, "but could you tell me when the library will be open?"

"When I say so!" Miss Voss growled as she pulled wads of newspaper from the hole she had torn in the box.

This woman was starting to annoy him. Simon was hoping to use this place, both for sorting mail and perhaps to find out a little bit more about Festeron, especially about exits from the island country. But this particular librarian apparently wanted to use this building as her private domain.

"Pardon me," he ventured again, trying to keep his own temper in check, "but is the library ever open?"

"It can't be!" Miss Voss snapped. "Not now. There are certain changes that have to be made—renovations that are far overdue—" She paused, glaring once again at Simon. "But why am I explaining this to a *postman?*"

She reached into the box and pulled forth a thick book with a lurid red cover. The title flashed before Simon's eyes: *Love's Savage M—*

"But what are you doing, gaping at me?" she demanded. "Your job is done here. Get out—" she paused and pointed back at the dingy corridor, "—the way you came in!"

This was too much! No librarian, or anybody else, was going to talk to Simon that way!

"Oh, yeah?" he began angrily, only stopping when he felt something tugging against the back of his jacket. He turned around to see Sneed frantically shaking his head no and pointing toward the corridor out. The little man looked even more upset than he usually did.

"Did you have something to add?" Miss Voss asked, her voice the temperature of your average iceberg.

"Oh, yeah," Simon replied somewhat more affably as Sneed pulled frantically on his sleeve. "Oh, yeah, that is the way out, isn't it? Well, I guess I'll be seeing you around."

"I don't expect to see you back here," Miss Voss barked at Simon's back, "unless you have business."

"Or unless I need to use the library!" Simon called as he slammed the delivery door behind him. He just couldn't help himself. People like Miss Voss, who acted like they owned the entire world with you included, always got on his nerves.

The door opened again. Simon spun around, ready for whatever Miss Voss had to say. But it was only Sneed.

"Oh, dear," the little man said. "I don't know if it's very wise to anger the librarian."

"I don't know if I angered her exactly." Simon paused to adjust his cap. "I might have talked back to her, but a postman's gotta do what he sees fit."

"But that's the problem," Sneed insisted. "You see, Miss Voss is a very special friend of Mr. Crisp."

"Very special?" Simon's heart sank. Was Sneed inferring what Simon thought he was?

"*Very* special." Sneed nodded unhappily. "I should say no more."

"Very special," Simon whispered. That meant that Crisp and Voss had a thing going, didn't it? He couldn't imagine how anyone as hyperactively strange as Mr. Crisp or as shrewishly sour as Miss Voss could appeal to anyone—but then again, perhaps they were made for each other. Hyperactivity and sourness could complement each other, he supposed, although Simon decided he wanted to be nowhere in the vicinity when and if they did.

Still, that probably meant he had started his new postman job by making one of the worst enemies imaginable. It figured. As cheerful as everyone had been since he had come to Festeron, every time he tried to do anything on this island, it seemed to come out instantly wrong. Maybe, Simon thought, he and this island were like things never meant to mix, like fish and bananas, or mashed potatoes and chocolate sauce. If it wasn't for Gloria, he would get off this island as fast as his postman shoes would take him.

But there was Gloria. And he had mail to deliver to her.

He sighed. "Come on, Sneed. Let's get out of here. We have a job to do. Besides, what can a librarian do to me?"

"Nothing, now." Sneed looked around furtively, as if every bush might hold a spy. "But later—" His mouth snapped firmly shut, as if his jaw muscles decided of their own accord not to let him finish the sentence.

"Later?" Simon prompted.

"Oh, dear." Sneed cowered, waiting for the spies to pounce on him at any second. "I should say no more."

Simon sighed. Sometimes, it seemed, talking to Sneed managed to get you less information than talking to yourself. He stuck his hand into the mail sack and drew out a handful of letters. Scanning the addresses quickly, he found that three of them were for places in the middle of town. He stuffed the remaining envelopes back in the sack, placing the three local letters in his pocket with the missive for Gloria. He'd have to find some other place in downtown Festeron to sort the mail, but he might as well get rid of a few letters while he looked around. He checked his map. One of the local letters would get delivered right down the street, across from the circle with the statue.

He threw the mail sack over his shoulder and headed toward the next delivery. Sneed hurried after him. In less than two minutes, they stood looking up at the statue of Phineas T. Fester. Simon pulled the envelopes from his pocket. Here was the one he wanted:

Hortense D. Fester
3 Festeron Circle
Festeron Village, Festeron H7632WWWT3-2134X

That should be right around here someplace. He scanned the stately brick homes that faced the circle. This was obviously where the big money of Festeron lived. There was Number Three, across the street from the movie theater. Simon noticed that the features had changed since he spent the night in jail. The Festeron Palace was now showing *Gidget Goes Jamaican* and *Pollyanna Meets Pippi Longstocking*. The new postman made a face. He turned to Sneed.

"Don't they ever show any real movies around here?" he asked.

"Pardon?" the little man asked nondescriptly.

"You know," Simon explained, "movies with bombs and guns. Non-stop blood-and-guts action. Vampires and zombies."

"Oh, dear." Sneed sighed. "Oh, no, they won't show those until—" He paused to clear his throat. "They show nothing but that sort of thing, I suppose, after—" His voice died in his throat. He looked miserably at Simon. "I should say no more."

Simon repressed the urge to scream at his soft-spoken companion. Wasn't Sneed tagging along to give him some answers? Whatever the small man wasn't talking about seemed to be too much for his mild-mannered mind to deal with. Better, Simon guessed, that he should deliver the mail, and find out about Festeron for himself.

He walked across the street and up the steps to Number Three. There didn't seem to be a mailbox. Come to think of it, there hadn't been a mailbox anywhere around the library, either. That was odd. He considered asking Sneed if there was any reason for this, but thought better of it. He rang Number Three's doorbell instead.

The door opened a moment later. An elderly woman smiled out at him.

"Yes?" she began. "Oh, what a nice young man!"

Simon smiled back at her. "I have a letter for you, ma'am."

"Oh, you're the postman?" Her smile fell to a look of total dismay. "Oh, dear. I'm so sorry."

She was sorry, too? Because he was a postman? What was going on here? Simon wondered if there was some way he could get this woman to give him some answers.

He decided the best thing to do would be to keep her talking.

"Oh, being a postman isn't so bad," he remarked, the smile still on his face. "Especially on a nice day like this."

The old woman nodded grimly. "Oh, it wouldn't be bad to be a postman now. No, not at all. At least not yet." She made a clucking sound with her tongue. "Wait there a minute, young man. I have something for you." She walked away from him down the hallway, then turned out of sight.

Simon glanced at the letter still in his hand, then looked through the screen door into the empty hall. Somehow, the two stops so far on his route had both turned into major productions. If this was the way his job was going to go, it would take him days to deliver anything. Maybe that was the curse of being a postman; that the work was never-ending. Somehow, though, Simon had the feeling that this was still not the answer.

"Here we are!" The old woman appeared in the hall once again, and bustled toward Simon. The screen door creaked as she pushed it open.

"Here you are," she said, thrusting a small box into Simon's free hand. "This is for you. The very thing."

"Oh," Simon replied, perhaps even more dumb-founded than before. "Don't you want your letter?"

"What? Oh, most certainly." Her hands fluttered wildly at her sides, as if they might sprout wings at any moment. "I just haven't had one in so long."

"A letter?" Simon smiled again as he handed her the envelope.

The old lady shook her head. "No. A visit from a postman. It's been so long, you know, after everyone found out—" She hesitated. "But I shouldn't be talking about this, should I? May I say again that I most certainly and fervently hope to see you again. And please use what I gave you. There's an instruction booklet inside."

The woman gave Simon a final smile as she shut the door. He looked at the box in his hand.

ACME KITCHEN WONDER, the box proudly proclaimed, yellow letters on a blue background.

He turned to Sneed.

"What—" he began.

"Yes?" the little man prompted when Simon couldn't find the words to continue.

"Never mind," the new postman muttered. He doubted that Sneed's answer, if indeed the little man did deign to answer him this time, would make any more sense than anything else going on in Festeron.

CHAPTER EIGHT

AT LEAST HE HAD found a place to sort the mail. The door to the First Church of Festeronian Science had been wide open. Simon had waited for Sneed's reaction as he dragged the mail sack up the church steps, but while the little man had not been wildly enthusiastic about sorting the mail inside, at least for a change he had not been totally negative. Now they sat side by side on a mahogany pew, Simon sorting the in-town mail by street while Sneed arranged those letters that went to the rest of the island in what he described as "an orderly fashion."

So the mail would finally get delivered. Now all Simon needed were some answers. He looked up at Sneed, who was humming some popular song or other, something that Simon couldn't remember the name of.

"Is there something you'd like to tell me?" Simon asked.

Sneed looked up from his letter sorting. "Oh, dear." He glanced quickly about the church. "Why do you say that?"

"Because otherwise I have no idea why you're following me around." Simon shook his head.

"Oh, my." Sneed looked as though he wanted to fade

into the woodwork. "Well, yes, there are things—that is, I feel you would be better prepared if—oh, dear, not here! Not yet!" He began to sort the mail with renewed vigor. "I should say no more."

Simon threw his mail down on the bench beside him. This was ridiculous. Everyone he had talked with since the trial had seemed to be avoiding something, changing the subject or turning away whenever he tried to lead the conversation toward anything specific. Simon couldn't get anyone to admit to anything but vague generalities, leaving him with nothing but the all-too-certain feeling that whatever that something was that everyone was trying to avoid, it was going to happen to him.

All three people to whom he had delivered mail in town had been quick to offer their condolences, and Miss Voss had dismissed him in a manner that seemed to suggest she would never have to bother dealing with him again. What was happening here? Simon hated to admit it, but he was no longer simply annoyed at the situation. He was starting to get a little afraid. Why had the judges made him a postman, rather than sentencing him to death? And why were the townspeople so sorry when he delivered the mail? Was he due to be sacrificed to appease the postal gods? Simon would have laughed at such a thought if he hadn't suspected it might be true.

"Not now, you say? Not here?" He spoke to Sneed between clenched teeth. "Then *when* can you tell me?"

"Oh." Sneed sighed, using a corner of his raincoat to mop the sweat from his forehead. "Oh. Yes. Certainly. Out of town. When we are alone. Truly alone. Someplace far out of town."

"Good. Let's do it, then." He stood up, tossing his mail back in the sack. The in-town letters would have to wait for later. He reached into his pocket and pulled out Gloria's letter to check the address. "I want to start in the direction of River Road. Can you give me any mail to deliver along the way?"

Wishbringer

"Certainly," Sneed assured him. "I have everything nicely sorted. It's the least I can do."

Simon grunted, and pushed Gloria's letter back into his pocket. His fingers hit something else, a small box. He'd almost forgotten about that. No one had answered any of his questions, but that old lady on Festeron Circle had given him something instead.

He pulled the bright blue box from his pocket and read the label again:

THE ACME KITCHEN WONDER!
1001 uses, inside the home—and out!

He opened the box and looked inside. It only occurred to him then that there might be something within other than what was advertised without. Simon frowned. He should have thought of that right away. Any self-respecting thief would. This postman gig was upsetting him more than he realized.

He reached his thumb and forefinger into the box and pulled out a metal and plastic cylinder that looked like some odd combination of screwdriver, knife handle, and calculator, with buttons and holes for small attachments all over the place. It looked to Simon like it was probably a Kitchen Wonder. He put it back in the box.

He still had no idea why that old lady had given him this. He had half thought of throwing it away, but Sneed had fervently urged him to keep it, saying, cryptically as always, that he never knew when he might find a use for it. After all, Simon thought, if he stuck around Festeron long enough, someday he might even get a kitchen.

Simon swore softly to himself and thrust the box back into his pocket. It was time to find Gloria's house, and Gloria too. Somehow, if he could see her, all the rest of this would no longer matter.

He stood, hefting the mail sack and throwing it over his shoulder. Sneed still had a pile of thirty or forty letters neatly stacked before him. Simon told the little man to bring them along as well. He marched out of the church as Sneed stuffed the remaining letters into his raincoat.

Sneed caught up with the postman on the church steps, where Simon was consulting his map. The postman frowned as he looked up to get his bearings.

"Let's see. We turn left here, don't we?"

Sneed nodded rapidly. "Straight down Western Avenue. There's another reason I'm here, you know."

Simon glanced back at the little man before he started down the steps. "Something you can tell me about?"

"Oh, dear. Most certainly." The little man nodded again. "You did a very noble thing."

There Sneed went with the nobility stuff again. That was another thing he couldn't figure out. All he had done was to keep a sucker from losing all his money. Simon looked at the other man skeptically. "Don't a lot of people do noble things in Festeron?"

"Most certainly not!" Sneed insisted. "There's a lot of niceness in Festeron, but very little nobility."

"Really?" Simon mused as they both descended the steps. "Well, I certainly hope you can tell me about it—" He paused when he saw the frightened look pass across the other man's bland features. "And we'll talk about it just as soon as we're far enough out of town."

Sneed smiled and nodded. They turned left and walked away from Festeron Center.

"In the meantime, we have mail to deliver." Simon looked critically at the small man's crumpled attire. "You have anything in that raincoat of yours addressed to Western Avenue?"

The landscape changed quickly as they left the center of the village. The stately homes and municipal buildings that clustered around Festeron Circle soon gave way to more modest dwellings, small one- and two-story homes, always, it seemed, recently painted white so that the wood shone in the early afternoon sun, with shutters and doors painted dark red, or blue, or green. This looked a lot like the sort of place in which Simon had grown up. Except that, somehow, it seemed much nicer.

The farther they got from the center of town, the more Sneed began to talk. Not about anything really important, at least not yet. But at least he began to tell Simon about some of the customs, and peculiarities, of the island republic. Simon had to admit he'd never heard of another place that held a week-long "Have a Nice Day" festival.

And, as Sneed talked, Simon delivered mail. The houses grew farther apart, often separated by gently rolling hills so that each home seemed to stand alone, isolated from its neighbors. Simon noticed another change as well: Some of the houses out here did have containers of one sort or another that could pass for mailboxes. If not, Sneed explained, you just left the mail on the front step. People were so nice in Festeron that no one would even think of disturbing another person's correspondence.

That same theme seemed to run through most of Sneed's explanations: How nice everything was in Festeron. Simon simply listened, trying to remember the occasional tidbit of information that seemed important, and ignoring most of the rest for what it was, nervous chatter on Sneed's part until the little man felt safe enough to tell Simon what was really bothering him.

They came at last to the end of Western Avenue, and the end of the island as well. Simon looked out at a vast expanse of pebbled beach, with the blue-gray ocean beyond. The day was crystal-clear, and he could see the jagged shape of another island in the distance. He asked Sneed what it was.

"Oh, dear," was Sneed's reply. "It's called the Misty Isle."

"The Misty Isle?" Simon asked. "What's the Misty Isle?"

"Oh, my," Sneed answered shortly. "It's the kingdom of the platypuses."

Simon glanced at the little man. He seemed, suddenly, to have reverted to the noncommunicative companion he had been in the middle of town. Certainly, after the endless stories about the niceness of Festeron, Sneed must have an anecdote about someplace as strange as the kingdom of the platypuses? But the little man seemed preoccupied at the moment with studying his shoes. Simon turned his attention back to the island.

Maybe, if he could get over to the Misty Isle, he could escape from Festeron once and for all. But how could he get there? Simon had never been much of a swimmer, and he still remembered what the cops had told him about the sharks on the island's other side. There seemed to be no way to reach the Misty Isle, then, without a boat. Well, someone on Festeron must have a boat. (And, Simon reflected, it was probably a very *nice* boat.) Once he found a means of transportation, he now had somewhere to go.

Simon pulled out his map to see if it might show some method of access to the other island, but there was no indication of the Misty Isle in the map's depiction of the Western Sea. Well, at least that meant it wasn't on his delivery route. He decided that, for the moment at least, he didn't have time to worry about it.

The map also showed him that they now stood at the junction of Western Avenue and River Road. If they turned south, they would soon come to the large expanse of the Festeron Cemetery. Simon assumed that Gloria's house had to be to the north.

As they turned right, Simon asked Sneed why they called this highway River Road.

"Pardon?" Sneed replied, cowering ever so slightly.

Simon decided to ignore his companion's overt flinching. "I mean," he continued, "here we are, right by the open sea. Shouldn't this road be called Ocean View

Drive or something like that? Where is this river, anyway?"

Sneed looked behind them and to either side before replying. "It's hidden."

"Huh?"

"The river. It's hidden." Sneed glanced down at his shoes.

"Hidden?" It was Simon's turn to look around. "Where?"

"Underground," Sneed replied. "There is much in Festeron that is hidden. But I should say no—say, isn't that the house you were looking for?"

Simon looked to his right. There, set back among the trees, was a brown-and-white gingerbread house that looked as if it had jumped straight from a book of fairy tales. It was also, by far, the nicest of all the houses Simon had seen. Not that all the other houses weren't nice. It was just that they had been nice and ordinary. This place, however, gave the word "nice" an entirely new meaning altogether.

Simon saw the number painted on the cheerful yellow door: 114. He pulled the envelope from his pocket. There was the address: 114 River Road. Sneed was right. This was the place, then. So why did his feet feel like they were rooted to the pavement?

It couldn't be because he was going to see a girl. When he was a lot younger, maybe, he might have had that sort of problem, but over the last few years he had spent a lot of time with a lot of young women. By now, he knew just what to do, what to say. He had all the moves just the way he wanted them.

At least he thought he had before he had come to Festeron. There was something about this place that was very odd, to say the least. Something that threatened to throw him off his stride in everything he did. Maybe that was his problem. Yeah. He should be able to march right up there, knock on the door, and talk to Gloria. No problem.

"Pardon me," Sneed interrupted his line of thought. "If you're going to stand there all day, I could go and deliver the envelope."

"Hey!" Simon protested. "I'll deliver it. I was just admiring the house. A postman has to take a minute out once in a while, doesn't he?"

Properly chastened, Sneed nodded rapidly, then stared down at his shoes. Simon felt a little guilty. He shouldn't take out his feelings on somebody who was trying to help him. But what were his feelings? And why was he worried about feelings at a time like this? His only job here was to walk up to that front door and deliver this letter. Of course, he'd have to knock on the door, and maybe somebody would answer. Somebody like Gloria.

"Excuse, me," Sneed interjected again, "but there's a little box out here at the end of their sidewalk. If you're feeling overworked, I'm sure they wouldn't mind if you simply left the letter there and proceeded on your way."

"What?" Simon cried. "I can't just leave the letter—" He paused, willing himself to calm down. "No, Sneed, I don't mean to shout. And I thank you for your suggestion. But if I'm going to be a good postman, I will have to do my job to the fullest. And in Festeron, that means delivering the mail in person."

There! He'd said it. He was going to walk up to that house and deliver the mail. He turned toward Gloria's home, the house where Gloria lived, that place where— why, Gloria was probably somewhere inside that gingerbread frame at this very minute!

He willed his legs to move. He was having a bit of trouble remembering how to walk. But he knew if he stopped now, Sneed would offer another helpful suggestion.

Simon took a deep breath, and began the long walk up to that front door. What was the matter with him? He had sort of lost track of his birthdays over the years. But he had to be nineteen, at least, or somewhere near that. And here he was acting like some overgrown kid!

It must have something to do with the unrelenting niceness of Festeron. Yeah, that had to be it! Well, all that niceness wasn't going to change old Simon. He increased his pace, his anger giving a spring to his step. He pounded on the front door as soon as he reached it.

"Coming!" a young woman's voice called. Simon staggered, as if every muscle in his legs had disappeared from his legs. But no, he had a job to do. He held the letter before him as he peered through the small glass window in the center of the door.

Did he see someone moving through the darkness inside? He heard footsteps! Yes, someone was definitely coming. He saw long hair swing through the shadows. Gloria! What would he say to her?

The door swung open.

CHAPTER
NINE

IT WASN'T GLORIA. IT was her sister.

"Oh, it's you," Gloria's sister said with a frown. "I heard they made you a postman."

"Yes, they did." Simon tried to smile, hoping desperately to remember the sister's name. It was gone, crowded out by that single, glorious name that filled his head. The girl-with-no-name's frown deepened as he stared at her. Apparently, she wasn't about to make small talk.

"Is your sister here?" he blurted at last.

The younger sister folded her arms in front of her. "Why?"

"I've got a letter for her." He waved the envelope before her nose.

"Oh, I'll take that." Her hand reached out, quick as a cobra. Simon barely snatched the letter back in time.

"No!" he replied with surprising vehemence. "I'm afraid I have to deliver all my letters personally."

"Personally?" The girl's lips curled upward into the cruellest hint of a smile. "Well, what if she's not—"

"Shirley!" another woman's voice called. "Who is that at the door?"

Simon recognized that voice.

"Gloria?" he shouted.

"Simon?" her voice rose in turn. He heard a drumroll of feet descending the steps. Shirley scowled and looked behind her as she was pushed aside.

And then Simon was looking at Gloria. And Gloria was looking at Simon. He thought fast, trying to come up with just the right thing to say.

"Oh . . . hi," he managed at last.

She smiled, and his heart pressed against his ribcage like some animal yearning to be free.

"Well," she replied, "it's nice you got out of jail."

"Yes, it is," Simon answered.

"And it's nice you can walk around on such a beautiful day," Gloria offered.

"Oh, it is a nice day, isn't it?" Simon replied, struck by the thought.

"I think I'm going to be sick," Shirley interjected. "Would you listen to you two?"

"Well, you certainly don't have to." Gloria turned to Shirley. Her smile, while still there, had gone hard around the edges. "Why don't you be a good little sister, and run along and play with—" she paused, her eyes drawn back to Simon, "—well, whatever it is you play with?"

"Wow." Shirley rolled her eyes up toward the heavens. "Wait until I tell Brad about you two."

"Oh!" Simon exclaimed, holding up the envelope as if he had never seen it before. "I've got a letter for you."

"For me?" Gloria clapped her hands like a three-year-old. "How wonderful!"

"Maybe I'll be sick all over your letter," Shirley suggested.

Simon handed Gloria the letter. Their fingers touched. Gloria put the envelope down on a table in the hall without even looking at the address.

"I'll read it later," she explained. "It's much too nice a day to be shut inside reading letters."

"Oh, yes," Simon replied. "It is a nice day, isn't it?"

They gazed into each other's eyes for a long moment.

Shirley groaned. "You've delivered your letter," she remarked. "Isn't it time you delivered something somewhere else?"

Both Simon and Gloria glanced disdainfully, and ever-so-briefly, at the youngster.

"I suppose I should be going soon," Simon said after a moment.

"Oh, yes." Gloria's smile faltered. "All that mail to deliver."

Simon nodded grimly. He had to leave, or he would risk the wrath of Mr. Crisp, and possibly the High Court of Festeron. But now that he had seen Gloria again, he was not going to lose her!

"They can't have me delivering mail around the clock!" he said with new conviction in his voice. "Could I stop back to see you tonight?"

"Tonight?" Her smile was gone completely, now. Had he said something wrong? "Oh, dear, that might not be such a good idea."

Not such a good idea? That must mean she had other plans. He should have known, when she got a letter like that, that there had to be somebody else. Well, Simon didn't give up that easily.

"How about tomorrow night?" he suggested.

"Oh, dear," Gloria said again. Shirley smirked at her side.

"Tomorrow night?" Gloria bit her lip. "Well, we never know. The nights are strange around here sometimes."

"Strange?" Simon replied. He thought about his last night in the jail. It had been quiet, save for the gentle chirping of crickets.

Gloria brushed back her lustrous hair with one perfectly formed hand. "Well, how do I explain it . . ."

"You don't, Sis!" Shirley hissed in a stage whisper. "Especially not to him!"

"Oh, my," Gloria whispered. "How can I say this?" When she looked up at Simon, her expression of misery was the equal of anything that had crossed Sneed's face. But when she spoke, her voice was clear and decisive:

"If nothing changes, I'll be glad to see you tonight."

"If nothing changes?" Simon blurted out. "How am I supposed to know—"

"You'll know," Gloria replied shortly. "Oh, Simon!" She stepped closer to him. Their faces were mere inches apart. All Simon had to do was lean forward slightly, and their lips would meet.

"Gloria!"

Simon jumped back. It was a man's voice.

Gloria looked behind her, her hair swinging out in a great arc, almost touching Simon's nose.

"Yes, Daddy?"

A tall man with a full mane of wildly unkempt white hair walked up behind the two girls. "Have you seen my *Treatise on Festeronian Philosophy*? Or my hammer, for that matter?"

"Oh, Daddy!" Gloria chided. "I think I saw the *Treatise* down on your workbench."

"And your hammer's up in your study," Shirley added helpfully.

"Good, good." Their father squinted as he peered out into the sunlight. "But who do we have here? Why doesn't someone introduce me to this nice young man?"

"Oh, Father!" Shirley laughed derisively. "It's only the postman."

"Oh, my. Really?" He nodded his head soberly at Simon. "I'm so sorry for you, old chap."

"No, Father," Gloria insisted. "This is no ordinary postman. You remember the young man I told you about, at the Fun Pier, and then at the jail? This is he, Father, our postman, Simon."

"Really?" Her father scratched at his white mop of hair with a long-fingered hand. "Then could this be—"

Gloria glanced shyly back at Simon. "I don't know, Daddy. I'm not sure if this feeling—"

"I think I'm going to be sick," Shirley remarked. "You think he's—"

Simon couldn't stand it anymore.

"What?" he shouted. "You think I'm what?"

All three members of the Magnifico family turned to look at him. From their expressions, it was apparent that they were not pleased with his outburst.

"I'm afraid there are certain things we should not speak about," the father intoned.

"But Daddy is someone who would know about those sorts of things," Gloria added enthusiastically. "He's a professor at the University of Festeron."

"Part-time," her father added.

"Oh. You're a part-time professor?" Simon figured that if he could keep them talking, they might finally give him some clues as to what their great secret was.

"No, actually it's a part-time university," their father replied sadly. "Festeron is very small, as you've no doubt noticed. Because of our size, we can only afford to keep the university open every other year, I'm afraid. But I fill in between times as best as I can. Odd jobs. Mechanical repairs."

Simon saw what the old fellow was getting at. "Oh, you mean you fix washing machines, lawn mowers, that sort of thing?"

"Oh, dear me, nothing so large! No, I've always been a specialist, looking at the minutiae of existence. That is the direction I have taken in my scholarly pursuits. It is therefore the direction I have taken in my repairs."

"Father does watches and clocks, blenders and can openers," Gloria explained.

"I do my best," the old man said humbly.

"Nonsense! Don't listen to him. Father is a master of the Small Appliance!" Gloria said proudly.

"I will have to remember that," Simon said cheerily.

It was time to steer the conversation back to matters that concerned him. "I was wondering, could I ask you a couple of questions about the operation of the post office?"

"My, my." Professor Magnifico made a *ts*king sound with his tongue. "It's getting awfully late in the afternoon."

"Yes, it is," Gloria all-too-readily agreed. "Simon, don't you think you should get on with your mail delivery?"

Simon blinked. What was this?

"But Gloria—" he began.

"If this goes on any longer," Shirley announced, "I'm going to be sick."

Gloria put her hand on the door and began to close it.

"I'm sorry, Simon, but you have to leave now. Please try to understand."

Understand? How could he understand if no one would tell him anything?

"But Gloria," he added hurriedly, "I'll still see you tonight, won't I?"

Gloria managed a tenuous smile. "Sure you will, as long as—we'll meet unless something—" Her smile fell, and her eyes were full of despair. "Oh, Simon, you'll know!"

The front door closed with a slam.

CHAPTER
TEN

IMON WALKED BACK
out to River Road like a man condemned.

"Oh, dear," Sneed remarked as the postman retrieved
his mailbag. "If you take that long to deliver every letter,
you'll never finish your route."

Simon hoisted his mailbag over his shoulder and
walked away. He didn't care anymore about Sneed's helpful criticisms. He didn't care, actually, about much of anything.

How could he care about things, after all, if no one
in Festeron would tell him about anything? Oh, he supposed he could understand some of their reticence. He
had been arrested for gambling on the Fun Pier, after all,
and his donning this postal uniform wasn't a job, it was a
criminal sentence. Still, he wished the people around here
would stop being so polite and actually tell him something. Simon sighed. He didn't know. Maybe everyone
around here was just too *nice* to tell him the truth.

Whatever that truth was.

Still, Simon had to admit, that wasn't what was really
bothering him. It was one thing when perfect strangers
offered their condolences and then refused to explain. But
when Gloria wouldn't talk to him either . . .

78

"I give up!"

Simon threw his postal cap to the ground. Why should he even bother delivering the mail? Why not just sit down here and wait for whatever it was that was going to get him to hurry up and finish its job?

Sneed scurried up to his side.

"Oh, my!" the little man exclaimed, new excitement in his voice. "I think we're almost far enough away from town!"

"Really?" Simon replied, not truly listening.

Sneed nodded conspiratorially. "Oh, dear, yes! And we do have more mail to deliver on River Road."

"I suppose," Simon muttered. "To be honest, Sneed, I don't know if I even feel like delivering it."

"Oh, but you must!" Sneed insisted. "It is your duty, after all. Besides which, it gets very interesting farther up River Road." Sneed pulled urgently at Simon's sleeve. "You'll be amazed just what kind of things you might hear when you're walking *that* far away from town!"

Simon stared at the little man. Wait a moment! Sneed was trying to tell him something. His companion had been hinting all along that he would tell Simon the secrets of Festeron when the time was right. Well, now Sneed was telling him that the right time was almost here! And Simon had been so lost in his lovesick funk, he almost hadn't heard him.

"Let's go," Simon remarked shortly as he shifted his sack to a more comfortable position on his shoulder. "We've got mail to deliver."

He walked quickly down the road, Sneed jogging at his side.

It was all the fault of that woman. Why did he let her get to him that way, anyway? And here he had started thinking that he wouldn't even escape from this crummy island, unless he could take her with him.

Well, maybe it took her slamming the door in his face, but Simon was finally coming to his senses. If Gloria didn't want to come along, he'd have nothing more to do with her.

Then again, she did say she might meet him tonight, if nothing changed.

If nothing changed? What was that supposed to mean? Sneed would have to answer some tough questions once they got far enough up the road to talk. Simon was going to find out about everything.

And then, once he knew what was going on around here, he'd know the most important thing of all—the best way to escape. And once he figured out his escape route, Gloria or no Gloria, he was out of here.

"Almost there," Sneed reassured him.

"Stop where you are!" A blue-clad figure stepped out of the woods. "I've been looking everywhere for you!"

One glance at the epaulets told Simon who it was, even before he looked up into the self-satisfied smile. Mr. Crisp had found him.

"I hope you're enjoying your first day as a postal carrier," the postmaster chuckled.

"We're getting along all right," Simon replied, wondering what Crisp was getting at.

"We?" Crisp raised a single eyebrow. "Ah, that already means you consider your mail sack as a personal friend! Yes, it's better if you accept things that way. It makes your lot so much easier!"

His mail sack? Simon had been talking about Sneed. He wondered if he should disabuse his boss about his fantasies of happy mail carriers, but thought better of it. He had the feeling that any time he objected to anything Crisp had to say, he would automatically be threatened with a return to the High Court of Festeron.

"Well, it's awfully nice to chit-chat with my employees, but that's not why I'm here," Crisp continued. "I want you to drop everything you have for a very special task."

Drop everything? How would he get to talk with Sneed?

"But the rest of my mail—" Simon began.

"Oh, we have objections, do we? Well, I'm sure the

High Court of Festeron would like to hear—" Crisp shook himself. "But I am overreacting. It is commendable that you care so much about your delivery route that you do not want to leave it until your work is through. Still, I am telling you the job I have for you now is more important. Give me your sack. I will keep it safe, back at the office. You will be able to finish your deliveries, well—" Crisp chuckled softly to himself, "—whenever you get back. Come on, now. Hand over the sack."

Simon did as he was told.

"That's a good postal carrier. Believe me, if you keep an attitude like this, we can really learn to work together!" Crisp pulled the sack away from Simon and let it fall to the ground.

"Now." Crisp reached into the inner pocket of his uniform. "This is what I've marched halfway around Festeron to give you." He pulled out an envelope. "It's special delivery."

He handed the letter to Simon, who turned it around to read the address:

Proprietor
The Magick Shoppe
Way-Up-On-Top-Of-The Hill
North Festeron, North Festeron YYZ3WWX45T-8974G

"Do you still have your map with you?" Crisp demanded.

Simon nodded, pulling the folded paper from his pocket.

"Good," Crisp replied. "The Magick Shoppe is across the bridge to the north, at the end of River Road." He glanced at his watch. "It closes in a little more than an hour, so you'd better hurry!"

With that, Crisp disappeared back into the woods, dragging the mail sack behind him.

Simon looked at the letter in his hand. Crisp had said

he would have to travel north to deliver it, the same way he had planned to walk up River Road in the first place. That wasn't so bad, then. Sneed could still tell him the secrets of Festeron while they walked.

But where was Sneed? Simon turned completely around, looking up and down the curving road, then deep into the forest on one side, and out to the beach on the other. But there wasn't another human to be seen, in a raincoat or otherwise attired.

Sneed must have scrammed when Crisp showed up. Well, Simon could understand that. He'd like to avoid Crisp whenever he could, too. Still, he wondered why the little man had made himself scarce. Could Mr. Crisp have something to do with Festeron's dread secret?

And where could Sneed have gone? Knowing the little man's physical peculiarities, Simon wouldn't have been surprised if he had simply evaporated where he stood. More likely, though, he had run farther up the road, heading toward that safe area where he would have told Simon his secrets.

Simon decided he'd go that way, too. With any luck, Sneed was out there waiting for him. And if not, at least he'd get this letter delivered. He'd find Sneed when he came back.

He pushed the letter into the same pocket that held the Acme Kitchen Wonder, and walked north up River Road.

He heard music up ahead. Rock and roll music, with lots of drums and guitars.

He realized this was the first time he'd heard any hard and fast music since he'd arrived here. Oh, sure, there'd been that wimpy pop stuff that they had played on the Festeron Fun Pier, and the soothing background music in his jail cell. And then there was that ridiculous Festeron National Anthem that seemed to get played everywhere. But this? Simon punched his fist in time to the power chords. This was a surprise. Festeron seemed like too nice a place for music like this. Simon started walking to the beat. This was the kind of music he could really get into.

The music got louder as he moved up the road. It was coming from the beach. Simon walked off the road, across the thin strip of green to the mix of pebbles and sand beyond. Something ahead of him shone in the late afternoon sun. Simon reached it just as the song ended.

It was a radio, small and silver, with a bright red dial. It fit in the palm of Simon's hand, and seemed to be made of some lightweight plastic with a thin coat of metallic paint. Simon wondered how old this thing was. He remembered radios like this from when he was a little kid, but he remembered the sound that came from their little speakers to be so tinny that you almost couldn't make out the music in the songs. This little radio put out more noise than a boom box. Just another example of the wonders of modern electronics, Simon guessed. But where had the radio come from?

An ad for pimple cream came and went as Simon stared at the tiny box. The announcer's voice boomed deeply from the minuscule speaker:

"You may already be a winner!"

It was another one of those midsummer contests. Simon guessed that radio stations were the same all over.

"That's right. You're entered in our WFES Winning Contest just by listening to WFES! And now it's time to announce this hour's lucky winner!"

The announcer's voice was replaced by a dramatic flurry of trumpets. The deejay came back on with a laugh.

"Well, let me dip my hand into the WFES Winning Contest barrel here. Let me get down deep. Okay. The lucky WFES winner for this hour is—let me turn the card over here so I can read it—Simon the Postman!"

The trumpets flurried again. Simon almost dropped the radio. What had the deejay said?

"That's right, Simon the Postman!" the announcer continued. "You're this hour's lucky WFES Winning Contest winner! Now all you have to do to win your very special prize is to visit the Festeron Magick Shoppe before it closes today! And, when you claim your prize, you'll be automatically entered in the WFES Winning Contest Grand Prize Drawing! That's right, Simon the Postman, you *could* win it all! And now back to more music. Here's Heavy Metal Thunder singing 'My Pants Are Too Tight'!"

Bashing guitars blared forth from the radio's tiny speaker, but Simon was no longer listening. This whole thing had passed beyond strange now, and had entered the totally weird. He had just won a contest which had him going someplace to which he was already delivering a letter. Simon didn't believe it could be a coincidence. At this point, he didn't quite believe anything Festeron had to offer. Someone must really want to get him to that magic shop.

Well, he guessed he should go, and quickly, too, before the place closed. He looked at the radio, and for a second considered putting it back down on the beach where he'd found it. Instead, he stuffed it into another one of his pockets. Someone had abandoned it out here, he reasoned. If they had wanted to keep it, they could have taken it with them. If it belonged to somebody else, Simon was sure he'd hear about it sooner or later; Festeron was that small. Besides, the way things were going today, he wouldn't be surprised if he had been meant to find and take this little radio.

But then, what did he know? Simon wished Sneed could have stuck around a little longer before disappearing.

He climbed back onto River Road and started walking north.

Miss Voss rose eagerly from the checkout desk when she heard the pounding on the door. She'd know that knock anywhere. She moved quickly to the front of the library, unlocking and opening the door in a single, fluid motion.

Mr. Crisp bounded into the room. She closed the door smartly behind him.

"It's done!" Crisp shouted, not quite suppressing a giggle. "He has the letter!"

Miss Voss was not so ready to celebrate. "I have met the young man. Are you so sure he will deliver it?"

Crisp sobered suddenly, as if the thought had never struck him. "He has to. It is a postal officer's duty!" The hint of a smile worked at the corners of his mouth. "And if he doesn't, there is always the High Court of Festeron!"

Miss Voss laughed girlishly, a somewhat disconcerting sound coming from one so prim. "It's so silly of me to doubt you, Corkie. You've thought of everything this time, haven't you?"

Crisp nodded, supremely self-satisfied. "Yes, my dearest. There is no way for him to escape. And, even better, once the wheels have been set in motion, he is not of sufficient moral fiber to do anything about it!"

"Oh, you have thought of everything!" she whispered fiercely.

"I've only done it for you, dearest," he replied, taking a step closer. His hand reached out for hers

She backed away. "No. You know it isn't right. Not yet."

"Forgive me." He withdrew his hand, clasping both hands together as if he might pray. "I was temporarily overcome. But soon it will be different."

"How I long for that moment!" she whispered passionately.

"I, too," he agreed. "But this time, all our preparations will bear the fruit we so richly deserve. This time, when our moment comes, it will last—"

"Forever!" she finished the sentence for him, their eyes meeting in a way that their bodies could not.

But everything would be very different, very soon.

PART TWO

"The Middle"

CHAPTER
ELEVEN

WHEN SNEED DISAP-
peared, he did it wholeheartedly. Simon didn't see anyone
at all for the whole length of River Road. He was doubly
glad now that he had taken the radio. It was the only
company he had.

He had been walking for a good twenty minutes or
more, as River Road had curved gradually to his right, so
that now he was walking almost due east. A couple of
minutes ago he had first spotted North Festeron Island to
his left. Now the new island crowded close to the main
body of Festeron, so that only a narrow channel of water
separated the two. Simon thought he saw something moving against the swiftly flowing current; fins of some sort,
maybe. He remembered the sharks. Well, swimming was
the last thing on his mind. He must be getting close to
the bridge Crisp had told him about.

The song on the radio ended, the last of "seven heavy
metal bashers in a row!" The announcer's voice shouted
in Simon's ear.

"That was the Boys Who Like to Dress Like Girls
singing 'Baby, Squeeze My Avocado'. And—this just in—
we understand that the Festeron Magick Shoppe has not
yet heard from our lucky contestant! WFES, the station

with that boom-boom sound, would like to remind Simon the Postman that he only has thirty-eight minutes left! And now for this—"

Simon turned the radio off. He didn't need to be reminded of how little time there was left before the magic shop closed. Besides, he had spotted the bridge to the other island ahead. There was someone standing at his end of the bridge, looking down River Road. Someone waiting for Simon.

He wondered for an instant if he had finally caught up with Sneed. But even at this distance, the person waiting looked altogether different. He stood up straight, with none of Sneed's characteristic slouch, and his dark uniform had none of the wrinkles held by the nondescript man's dirty raincoat. Besides, Simon didn't think Sneed would be caught dead wearing storm trooper boots.

"Vermin!" the distant man called. "Toadstool! Yeast infection!"

Simon would recognize that name-calling anywhere. It was Sergeant MacGuffin.

He quickly pulled the letter out of his postal uniform.

"Sorry, Sergeant MacGuffin!" he called as he approached, waving the letter before him. "Don't have time to talk! This is special delivery!"

"And you'd better get it there on time!" The policeman ran forward, grabbing Simon by the collar and propelling him toward the bridge.

"Yes, sir, Sergeant MacGuffin!" Simon called as the policeman gave him a final push.

"Lackey!" the sergeant called out after him. "Nosehair! Wombat feces! Just get that letter there—or else!"

Simon walked quickly across the bridge. To his relief, the policeman did not follow. The worn wooden planks creaked beneath his feet; there was no sound of any other footsteps following. When he reached the gravel path at the bridge's other end, Simon turned to look behind him.

Wishbringer

Sergeant MacGuffin had disappeared. Simon decided it was safe to turn the radio back on.

"Only twenty-seven minutes left for our lucky post-man to claim his prize!" the radio announced. Mr. Crisp, Sgt. MacGuffin, the radio announcer; everybody really wanted him to deliver this letter. Simon looked around at this new island, far more barren than Festeron. There was nothing around him here except dirt and dead trees. Simon seemed to be standing at the end of a well-worn path, or perhaps a dry stream bed, that wound its way towards the island's interior. Well, it was as good a way as any to look for his destination. Simon began to climb.

A moment later, he saw the first hint of color ahead. It was a sign, with blood-red letters painted on a glossy black background: "Magick Shoppe—This Way".

The sign pointed straight up.

Simon looked up at the sheer cliff before him.

It looked like he had a long, hard climb in front of him. Simon decided that he might as well have some music. He turned the radio up loud.

The radio was playing a golden oldie: "Stairway to Cleveland" by Roger and the Ramjets. Simon decided it was good climbing music.

It took him a good ten minutes, complete with two more songs, five commercials (two for soft drinks, one for the Fun Pier, another one for acne medication, and one set to a marching band about being a man's man in the Festeron Armed Services), and lots of deejay patter, before he reached the top of the hill.

Before him stood a single house, which dominated the flat plain around it, more of a rocky plateau than a hilltop, a jumble of gray slabs of weathered granite. Nothing grew up here, save for some sickly-looking scrub-brush that peeked out here and there from among the rocks, and a couple of stunted trees partially protected from the elements by the great bulk of the house.

And what a house it was: a great, hulking Victorian

structure, the same gray as the rock that surrounded it. It was a good three stories tall, four if you counted the cupola and widow's walk at the house's peak, and it seemed to lean toward Simon, as if, at any minute, the whole structure might pull itself free of its foundation and lumber straight for the startled postman. The house looked slightly out of place against the late afternoon light and almost-setting sun. Simon decided the place would look at home only under rolling clouds and streaks of lightning.

Part of the house had been converted into a store, for the corner of the structure nearest to Simon featured an oversized window displaying multicolored wares, above which hung a wooden sign that swung back and forth in the wind. Simon read the ornately produced words, golden on a field of royal blue: "Ye Olde Magick Shoppe".

The announcer's voice broke in to the middle of a song on the radio: "Time to remind Simon the Postman that he only has twelve more minutes—"

Yeah, yeah. Simon had had enough of that. He turned off the radio and walked over to the door beneath the sign.

The door opened with a squeal of hinges as he approached. Simon guessed he was expected. He walked into the shop. There was no one behind the door.

"Hello?" Simon called.

The door slammed shut behind him. There was no other sound, save for the wind outside. Simon, who was determined not to be startled by anything else that happened to him, decided to take a look around.

There was a small counter at the back of the store, behind which was a heavy black curtain that Simon assumed led to a storeroom of some sort.

"Hello!" Simon called again as he reached the counter. "I have a letter for you!"

There was still no reply. Would the proprietor leave the shop unattended? Simon decided to look behind the curtain. He stepped around the counter and reached for the black cloth with his free hand.

"Ow!" he exclaimed, for his fingers, instead of hitting cloth, had come up against something as hard as stone. What was this, a piece of granite carved to look like a curtain? He blew on his bruised knuckles. There obviously wasn't anybody hiding back there. He wondered if there were another storeroom door hidden somewhere around the shop.

He stepped back out from behind the counter to get a closer look at the stock. The place was filled with colorful displays, most of them novelties rather than magic tricks. He glanced at a pile of something called FUNTIME PEPPER GUM!—First they start chewing, then they start sneezing! He let his gaze wander up the wall, past the JOKE THROUGH-THE-HEAD ARROW! and the AMAZINGLY LIFELIKE PLASTIC BAT GUANO! Amuse your friends. Be the life of the party. He stopped to look at something called THE AMAZING SHELL GAME!—with enclosed instruction booklet full of helpful hints!—a package containing three plastic cups and a plastic pebble. He was the slightest bit disturbed that someone was merchandising his livelihood. Still, his setup somehow had a funky charm that you could never get in a package, and besides, it was all in the patter. He wondered if the enclosed instruction book included any helpful hints he hadn't used yet.

The wind blew against the house with redoubled force. He felt a breeze push against his postman's uniform and almost lift the cap from his head. It was surprisingly drafty in here.

"Hello?" he called one more time. There was still no answer.

A burst of static boomed from the radio.

"Just over a minute left for Simon the Postman to claim his prize!" the announcer's voice blared. Simon stared at the small box in his hand. Hadn't he turned that thing off?

The wind returned, this time with such a force that Simon could have sworn it originated within the shop rather than on the breezy hilltop outside. He found himself pushed back a step by the force of the gale.

"All right, okay!" an aged woman's voice called from behind the fluttering curtain. "I'm coming already!" The wind redoubled, blowing the heavy black curtain aside—the same curtain that had felt as hard as stone a moment before. A gray-haired lady stepped out into the shop, still fussing with the cameo that joined together the top of her starched white blouse. "Can't an old lady have any peace?"

"Hello!" Simon greeted her, once again turning off the radio. "I have a letter for you."

"How are you so sure it's me?" the woman demanded.

He pulled the special delivery letter from where he had stuffed it back in his pocket. "You are the proprietor, aren't you?"

"I suppose so." There was a weariness to the woman's reply. "If I wasn't, I suppose they'd find some other way to get that message to me. Whenever they start these things, they get awfully persistent."

Simon held the letter out to her. "So, are you going to take it?"

"I wish I didn't have to." The old woman sighed. "But weren't you going to tell me something about WFES?"

"You mean about the Lucky Winners' Contest?" Simon had almost forgotten about that.

The radio crackled to life. "You're a winner!" it exclaimed, before Simon turned it off again.

"Exactly!" The woman actually smiled. "That makes all this an entirely different matter. Why don't you open the letter for me?"

Simon looked at the envelope still in his hand. "Certainly, if you want me to. Did you forget your reading glasses or something?"

"Nonsense. My eyes are as sharp as the day I was born. It's just tradition. The postman always reads the message."

Simon dutifully ripped open the envelope, and pulled out a short, almost illegible handwritten note. He struggled to read it:

Dearest sister:

I have you now. Even as you read this, my minions (or manions, Simon wasn't quite sure) are taking over the country. And I have found the stone. There is no way you can stop me. By dawn tomorrow, Witchville will be forever!

Yours Cruelly,
The Evil One.

"The Evil One?" Simon asked.

The old woman nodded grimly. "She prefers it to her given name of Gladys. You read that very well. Her handwriting is atrocious."

Simon studied the letter in his hands. The writing was exceptionally blotchy and ill-formed, with letters slanting every-which-way. "Does it have something to do with her evil nature?"

"It has more to do with her having spent two years in medical school. But that was before she realized her true calling—supreme nastiness!"

"Really?" Simon mused. "I guess you can't do that if you're a doctor."

"Well, you can sometimes if you're a surgeon. But you're right. Nastiness does not generally make for a good bedside manner. So she turned to her new vocation— freelance dictatorship!"

"Around here? In Festeron?" Simon asked. What was she talking about? How could you dictate niceness?

"Not yet," the old woman replied, glancing at an ornate grandfather clock set up near the front door of the shop. "Festeron will still exist for another fifteen minutes or so. But when that clock strikes six, then she takes total control."

Festeron was only going to exist for another fifteen minutes or so?

"What happens at six?" he asked.

"Oh, the change occurs," the proprietor replied conversationally. "I could see it coming. This process has been going on for weeks. In a way, I suppose it's been going on for years. But I would suppose you would like some explanation?"

Simon simply nodded his head.

"Why don't you sit down?" the woman suggested, indicating an overstuffed chair crammed between a shelf of festive paper plates and a display of party hats. "This may take a while."

Simon sat, amazed that someone was finally going to tell him the truth!

"Very well." The old woman closed her eyes for a moment, as if ordering her thoughts. "Years ago, Festeron was naught but another sleepy island community. But there was a family in town that raised three young sisters. I was the eldest of the three. The youngest, and scrawniest, was Gladys, who now styles herself The Evil One.

"What can I say about those formative years? Gladys was a sickly child, and an unhappy one as well. She claimed that my mother and father, my sister Hortense and myself, in fact the whole town of Festeron, would go out of their way, any time, day or night, to pick on little Gladys. How much of that was real? Oh, you know as well as I that any family contains a certain amount of sibling rivalry, and perhaps parents aren't as fair with one child as with another. And true, there were a couple of bullies at school that picked on Gladys because of her size."

She paused, glancing from Simon to the grandfather clock, then back to Simon again.

"I guess what I'm trying to say is that we all share part of the blame for The Evil One's actions. But Gladys was always so melodramatic. From the time she was little, she always had a way of blowing things way out of proportion. And that, I am afraid, is what she will do again tonight." She paused again, her eyes returning to the clock.

"If you don't mind my asking," Simon went ahead and asked, "what is Gladys going to do?"

"Before I explain that, I'm afraid you'll need a bit more background." The proprietor clasped her hands behind her back, and paced down the aisle before him. "I have to tell you about the stone."

She stopped, staring beyond a display of joy buzzers and X-ray glasses. "There is something special about the two islands that make up the republic of Festeron. There is something here, whether it is location, or climate, or some element in the soil, or perhaps a combination of all three—and that something makes this place magic!"

"Magic?" Simon replied in disbelief.

"Oh, not like this!" She waved at the card tricks and scarf-producing cups before her. "Real magic. And one of the main sources of this magic is a stone, found upon this very hillside. The Wishbringer stone. The Evil One has wanted this stone for years for her own foul purposes; mainly, the conquest of our islands, then of the world beyond."

"The whole world?" Simon asked.

The proprietor nodded. "Gladys always did think big. That's why it will do you no good to escape. Once Gladys gets her way, she won't stop with Festeron, but will take our neighboring countries, and then their neighbors in turn, until she controls everything upon the surface of the Earth!"

Simon stared at the old woman. How did she know he was thinking about escape? Could she read his mind?

"Only when your thoughts are particularly transparent." The old woman laughed. "It's a talent my sisters and I have, but it's not as remarkable as it first appears. Quite frankly, if I were stuck working for Mr. Crisp at the Post Office, I would think about escape as well."

Simon shivered. Was this an example of Festeron magic?

"But I haven't really told you about the stone," the old lady continued. "You see, the one who possesses the Wishbringer stone is given certain magic powers, certain wishes, if you will, for luck, or freedom, or darkness, various things like that, useful when fighting The Evil One's minions. Generally, when I get one of The Evil One's notes, I give the stone to the postman or postwoman who delivered the letter to me. Then he or she gets to foil my sister's plans all over again."

"Generally?" Simon asked. "All over again? So this sort of thing happens often?"

"More than I like to think about it," the proprietor replied wearily. "This whole thing is like a game to my evil sister. She never seems to tire of it."

Simon nodded, trying to put his thoughts in order. The shopkeeper had dutifully answered every one of his questions. Why, then, did he feel even more confused than when he had walked into this place? He frowned at the flies-in-the-icecubes display by his left hand (Put them in your friend's drinks! A laff-riot at parties!) then looked again at the old woman. Perhaps, with a bit more explanation, everything would fall into place.

"So, let me get this straight." He spoke slowly, careful to choose just the right words. "Since I am the postman, it is my job to take this stone and somehow defeat your sister's plans?"

"Normally, that would be the case," the old woman replied. "You would be the guardian of the stone, which is the thing my evil sister desires most. For if she can take that stone, and, at the precise stroke of midnight place it in the forehead of the statue from which it originally came, her power will increase a thousandfold, and she will become virtually unstoppable."

"Normally?" Simon prompted.

"But not in this case," she explained. "You see, we no longer have the stone." The old woman laughed again. "Oh, they thought they were so clever! First, they steal the stone by subterfuge, then, with the aid of the High Court, they choose a postman who, in their opinion, was doomed to failure!"

"Failure?" Simon repeated. They thought he was a failure?

"Yes! Can you imagine their shortsightedness? They thought you a common criminal, a lowlife who would run at the first challenge. And that is where they made their first mistake."

"They thought what?" Simon exploded. Was that what the goody two-shoes in Festeron had thought of him? The nerve of those hypocrites. Sure, he had been in jail a time or two, but he was anything but a common criminal. And being called a lowlife because he ran a shell game? Simon had always considered himself an independent businessman.

"Exactly," the old woman continued. "But both you and I know that you are made of sterner stuff. Stuff that can defeat The Evil One and her minions for good."

So precisely what was this old woman proposing? Simon frowned. Whatever it was, it sounded difficult, perhaps deadly.

"Are you sure I just can't run away?" Simon ventured.

"There is no place you can run. You are the hero now, whether you like it or not. Besides this, there are other reasons you will not flee, but I will let you discover those for yourself."

"And I have to be a part of this?" Simon continued.

"There is no other way. Once the process has begun, I know of no way to change it. There is no turning back."

And with that, the clock by the door struck six times.

"That's it," the old woman intoned. "Festeron is no more."

CHAPTER
TWELVE

FESTERON WAS GONE?

"What happened to it?" Simon demanded. "Where are all the people?"

"Oh, the people are still there, along with the buildings, and streets, the whole island, in fact. But none of it is the same as it was before. The Evil One has transformed Festeron into Witchville!"

"Witchville?" Simon repeated in disbelief.

"I know, I know." The old woman nodded her head sympathetically. "My sister Gladys never was very good with names. But she calls it Witchville, and, through her power, it *is* Witchville!"

"And what, exactly," Simon found himself asking, "is a Witchville?"

The old lady moaned softly, deep in her throat. "It is an evil place. It is a vile place. It is a place you will not recognize."

Simon felt a panic rising within him. "But what about the people there?" He stumbled over his words in a vain attempt to control his emotions. "I—I haven't been here long, uh—but I've made some friends." Oh, heck. He might as well get it out in the open. "What I want to know is, what about this girl I met—her name is Gloria?"

"Gloria?" The old lady paused in thought. "Oh, the sweet young daughter of that professor."

So she did know Gloria! Simon wondered for an instant if the proprietor of the Magick Shoppe knew everyone in Festeron, and everything that ever happened there besides. He looked at the woman's clear, gray eyes. With a gaze like that, anything was possible.

"Yes, even she will be be profoundly changed," the old woman continued solemnly, her gray eyes boring into Simon's soul. "Sweetness and light cannot exist in Witchville. I suggest, in fact, that you avoid seeing her until Festeron has been rescued."

Not see her? But if Witchville was as evil as this old woman said, wouldn't Gloria be in danger? Simon realized he had to learn the odds before he tried to rescue her.

"And everyone is changed?"

"Some more than others." The old woman raised her eyebrows meaningfully. "Postmaster Crisp, Librarian Voss, Sergeant MacGuffin, and a few others will be more or less as they were, only more so. It is only when the island has been turned to Witchville that they may allow their natural proclivities free reign."

"Proclivities?" Simon wasn't quite sure what that meant, but he didn't like the sound of it.

"With them, nastiness becomes an art. Avoid them if you can. Besides that, remember: Nothing is the same as it was, and people who were your friends will be friends no more."

Simon pushed back his postal cap. "Then there's no more Gloria? And no more Sneed?"

The old woman looked at him oddly. "Sneed? What's a Sneed?"

Oh, Simon thought. So she didn't know everyone around here. He had been reading into this old woman's powers, making her omnipotent when, perhaps, she was merely knowledgeable with her years of island living. After all, what proof did he have of this so-called magic around her except for her telling him about it? Maybe, he thought, he should be a little more skeptical of her explanations.

"Just a little man I met," he replied when he realized she was still waiting for an answer.

"In Festeron?" She shook her head vehemently. "That's impossible. I know everybody in Festeron. I know what everybody does in Festeron, every minute of every day! There hasn't been a Sneed living in this town for twenty years!"

Really? Simon decided to let the comment go. There were still too many things he needed to learn from the old woman. He didn't have time to contradict her.

Besides which, he thought this was a very interesting development. Maybe there were things the shopkeeper didn't know after all. Simon wondered if The Evil One would be equally ignorant. Perhaps their blind spots would give him a way to triumph. Or perhaps he could find a way out of this place after all.

"You're thinking about escape again," the proprietor informed him. "I can see it in the way your eyes shift all over their sockets. I suppose I must tell you one more thing about The Evil One."

She stopped her pacing, and pointed at Simon with a magic wand that had somehow appeared in her hand. "You, as the postman, are a central figure in this little drama, and it is even more important to my sister than to me that you play out your part. If she captures you, you are in trouble. If she captures you and discovers that you have been trying to escape from the island—well, trouble is no longer a strong enough word for what you'll have gotten yourself into. Let me just say that you'll find yourself wishing you had a less painful death, say, being nibbled slowly, over a period of hours, by the sharks in Festeron Harbor. Do I make myself clear?"

Simon nodded. Apparently, he was in the post office for good.

The old woman nodded back, satisfied that she had made her point. "So that's it in a nutshell. Festeron is under the spell of The Evil One, and only you can save us."

"But how do I do that?" Simon asked. "You mentioned a stone?" But hadn't she also said that the stone was missing?

"Ah, the Wishbringer stone." The woman pulled back the wand and let it tap across the bridge of her nose. "Yes, there's real magic there."

"Real magic?" Simon repeated, intrigued despite himself. "Where would something like this come from?"

The old woman looked at him conspiratorially. "Well, there's this legend about knights and fairy princesses, but I think it's all a bunch of bullhooey. In my opinion, the stone came from outer space.

"But I forgot." She rapped the wand against the counter in consternation. Scarves erupted from the plastic cylinder, shooting up to the ceiling. "You're a winner!"

Simon's radio came to life again.

"That's right, Simon the Postman is this hour's big WFES winner!"

Simon stared at the small plastic box. It was getting so he expected the radio to turn itself on.

"And let's ask the proprietor of the Magick Shoppe," the announcer's voice continued. "What has this hour's WFES Lucky Winner Contest winner actually won?"

"Why, thank you, radio," the old lady replied. "Let's take a look and see." She leaned over the counter, grabbing a brown paper bag from a shelf built against the back wall. She stood and handed the bag to Simon.

"Open it," she instructed.

Simon opened the bag and reached inside. He pulled out something that felt like molded plastic.

"That's right!" the old woman exclaimed. "The lucky

WFES winner has won an official pair of Festeron Magick Shoppe Magick Glasses!"

The radio cheered.

Magic glasses? Simon looked down at what he held in his hand. Black plastic frames, complete with brown eyebrows, attached to a pink plastic nose and a brown plastic mustache beneath. These were magic?

The radio cheered again.

"That's enough, radio," the old woman chided.

"This is WFES, signing off!" the radio replied cheerfully, followed by a loud click, then silence.

"There," she remarked with finality. "Unfortunately, small appliances must sometimes be reminded of their functions. It's not their fault, exactly. They simply get overly enthusiastic."

She pointed at Simon's prize. "But why don't you try them on?"

Well, what did he have to lose? Simon slipped the fake plastic nose over his own, tucking the earpieces of the frames behind his earlobes.

"Now look around the shop," the old woman suggested.

Simon did as she asked, turning away from her to look down the nearest aisle. It did look different. Most of the brightly colored merchandise that filled the shop had turned to a dull brown. There were a few things, though, that appeared to glow with an inner light. A mask on the wall was bright pink, a box on the counter a brilliant turquoise, a package down the aisle a softly pulsating salmon.

"What is it?" he asked in an awed whisper.

"These glasses show you the world as it really is," the old woman explained. "Most of the novelties in this store are not worth the ingredients that went into them. You therefore see them represented as brown—a perfectly symbolic color. There are a few things in this shop, however, that are truly magic, and the glasses will show you every one."

It was true. The radio glowed yellow at his side. But there was another light, coming from below. Simon yelped. He realized his coat pocket was glowing bright green. He pulled out the Acme Kitchen Wonder. It gleamed fluorescently.

"Oho!" the proprietor exclaimed. "Hortense is in on this, too?" she chuckled. "Gladys doesn't know what she is in for."

"Hortense?" Simon asked.

"The woman who lives on Festeron Circle," she explained. "My sibling—the middle of the three sisters. But I would suggest you put the Acme Kitchen Wonder back in your pocket. And take off those glasses as well. They can be very useful at times, especially when you believe someone is trying to hoodwink you. They are, unfortunately, fairly fragile, and you would not want to break them at an inopportune moment."

Simon repocketed the Kitchen Wonder and took the glasses off. The shop returned to multicolored clutter.

"So now what happens?" he asked. "Do you give me the stone? Or tell me how to get it? You said it wasn't here?"

"Normally, that would be the case. The postman gets the Wishbringer stone, and must make sure it is not delivered into the wrong hands. This time, however, we have changed the rules. You see, The Evil One already has the stone."

"What?" Simon blurted out. "She's already gotten what she wants? How did she get control of something so powerful?"

"I let her have it," the old woman replied smugly. "She, of course, thinks she stole it from me."

That was it. That was enough. Something in Simon snapped.

"Wait a moment," he demanded. "I was made the postman, which means I'm somehow supposed to save Festeron from this Evil Person, and if I try to do anything else, I'll die a slow and painful death. But the way to save Festeron is to keep her from using this Wishthingy stone. Except you've given the stone to her already! Tell me, do you like to fail?"

"There, there," the old woman replied reassuringly. "No one's going to fail, especially not you. I saw that special drive in you as soon as you set foot in Festeron, and I'm never wrong. Well, hardly ever, and those few times were caused by extraneous circumstances. I mean, how could I know that one postman could die a hideous—but I'm wandering. The Evil One has the stone, this is true. But when Gladys swiped the magic rock, she also swiped a little extra spell I placed upon it, a spell that becomes activated only when Festeron is turned to Witchville."

She chuckled again. "Oh, what a clever Magick Shoppe owner am I. The minute Witchville appears, the stone disappears. It becomes invisible, you see, and furthermore moves three feet to the left of wherever it had last been in Festeron. So Gladys will have cast her spell with no way to complete it! For no one can see the magic Wishbringer stone, unless they use the magic glasses."

"These?" Simon waved the plastic frames he still held in his hand.

"Exactly." The old woman smiled gleefully. "They thought they could win by choosing a postman of ill repute, then stealing the stone from under my nose. But nothing is quite as it seems, is it? They decided to change the rules on me, so I simply changed the rules back on them. And this time, we are going to win."

Simon was glad the old woman was so happy about all this. Still, he had a couple of problems with this whole setup.

"And what am I supposed to do?"

"Simply capture the stone from her before the night is through. Without the stone, Gladys is helpless, and Festeron will return with the dawn."

The large grandfather clock struck once. Simon

looked at the painted dial. Half an hour had gone by in explanation.

"But I have spoken enough," the proprietor declared. "On your way, postman, you have much to do before dawn!"

"But—" Simon began. Before he knew what happened, he was walking through the front door of the shop.

"Oh, yes!" a voice called over his shoulder. "Don't forget your radio." He felt the small plastic box shoved into his free hand, then heard the door slam behind him.

He couldn't tell if the world outside the magic shop had changed or not. In fact, he couldn't see a foot in front of him. The world outside the shop was blanketed with a thick gray fog.

CHAPTER
THIRTEEN

WHAT SHOULD HE DO now? The old woman had given him a task, and not given him a single clue on how to go about it. He had to somehow rescue this Wishbringer stone, or Festeron, and perhaps the rest of the world beyond Festeron, would soon be subjugated beneath The Evil One's dictatorial cruelty. And, if he did not rescue the stone, and was captured instead, he would be subject to a death too hideous to comprehend. Simon thought for a moment. Yes, that seemed to sum up his options.

How did he always get himself into these things?

More to the point, how was he going to get himself out of this?

He looked out into the fog; it was opaque and still. He supposed his only option was to venture out into the grayness, and somehow get back down to the other island. He took a tentative step over the uneven rock of the plateau, then another and another. At least he could see where he was putting his feet, although the terrain grew hazy a few inches beyond his toes.

Simon stopped. It was so still. The only noise was the sound of his running shoes scuffing against the rocks.

There was no wind, no rustle of branches or bushes. Why, then, did he feel as if someone was watching him?

Simon turned around so quickly he almost lost his balance. There was nothing around him but gray. No landmarks, no setting sun or rising moon. Even the house that held the magic shop had disappeared. Everything was lost in the all-conquering mist.

Simon forced himself to laugh. This was nothing but his imagination, combined perhaps with this strange weather. How could anyone see him when he could barely see his hand at the end of his arm?

How indeed? His laugh had sounded awfully hollow, as if the noise had been swallowed by the fog the instant it emerged from his mouth. This fog didn't seem natural. Could it be a part of The Evil One's plans, some extension of whatever had happened to Festeron? He remembered now what the shopkeeper had called it: Witchville. Maybe, then, this fog had been caused by witches. Or by just one witch, who was watching him now?

Simon dismissed the thought as soon as it entered his head. He had no rational reason to believe anything of the sort was happening to him.

Then again, he had no rational reason to believe anything that had happened to him in Festeron, either.

The fog, if anything, seemed even more solid than before. He could see tendrils of it reaching out to caress his fingers and twist around his arms. The fog was cold where it touched his skin; far too cold. He felt isolated, lost in the silent, icy fog, the grayness closing in about him, a fraction of an inch closer here and there, almost touching his head, fondling the laces of his sneaker. He wondered, when the fog closed him in completely, if it would silence him as well.

Maybe he should whistle. Anything to fight this silence.

But he could do better than whistling. He was letting this fog get the better of him, getting between Simon and his common sense. He had resources: things given to him by the proprietor of the magic shop, not to mention his own quick wit. And he couldn't think of anything that could better dispel the mood of the fog than a little head-bashing music.

He turned on the radio, twisting the volume knob toward maximum. It came to life with a burst of static. And then, nothing but white noise.

He frowned. Where was WFES? Maybe it went off at sundown. For all Simon knew in this fog, it could be sundown. But there had to be other radio stations around here. He twisted the dial slowly. There was nothing but more static all the way to the low end of the dial. He turned the knob the other way, and was rewarded at last by a burst of music.

He turned back to the strong signal. The music was fading. Did he hear violins? An announcer's voice came on, smooth and deep:

"And that was the Million and One Strings, performing the Chuck Berry Medley. And this is 1313 on your radio dial, WTCH. Now that you've got us tuned in, you'd better listen!"

The announcer's voice was replaced by commercials for house siding and insurance.

Violin versions of rock and roll? The horrendous face that Simon made was masked by the fog. He hated that sort of thing; syrupy swirling strings that sucked all the original spirit from the music. There had to be something else on this radio.

There wasn't.

Simon twisted the dial back and forth three times before he gave up. At least up on this plateau, his choice of radio stations was limited to one.

"Welcome back to WTCH," the announcer's oily voice remarked. "The music you're going to hear, whether you like it or not. And now, here's the Ray Gandalf Singers, and their version of 'Land of a Thousand Dances'."

The music began with a percussive throb—castanets clacking against the beat of a large bass drum. Maybe, Simon thought, this wouldn't be so bad. He was still amazed by the amount of sound the radio's tiny speaker put out. Then the syrupy strings began to whine, followed by the even more syrupy voices.

"No one can boogaloo, like I do—"

Simon saw movement at the edge of his vision. His head snapped up. It was the fog, pulsating in time to the music. The Ray Gandalf Singers were making the cloud tendrils go wild. The fingers of fog thrashed against each other over and over again, precisely on the beat. It was as if the bits of mist clacked together, rather than the castanets.

Simon wasn't sure if this development was good or bad. True, the fog was no longer quietly creeping. Violent thrashing, however, could not necessarily be categorized as an improvement. He did not relish having to walk through a pulsating weather pattern.

If only he could see through this murk!

And then he realized that maybe he could. He was carrying more than just a radio. He reached into his pocket and retrieved his magic plastic glasses. Slipping the still-broadcasting radio into his recently vacated pocket, he put the glasses on with both hands, careful to place the artificial pink nose securely over his own.

He blinked. The fog was gone, replaced by the early evening sky, the sun low in the west.

The Ray Gandalf Singers faded. The silence was broken by the announcer's overly-smooth tones.

"And now it's time for a little traveling music. Here's Peggy Como, with her version of 'I Can See Clearly Now'."

Huh? Simon shook his head. The choice of that song had to be a coincidence. Still, there was something about this radio that made him vaguely uneasy. There was something about everything here that made him uneasy.

He tilted the glasses down so that he could look over

the tops of the frames, and was confronted again by the impenetrable wall of gray. With the glasses back in place, though, he could see out to the edge of the plateau and across to the other island, underneath a cloudless sky. What was it that the old lady had told him? The glasses showed him only what was real? Something like that. So the fog wasn't real, but rather, he guessed, a product of magic. If the fog had itself been the source of the magic, he imagined he would have seen an impenetrable glow when he donned the magic glasses. Instead, he could now see it, or *not* see it, for the illusion it was. But who was producing this illusion? The Evil One? Was it part of this whole Witchville thing?

Simon decided he had had enough of this fumbling around in the dark. If he was supposed to save the fair island of Festeron, and his own hide in the bargain, he wanted to have some idea how to do it. He'd go back to the old lady and demand some answers. He turned around to face the magic shop.

It was gone. Oh, the house was still there, large and looming. But whatever corner had held the display window and sign had changed, and now held nothing more than weathered boards and peeling paint.

Did that mean that the magic shop had been an illusion as well? Or did the little store cease to exist as soon as Witchville took over?

Simon turned again, and thought he saw something in the cloudless sky, a great outline running from horizon to horizon. For an instant, he thought it might be some sort of reflection of the setting sun in the lenses of the glasses he wore. But then he remembered that the glasses he wore were nothing but empty plastic frames. He turned back to stare at the sky, and caught the image as it faded away into midnight blue. The disappearing form was huge, maybe fifty feet from top to bottom and a hundred feet across, and, because of its size, it took him a minute to register just what it was he saw. But the shape was familiar. And the movement.

The fading form blinked, and was gone.

It had been a pair of giant eyes, staring right at him.

Simon spun about wildly, trying to take in every point of the rapidly darkening sky. But he could see nothing but a band of color where the sun touched the horizon in the west, and the first faint glimmer of the eastern stars.

A noise came to him softly from very far away, a high, trilling sound. Maybe it was the wind, Simon told himself. And maybe it was an old woman's chuckle.

The song ended on the radio.

"That was 'I Can See Clearly Now', our traveling music," the announcer announced. "So why aren't you traveling?"

Simon reached into his pocket and turned off the radio. What the announcer had said was true; it wasn't doing him any good to stand around on this plateau and brood. He needed to do something, and fast. The first thing, he decided, was to get off this windswept hill. Then he would get over to the other island, and find out what happened to the one person that really mattered to him. Because, no matter what else he was supposed to do, his life here in Festeron began with Gloria.

PART THREE

"The End—Or Is It?"

CHAPTER
FOURTEEN

THERE WAS A KNOCK on the door, a firm knock, the kind that could only be made by a muscular, male hand with hard, virile knuckles. Violet's breath caught in her throat as she pictured that hand, and her heart stopped for an instant as she remembered how talented those long, male fingers could be. For she knew that knock, and the very act of fist striking wood filled her with an almost overwhelming desire.

The knock came again, and her perfect lips curled ever-so-slightly into a playful smile. She should let him wait for but another instant, and let his anticipation grow almost to the breaking point, so that, when she should open the door, dressed as she was in her daring scarlet gown with its tight bodice and plunging neckline, its full, flared skirt and three-quarter sleeves, with her long, ebony tresses pulled back behind her head and caught within the simple golden clasp, which was matched by the plain elegance of the large gold hoops she wore in either ear, earrings that gave her delicate, moon-shaped face a sense of mystery—when he saw her at last, in her beauty, could he be anything but overwhelmed—even helpless—before her, until he was forced by a power greater than intellect to rain kisses upon her face and neck.

"Coming!" Violet called as she slipped her dainty feet into her elegant black open-toed heels that added three inches to her height and gave her legs the sleekness and contour of a gazelle in full flight. She pouted at the mirror for an instant, tucking away an errant strand of hair, then moved quickly to the door. The brass knob felt sensuously cool to her touch as she twisted it with her long, tapered fingers capped by fashion nails. She pulled the knob toward her, and the massive oak door swung wide to reveal her love.

He stood on the front step, casually regarding her through half-closed eyes. His postmaster's uniform looked newly cleaned and pressed, so that the gold braid at the shoulders shone in the fading sunlight. The square cut of the cloth made his upper body look even more massive than she already knew it was, a great, sleek engine of power lurking within those post-office blues. He pulled off his cap and ran his free hand through his hair, tousling his mass of curly golden locks just barely tinged with gray.

His firm, broad mouth opened, and he uttered one word, his voice a mix of bass and gravel:

"Violet."

She gasped involuntarily. When he said her name like that, she felt as if her knees would no longer support her, as if the ecstasy that rushed through her form would turn every muscle to liquid, and she would collapse, helpless, before him.

But no. She forced herself to breathe deeply, conscious that, should she hold herself together, there would be greater ecstasy still to come.

She looked up into his stern green eyes, flecked with brown, and said his name in turn. No, more than just his name; her special way of calling him.

"Corkie."

He grabbed her shoulders violently, the force of his fingers sending shockwaves down her spine.

"It drives me mad when you say that," he breathed.

Her full, crimson lips smiled ever so slightly.

"Corkie," she said again.

His firm lower jaw trembled ever so slightly. "Oh, Violet." He took a ragged breath. "Violet."

"Corkie," she whispered throatily, knowing that every word was like a love arrow in his heart. "Corkie. Corkie. Corkie."

Neither of them could bear it a moment longer. They embraced, tenderly, passionately.

Violet felt a firm hand grasp her chin, guiding her face upwards, so that once again she gazed into the eyes of her beloved. His firm, manly lips were but a few inches from hers, so soft now, so pliant, so needful of his kisses. She breathed deep, filling her lungs with the masculine scent of the post office, as she felt her eyes close and lips part, ready to give herself totally.

"Perhaps," he whispered, "we should go inside."

Her eyes fluttered open to look at that assured smile and the faint gleam of mischief in his eyes. Oh, she wanted him more than ever now! But he was right. Festeron—staid, dull, dependable, blue-nosed, don't do anything because the neighbors might be watching Festeron—was no more. It was Witchville now. And in Witchville, you could do whatever you wanted. But in Witchville, you also had to watch your back. In Witchville, you could abandon yourself to your desires, but it was best to do it behind locked doors.

"Come inside, then," she whispered back, taking a step into the library. She clasped his hand in hers and drew him after her. Once they were both inside, she shut the massive oak door, pushing against the brass doorknob, so cold, so shiny, so hard. The door groaned shut, slamming with an exclamation that echoed through the long, narrow, empty corridors.

She looked around at the walls, the floors, the checkout desk. Everything in here was made of dark, dark wood. When this place was Festeron, it seemed quiet, reserved, respectful. But when this place was a part of Witchville, it changed, like everything on the island changed, and the wood-paneled walls and shining floors began to remind her of a pirate galleon, bound for Tortuga with a prize ripped from a Spanish merchant ship.

And what could that prize be? Rich silks, certainly, and chests full of gold. And perhaps a young, virginal maiden, sent across the ocean to marry a man—a governor perhaps—that she has never met. Oh, but it is not to be, for the pirates have taken her as a special prize, to be touched only by their Prince of Barbary, who stands at last, facing her, ravishing her with his eyes.

Her lover surveyed the room as well. He glanced quickly over the piles of books and card-catalogue drawers that littered the shelves, then paused when his eyes fell upon the large green couch that dominated one wall.

"What a soft couch," Violet remarked.

"What an ample couch," Crisp replied.

She could stand it no longer. She rushed into her beloved's arms, urging him back toward the waiting furniture.

"Everything I own is yours," she whispered. "Everything I am is yours."

Her man took half a step away, and looked at her with an intensity she had never known. The arms that held her trembled with emotion as he bent his head forward to kiss her.

There was a noise like a rusty cheese grater scraping unevenly across a blackboard. Both of the lovers looked up, the moment broken.

Maybe it was just the wind.

Or perhaps it was laughter.

"We have a job to do," he whispered.

"Now?" she replied. No matter how hard she tried to be brave, she couldn't keep her lips from trembling.

He made a sound, half sigh, half moan, as if it was a struggle for him as well. "You heard it as well as I. She's reminding us that there is work to be done."

But as soon as he had finished speaking, a shudder went through the length of his body, as if to release a flood of emotion that he could no longer hold.

"Why?" he railed at the ceiling. "Why must it always be like this? Why must we always wait? This time we have everything in our favor. She already has the stone, and the one we've chosen for postman is a dishonest fool. How can we help but win?"

The amorous librarian placed cool fingers upon her lover's cheek in an effort to calm him. "There is no way we can lose," she said soothingly. "Still, you cannot fault The Evil One. We have been close so many times. Somehow, despite all our efforts, that little thief we chose to be postman might succeed despite himself. She has to be sure."

"And what will it take her to be sure?" her lover replied, calmer now, but with his voice still tinged with despair.

"There is only one way," she replied firmly. "The postman must die."

He nodded grimly, a new resolve setting his firm and manly chin.

"I must do it myself."

"No, my love," she replied, again stroking his cheek. "We will do it together."

"Yes, together," he whispered, as if the word might give him strength. "Together."

And with that, he pushed away from her, a soft moan escaping his lips, an exclamation of pain that they must be apart. With a start, she realized that she had cried out as well.

"Together," he said one last time, looking down into her eyes, just beginning to brim with tears.

But she had to be brave!

"Just one last task," she whispered, nipping playfully at his long and manly nose with her delicate white teeth. "One last postman to be rid of, and we will be together forever."

CHAPTER
FIFTEEN

PEBBLES SHOT OUT FROM
beneath his feet. He staggered back, barely keeping his
balance, and heard the rocks he had dislodged fall fifty
feet below. Simon cursed. Even with his magic glasses, it
was hard to find his way down the path in the gathering
gloom. He had to keep his left hand brushing against the
sheer cliff-face as he inched down the narrow path.

At this rate, he was afraid he'd spend all night just getting down to the bridge between the islands. And it didn't
help that he had this distracting green light in his pocket that
he kept seeing out of the corner of his magic glasses.

Unless he could somehow use that green light—

Simon pulled the softly glowing Acme Kitchen Wonder box from his pocket and opened the flap at the top.
The box's contents were so blinding that he had to look
away for a moment. He reached inside the container and
felt cold metal and plastic beneath his fingers. He turned
back to squint at the Kitchen Wonder as he slowly pulled
it free. A small white booklet came out with it; the directions, Simon imagined, or perhaps a warranty of some
sort. He stuffed the paper back in the box. He would have
to read it when there was more light.

. The Kitchen Wonder itself still looked more or less as it did before, half jackknife, half raygun,. except that now it glowed with an amazingly virulent green, like a key lime pie left over from the kitchen at a nuclear accident. As Simon stared at it, however, he discovered that his eyes were gradually adjusting to the magical brightness, so that he could now discern details on the Kitchen Wonder's surface that he hadn't seen before: various bumps and grooves that all looked as if they had a purpose, including a button toward the bottom that looked very much like a flashlight's on-off switch.

Simon pressed the button, and the Wonder made a slight whining noise. What had he done? Things seemed to be moving on the kitchen object's upper surface. He hoped this Acme device wasn't dangerous. He had the sudden urge to drop it and back away. No, he was being foolish. This thing had been given to him by a nice old lady. Then again, wasn't The Evil One supposed to be an old lady?

He turned the thing over to get a better look at the moving parts and was almost blinded by a beam of yellow light.

"Oow!" Simon shouted, stumbling back up the path, stopping just as his left heel slipped from the edge of the cliff. The Kitchen Wonder almost fell from his startled fingers. He swung his free hand around to steady his grip, . careful to maintain his balance as well. Now that he knew the Kitchen Wonder did function as a flashlight, it wouldn't do to lose it (or himself, for that matter) off the side of the cliff.

He carefully stepped forward so that both his feet were firmly on the path, then decided he could resume breathing. Once he had blinked sufficiently to let his eyes again recover from the sudden flash of light, he allowed himself to experiment with the Kitchen Wonder's beam. It was a strong, narrow shaft of light, clearly illuminating the path some twenty feet ahead. In other directions, of course, it showed nothing but sheer cliff or empty air.

Simon decided it was high time he got down from here. With the aid of his magic glasses and the Kitchen Wonder's beam, he began to walk down the path at a more or less normal pace, ignoring the occasional pebble he kicked off the ledge as it fell through thirty seconds of silence before hitting softly, far below.

In a few minutes the path widened. A moment after that, the beam caught the movement of tiny waves. He had reached the bottom of the plateau, and now stood on the island's edge. Simon didn't know when he had been happier to see sea level. The flashlight beam picked up the dead tree ahead. He walked past it. In a moment he should reach the bridge. He turned the corner, past a final outcropping of rock.

The bridge had changed. It was no longer a simple wooden frame with a "You are now leaving/Welcome to Festeron" sign hanging above its center. It was much larger, more complicated, and heavily lit besides. Simon peered above the tops of his glasses, but the bridge looked no different than it had a moment before. Something had changed, though.

He realized he had left the fog behind.

Simon carefully took off the glasses and folded them, tucking them into the inside pocket of his postman's jacket. The woman in the magic shop had said the magic spectacles were very fragile. It would be best not to take chances. He expected he would need the glasses again.

The radio burst to life with a roar of static. He must have nudged it when he reached inside his jacket.

"—Love'," the announcer's voice began, "as played by the Cleveland Symphonic Polka Orchestra, from their new album 'Led Zeppelin in Polka Time'. But now it's time for our traffic report."

Traffic report? Simon had never seen a car in Festeron. But then again, looking at the newly overbuilt bridge in front of him, maybe there were cars, and a whole lot of other new things, in Witchville.

But the radio was distracting him. He turned it off, and, as quietly as possible, approached the bridge.

Actually, on closer inspection, it appeared that the original wooden bridge was still there. It had, however, been heavily modified, with a dozen steel girders that rose high overhead, each girder supporting a large glaring white light that shone down on the bridge below. There were other additions to the structure as well. An iron gate had been built across the midsection of the bridge, neatly bisecting it. Behind this closed gate was a small shack that somehow looked as if it had been there for years rather than hours. Simon guessed it was a guardhouse of some sort.

He didn't see any guards. Maybe he'd be lucky, and there wouldn't be any. Maybe he'd be even luckier, and discover that the iron gate, though closed, was still unlocked. Maybe he'd be luckier still and wake up from all this.

He waited a moment, but nothing changed. Just as he suspected, he was already awake and this was really happening. He guessed it was time to check out the no-guards and open-gate theories.

He stepped onto the bridge. The old boards made a hollow sound under his shoes. He tried to walk more quietly. Maybe, if there was a guard, he might be sleeping. He went up on tiptoes and stepped forward with exaggerated care. The next board creaked. Oh well, it was less loud than the pounding of his sneakers. Now, if he could just be a little more careful—

"BUT DON'T GO AWAY!" The radio turned itself back on with a rush of static. "THAT'S RIGHT! DON'T TOUCH THAT DIA—" Simon tore the radio from his pocket, almost ripping the jacket in the process, and managed to turn the volume level all the way down to off. Why did it keep turning itself on? And so loudly, too? It must have a loose connection somewhere.

"Ey?" a voice yelled from the direction of the guard-house. "Somebody say somethin'?"

Simon's heart sank. There was a guard here after all. His luck seemed to be running true to form. He suspected the unlocked-gate theory was shot, too. Oh, well. He stood absolutely still, waiting for the guard to appear. Maybe, just maybe, there was a way he could talk himself out of this.

Nobody moved. The guard didn't say another word. Everything was silent. Too silent, now that Simon thought about it. Weren't there any insects in Witchville?

After a minute, Simon took another cautious step forward. This board groaned as he put his weight on it. Simon froze, but there was still no response.

Maybe the guard had been sleeping after all. And maybe he'd gone back to sleep again. Simon certainly didn't see any movement around the guardhouse.

He crept as quietly as he could up to the iron gate.

"AND DON'T TURN US OFF AGAIN!" the radio screamed to life. "YOU STILL HAVEN'T HEARD THE TRAFFIC REPORT!"

Simon grabbed the radio again, twisting the dial to reduce the volume to a level that wouldn't puncture his eardrums.

"Whozat?" a gruff voice called from the guardhouse.

"That's better," the announcer's voice continued. "And here's Officer Glen with your traffic update."

"Thanks, Stan," another voice replied. "Well, things are pretty quiet in Witchville at the moment. Over in the graveyard, a few doomed souls are running for their lives—uselessly, I might add. And the Boot Patrol has begun their rounds. For those of you wishing to avoid them since, after all, the curfew is in effect, I would suggest steering clear of the Fun Pier for the next half hour or so, then staying off the roads to the north. Besides that, I really see only one potential problem, up on the north bridge, where Simon the Postman is about to get eaten by an ogre."

"Okay, Officer Glen," the first announcer's voice replied. "Thanks for that update. Keep listening to WTCH, Radio 1313. Your life may depend on it. And now a word from—"

"Whozat, I said?" the guardhouse voice bellowed even more gruffly than before.

Simon looked up from where he had been staring at the radio. Simon the Postman was going to be eaten by an ogre? How did they know? What sort of radio was this, anyway?

The door to the guardhouse swung open violently, slamming hard against the iron gate.

"Ey?" the guard continued shouting as he emerged from the shed. "Answer me! You know what happens to things that don't answer me!" His feet clomped across the bridge, ten times louder than any noise Simon had made. Simon was surprised that anything human could make such a racket.

And then he saw that the guard wasn't human. For one thing, he—or perhaps it—was eight feet tall, with bright pink skin that showed in a dozen places where the too-small guard's uniform had ripped. The thing turned to regard Simon, and the postman noted that, rather than teeth, the guard seemed to have two long tusks protruding from its lower jaw and rising to either side of its flat and wrinkled nose.

This, Simon thought, is the ogre the radio was talking about. The ogre that was going to eat him.

"There you are!" The ogre frowned at him. At least, Simon thought, it looked like a frown. With those tusks, it was hard to tell. "So speak up!"

"Uh," Simon replied somewhat lamely, not sure how to address an ogre. "Hello."

"Much better," the ogre replied. "You have to speak up to ogres." It took a shambling step towards Simon. The bridge shook as it shifted its weight. "Those that don't speak up get eaten."

"Oh, I see," Simon added hurriedly. "I'll speak up anytime. I'm quite a good conversationalist, really." He tried to smile at the creature, but the sight of those tusks seemed to make his facial muscles freeze. Instead, he added: "Now, however, I have to cross the bridge."

"Ey?" The ogre's tusks bounced up and down, as if the huge creature was silently laughing. "Oh, do you now? That's another matter entirely. This is a toll bridge, you know." The ogre took another step in Simon's direction. "Are you ready to pay the toll?"

"Toll?" Simon replied. "A money toll?"

"It's one way to pay it," the ogre answered, looking slightly disappointed.

Simon quickly dug into his pockets. Maybe he could still get out of this encounter unscathed. Yes, he did feel a few coins; the remains of his winnings from the Festeron Fun Pier.

He pulled the coins from his pocket and showed them to the ogre, still on the other side of the gate. At that moment, Simon decided he had never been so glad to see iron bars in his life.

"Here," Simon said. "How much do you need?"

The ogre's long taloned hand flashed though the gate, bending the bars to either side. It knocked Simon's hand aside with a single hairy pink knuckle. The coins went flying into the sea.

"That's Festeron money, worthless in Witchville. And it's all you have, hmm?" The ogre's purple tongue licked quickly from tusk to tusk. "Well, I suppose we might be able to make other arrangements."

Simon took a step away. "Other arrangements?"

The ogre nodded happily. "They don't feed me enough on this job, you see. I have to make up for it on my own."

"Then you want me to get you some food," Simon ventured.

"Ey? Oh, certainly not. I wouldn't think of putting you out. After all, the food is already here." The ogre's tongue showed itself again. "I won't ask for much, now. A hand and arm to the elbow, perhaps? Or maybe a foot to the knee. I'm not at all greedy, not me. I like to leave enough for my travelers to cross once or twice more. Good business, that's what I call it."

Simon could think of other things to call it, but he didn't want to upset his stomach any further than it was already. "Are you sure you couldn't take something else? I have a perfectly nice radio."

"AND IT'S A RADIO YOU WANT TO KEEP!" the small box in his hand shouted out, the volume once again sky-rocketing. "AND NOW IT'S TIME FOR AN EXCLUSIVE WTCH FEATURE, 'MUSIC TO DEFEAT OGRES BY'!"

"Ey?" The ogre replied. "I've never had a radio. Are they tasty?"

The announcer's voice was replaced by the sound of a harp.

The ogre made a face even more unpleasant than usual. "A harp?"

Violins swirled in behind the harp's sonorous chords.

"Violins?" the ogre whispered, genuinely upset. "Violins?"

"THAT'S RIGHT!" the announcer's voice spoke over the music. "AND NOW LET'S LISTEN TO THE NEW CRUSTY MONSTERS, AND THEIR VERSION OF 'THE MEN IN MY LITTLE GIRL'S LIFE'."

"No." The ogre's whisper held a tinge of fear. "Anything but that."

A men's chorus came on, speaking in unison rather than singing. This was one of those talking songs, apparently about a girl growing up, and how she related to men through her father's eyes. The violins redoubled their swirling as the chorus came around, the men's voices singing at last:

"The men in my little girl's—"

"No!" the ogre screamed. "No! Have you no mercy?"

But before Simon could answer, the ogre had run to the side of the bridge and jumped into the sea.

The song stopped abruptly.

"THERE!" the announcer's voice remarked smugly. "YOU CAN ALWAYS GET OGRES WITH TALKING SONGS. NOW AREN'T YOU GLAD YOU LEFT THE RADIO ON?"

"Do you mind if I turn you down?" Simon asked, twisting the knob before the announcer could reply.

"I quite understand," the radio continued reasonably. "Listening to 'The Men In My Little Girl's Life' at top volume can be a harrowing experience for anyone. Just be thankful that the ogre jumped when he did. If he didn't, we would have had to play 'Ringo'."

Simon thought he heard the announcer shudder. He would shudder, too, if he could imagine a song worse than "The Men In My Little Girl's Life".

"What should I do now?" Simon asked the radio.

"Better get on about your business," the announcer replied. "Unlike that song we play by the One Thousand Three Hundred and Forty One Strings, time is not on your side. You only have 'til midnight, after all. Oh, and turn off the radio for a while. You'll need to save the batteries."

"But what if I need your advice?" Simon asked.

"Don't worry," the radio replied. "We'll be around. This is WTCH, the station for postmen on suicide missions, signing off."

The radio turned itself off before Simon could touch the dial. The postman turned and looked at the iron bars in front of him. The guard might be gone, but he was on the wrong side of the gate.

Simon pushed on the metal bars. The gate swung open. It had been unlocked all along. He stepped through. Now that the ogre was gone and the radio had shut itself off, the Witchville night closed around him again, far too still.

Simon shook himself and stepped through the gate. He had a job to do. But more than that, he had to find out what had happened to Gloria.

CHAPTER
SIXTEEN

DULTS WERE SUCH
a drag.

Gloria, the real Gloria, puffed on her cigarette and
looked in the mirror. What right did her father have to
say anything about the way she looked? Or about anything she wanted to do, for that matter? She was sixteen
years old, after all, almost sixteen and a half, plenty old
enough to make her own decisions. If she wanted to bleach
her hair to a white blonde, who was going to stop her? If
she wanted to go out and party all night with the boys on
the Boot Patrol, it was her right!

She glanced a final time in the mirror, then smiled.
She had spent half an hour on her makeup until she had
gotten it just right. Who could say no to someone who
looked as tough as her? Certainly not that pantywaist who
called himself her father.

"Gloria!"

She frowned. It was that drag of a sister of hers. What
did the little creep want now? Gloria stubbed out her
cigarette on the edge of her vanity.

"Yeah?" she replied.

Shirley pranced into the room, wearing high-heeled
boots and jeans that looked like they had been sprayed on

her rear. She'd lightened and curled her hair, too, although on her it looked a little cheap, not anywhere near as sophisticated as the look Gloria had achieved. She was wearing a tight new off-white sweater, too. At least Gloria thought it was new. Even though she didn't remember seeing it in her sister's closet, it still looked oddly familiar.

Shirley pushed her sister out of the way to study herself in the mirror. "How do I look?"

Gloria looked at the cable stitching on the sweatered shoulder Shirley had stuck in front of her. She knew where she's seen it before—in *her* closet!

She grabbed her sister's shoulders and spun her around. "You're wearing my sweater! You little creep, who told you you could wear my sweater?"

Shirley sneered back at Gloria for an instant before turning back to the mirror to double-check her hair. "Hey!" she drawled matter-of-factly. "I gotta look right when the Boot Patrol shows up."

"Boot Patrol?" Gloria demanded. "Who said you could come out and party with the Boot Patrol? I want to have a good time tonight. I don't want my drag of a little sister along."

Shirley turned to face her sister, then, her face flushed with anger. "Hey, who introduced you to the Boot Patrol in the first place? Who's been going out with Brad MacGuffin anyway?"

It was Gloria's turn to sneer. "That was back in Festeron. This is Witchville. And who's Brad going to like in Witchville—" she paused, pointing at a pimple on Shirley's forehead, "—a bratty, snot-nosed kid—" Gloria turned her index finger around so that it touched her breastbone, midway between her two young breasts, held firm by a push-up bra, "—or a real woman?"

"Hey!" a quavering male voice shouted weakly from the top of the stairs. "Could you keep it quiet? Don't you have any respect for an old man's delicate ears?"

Their father wove unsteadily down the stairs, one

hand on the banister, the other clutching a Scotch on the rocks. Somehow, he made it to the bottom still on his feet. Gloria was surprised he didn't fall down like usual.

"Oh, shut up, Dad," Gloria and Shirley said in unison.

"Shut up? You tell your own father to shut up? Oh, if only your mother was here." The old man sobbed into his drink.

"But she isn't here, is she?" Gloria replied angrily.

"No, she hasn't been around for years, since she ran off with that portable-toilet salesman!" Shirley added viciously.

"Stop it," their father moaned softly as he took another stiff belt of his Scotch.

"I can still see the brochures he left behind," Shirley continued, a cruel smile upon her lips. " 'No matter where you are, you'll always have a flush.' "

"Stop it!" their father demanded more loudly, as if the belt of Scotch had given him a moment's strength. "Another word about your mother, and you're going to he grounded for the rest of your life!"

Gloria couldn't take any more of this.

"Will both of you just shut up!" she screamed. "You are both such drags. How did I ever get into this family?"

"How dare you say that?" Their father took another drink to keep up his strength. "The Magnificos have always been a proud—" The rest of his sentence was lost as he fell over.

"I don't believe either of you!" Gloria shrieked. "Oh, if only the Boot Patrol would come and take me away from all this!"

Somebody knocked on the door.

Shirley ran to answer it.

"Oh no you don't!" Gloria grabbed the back of the sweater her sister had stolen as she ran past. "This is my date!"

Shirley turned, looking at her sister as one might regard a toadstool. "With the whole Boot Patrol?"

"Nobody invited you along!" Gloria snipped.

"So I'm inviting myself!" Shirley sniped.

The knocking came again, louder and longer.

Gloria pushed her sister aside and strode forward purposefully. She smiled as she opened the door.

It wasn't the Boot Patrol. It was one skinny guy in a dark blue uniform.

"Gloria?" the guy said uncertainly.

"What's it to you?" she replied. Did she know this dweeb? What did he want anyway?

The guy tried to smile. Actually, he was kind of cute, in a dorky sort of way.

"I'm here for our date," he replied.

"*Our* date?" Gloria laughed. "Mister, are you even on the right planet?"

"No!" the guy insisted. "Don't you remember? We made a date this afternoon."

"This afternoon?" Where was this guy coming from? "Hey, this afternoon, we were all stuck in Festeron. This afternoon, I didn't even exist!"

"But I spoke with—"

"That goody two-shoes?" Gloria waved her hand dismissively. "Forget about her. She's dead and buried."

Shirley stuck her head in front of Gloria. "Have you seen the Boot Patrol?"

"Boot Patrol?" The guy frowned. "Last I heard, they were checking out the Fun Pier."

"Fun Pier?" Gloria hit her mini-skirted thigh in disgust. "Aren't I ever going to get out of here?"

"Sure you will." The guy tried smiling again. "You can come out with me."

Gloria frowned back at him.

"What are you, anyway?"

"You know, don't you?" He took a step closer, searching her eyes for any sense of recognition. "We met in Festeron. I'm Simon, the guy they made a postman."

"Postman?" She looked to the ceiling, imploring the heavens to get rid of this creep. "You expect me to go out with a postman?"

"But earlier today—"

"Listen, buster," she said firmly. "I may have been alive earlier today, but I wasn't living. Now that Festeron is gone and Witchville is here, my past is gone, too. I'm gonna live to party!"

"Yeah!" Shirley chimed in. "Bring on the Boot Patrol!"

"Pardon me," this guy who called himself Simon asked. "But what is the Boot Patrol?"

"You don't know?" Shirley asked incredulously.

"You'll know soon enough," Gloria added smugly. "Once you meet the Boot Patrol, you'll wish you'd never been born!"

"But, Gloria—" The guy looked really hurt. Gloria had to admit it. She actually felt a little sorry for the poor jerk.

"Hey, listen," she said, smiling slightly. "I'm busy tonight, but there's no reason you can't ask my sister—"

Shirley looked surprised and a little annoyed. Gloria waited for her to object. Instead, she looked the postman over critically. "Hey, he is kind of cute. You know, I could always go for a man in a uniform."

"Shirley?" The postman's face drained of color. "But, Gloria—"

She sighed. The creep was starting to annoy her again. That's what you got when you were nice to people. It was a real dragola.

"Listen, buster," she hissed. "Shirley's interested, so move it or lose it. I've got other plans."

"I think I'm going to be sick," Simon muttered as he backed away.

Shirley slammed the door. "What a weirdo. Cute, but a weirdo."

Gloria nodded, agreeing with her sister for a change.

"Hey," she added. "What did you expect? This is Witchville, after all."

CHAPTER
SEVENTEEN

IMON LOOKED BACK
at the Magnifico cottage, stunned. Witchville had changed
everything. He had hardly recognized Gloria when she
had opened the door. Then she had started talking, and
he had recognized her even less.

The proprietor of the magic shop had been right.
Everything was different in Witchville. Only now did he
realize how profound those differences were. Just as he
was getting used to Festeron, The Evil One went and
changed all the rules.

Simon also realized he had no idea what to do next.
Here he was, standing out on the northwestern edge of
Witchville. Total darkness had descended around him, the
sky so overcast that he didn't even have the company of the
moon and stars. And once again, total quiet enveloped him
as well. There seemed to be no movement in all of Witchville, save for a slight breeze that tickled his ear.

Simon looked around. It was actually a very odd
breeze, so localized that he didn't even feel it on his cheek,
the sort of pressure one feels against the ear lobe when
someone leans close to whisper the darkest secrets.

Wait a moment. Simon held his breath. There was a

fluctuation to that tiny breeze, a rhythm not unlike the cadence of syllables in a very soft, almost inaudible speaking voice. Was someone really whispering? He strained to hear the words.

" . . . par . . ." came drifting on the breeze. " . . . ex . . ." It certainly sounded like a voice to Simon.

"Couldn't you talk a little louder?" he whispered back.

" . . . par . . . Pardon," the breeze replied.

Simon would recognize that obsequious tone anywhere.

"Sneed?"

"Excuse me," the breeze replied, audible at last. "I'm still here, but I'm almost not."

"What?" Simon wasn't sure he had heard the other man correctly. "Where are you?" He pulled out the Acme Kitchen Wonder and shone its bright beam in the direction he thought the breeze had come from. There was nothing there.

"Sneed?" he called again.

"Talk to me," the breeze whispered back. "Human contact makes me stronger."

"Okay," Simon replied. "If you say so. Where did you go before?"

It took the Sneed breeze a moment to answer.

"I disappeared."

"I know that!" Simon insisted. "I couldn't find you anywhere. But where did you disappear to?"

"That's just it." Sneed's whisper was growing stronger, more impassioned. "I didn't go anywhere at all. I simply left."

"Left?" Simon tried shining the flashlight beam in an arc to see if he could pick up some sign of the quiet man. "But how did you leave?"

"I vanished," Sneed replied. "To put it bluntly, I discorporated."

"How could that happen?" Simon demanded. There was still no sign of him. Simon tipped the light upward to illuminate the trees, but there was nothing up among the leaves, either.

"Oh, I've been expecting it for quite some time. It's a stress reaction, I'm afraid." Sneed sighed. "Some people seem to lose their grip on reality. In my case, unfortunately, it's reality that's been losing its grip on me."

"So you just popped out of existence?" Simon asked.

"Well, it's not quite that simple." Sneed's rueful laugh had surprising force. "It happens when I get worried. The more fretful I get, the more I seem to fade into the background. And back there, when I felt it necessary to tell you about The Evil One's plans, I was as worried and upset as I've been since this whole thing first happened to me. The more I wanted to talk to you, the worse it became, until it got to the point where I felt I had to talk to you, that instant, there wasn't a moment to lose! Unfortunately, by that time, no one could see or hear me. I was completely beside myself!"

"It sounds terrible," Simon agreed. He took a moment to swing the flashlight beam in a complete 360-degree arc around the spot where he stood. There was still no one there, nothing but a wild variety of bushes and shrubs. The flashlight had picked up a thing or two he didn't recognize, but there was no movement beside his own. Sneed's words were all too accurate; even though his voice was here, he still didn't exist. Unless—

Simon turned the light back to something that had flashed before as the beam had swept past. He had dismissed it as a reflection of some sort, perhaps water on the leaves of a bush. But when he shone the flashlight on it again, he saw that it was something hanging in the air, like wisps of night fog, wisps that took a vaguely human shape, or perhaps the shape of a crumpled raincoat.

"Sneed?" he asked again.

The wisps of night fog bobbed affirmatively.

"I am solidifying again," replied Sneed's voice, stronger as well. "The Evil One hasn't won yet!"

Simon stared as the fog slowly coalesced before him. "So you have a tendency to vanish?" he asked the form as it grew arms and legs.

"I'm afraid so," Sneed replied as the fog began to sketch in the outline of his hat. "It does have its advantages. The Witchville spell seems to have overlooked me completely."

Simon supposed that was an advantage. At least now he and Sneed could work together to rescue the Wishbringer stone. Still, he was a little uneasy about his friend's resolidification process.

"Have you always been like this?" he asked at last.

"Oh, no," Sneed replied with another one of his sighs. "I was a completely normal human being, before they made me the postman."

This was the sort of thing Simon didn't want to hear. "Until they made you a postman?"

The solidifying mist nodded. "Well, not immediately after I became the postman. Things were fine until Festeron turned into Witchville. Even then, things were bearable, until The Evil One got ahold of me."

"The Evil One did this to you?" For some reason, Simon felt his own voice was fading now.

"Yes, she was much kinder to me than my predecessors, because of my meek nature." The mist had solidified now to the extent that Simon began to discern facial features, especially a pair of large and fearful eyes. "I understand she is merciless with most of those who wear postal uniforms."

"Oh," Simon replied, tugging absently at his own postal blues. He wondered if there were someplace around here that he might get a change of clothes.

"After that," Sneed continued, "I admit that I got a bit paranoid. I began thinking that The Evil One was everywhere, watching my every move. And, should I do anything else against her, I feared her retribution would be even worse!"

"Watching your every move?" Simon muttered more to himself than to the solidifying Sneed. He remembered the gigantic pair of eyes that had watched him as he left the magic shop.

"I'm afraid my paranoia became a bit unreasonable," Sneed went on. "After all, The Evil One's powers are rather limited when this island is still Festeron. Of course, now that the island has turned to Witchville, she is virtually omnipotent."

"Omnipotent?" Simon replied.

Sneed paused to consider. "Well, perhaps that word is a bit too strong. My paranoia, you know. Omnipresent, perhaps? No, still not quite right. Ah—I suppose 'completely unstoppable' would be a best possible phrase."

Simon could feel this dialogue going the way of most conversations he had had on this island: very badly. Still, he supposed it wouldn't hurt if he raised a logical objection or two.

"Then why," he logically objected, "if you are so paranoid, are you telling me about this now?"

"Oh, dear. There are a couple of reasons," Sneed replied grimly, his voice returned more or less to that same weak timbre that Simon had first heard on the Festeron Fun Pier. "For one, let me tell you that vanishing is a life-changing experience. It completely alters your outlook on things when you're not there anymore. I realized it was time to stand up and be counted, if anyone could see me long enough to include me in a count.

"But I realized something else, when Festeron changed and I did not: My insubstantiality might have a positive side effect. Perhaps I was worried for nothing about The Evil One's eavesdropping, for apparently I had become so transparent that not even The Evil One's magic could see me!"

Sneed actually chuckled. "I realized then that I might really be able to have a positive effect on our little drama, for I will be able to explore all of Witchville under her very nose without her even realizing I am there! In an odd sort of way I will be able to use The Evil One's sorcery against her." To Simon's amazement, Sneed smiled as he added: "Perhaps we can defeat her after all."

Simon was astonished. He never expected to see such a change in this rumple-coated fellow. Besides which, his solidification seemed to have completed, for what little color Sneed boasted—primarily dark brown grease-stains on his raincoat—seemed to have returned as well. Maybe it was only the effect of the flashlight beam, but Sneed looked more substantial to Simon than he ever had before.

They stood in the all-consuming silence for a moment as Sneed caught his breath—a silence broken by a high and distant cry.

"A woman's voice!" Sneed frowned, his face losing any color it had recently gained and perhaps (though it might have been Simon's imagination) becoming the slightest bit transparent. "Could it be *her*?"

They were quiet again, straining to hear the voice. It sounded like cries for help.

"No, it won't be *her*," Sneed decided after a moment, renewed confidence in his voice. "Cries for help aren't *her* style. *She* specializes in evil chuckles and demonic shrieks, things like that."

Simon turned south, the direction the cries were coming from. "Shouldn't we see who it is?"

"Oh, of course," Sneed replied, blinking as if waking from a dream. "But I would expect you to say something like that. You always make such noble suggestions."

Simon turned and ran toward the entreaties. In the still Witchville night, he heard Sneed's soft footfalls behind him.

"Help!" He could hear the voice clearly now. "Help me, please!" It was clear, high, and frightened, maybe a teenage girl. Whoever it was, she was in trouble.

Simon moved as rapidly as he dared. Everything beyond the limits of his flashlight beam was absolutely black, as if the coming of Witchville had snatched every bit of light from the sky. Consequently, he had to slant the light at the ground immediately ahead of his feet, so that he would not trip over some sinkhole or fallen tree. There was no way he was going to save anything, whether it was a woman in distress or the entire island of Festeron, if he managed to twist an ankle or break a leg.

He still managed a brisk jog in the direction of the woman's voice, which was quite close by now, joined by the gentle sound of waves breaking on the beach. His flashlight beam picked up the dirt ruts of River Road, then the pebble-strewn shoreline beyond.

"Help me!" the woman shouted again. "Oh, help me, please!"

He was almost on top of her now. He swung the light around and caught her in the beam.

She squinted in Simon's direction. "Are you here to help me?"

It wasn't a woman. It was something else. Something that was covered with long brown fur, with a tail like a beaver's at one end, and a duckbill at the other where her lips should be.

"Uh, yeah," Simon replied as soon as he had collected his wits. "That's what I'm here for."

"Well, it's about time!" the furry maiden replied. "Oh, sorry," she added when she saw the startled look on Simon's face. "I am a princess, and used to having my way."

Sneed came puffing up beside the postman.

"It's Tasmania!" he exclaimed.

"Princess Tasmania to you," she replied huffily. "But haven't I seen you someplace before?"

"I used to be a postman," Sneed suggested.

"Really?" the princess replied, not completely convinced. "But you're so, so—nondescript."

"I even rescued her a couple times," Sneed said to the postman, slightly hurt. "How soon they forget."

"Hey, you'd forget things, too, if you stumbled into one of those Witchville traps," the princess remarked shortly. "But why are we talking when you could be freeing me?"

"Trap?" Simon frowned. "Where are you caught?"

"Down here." She pointed at her rear leg with a webbed forepaw. "I was sunning myself on the Festeron Beach—those late afternoon rays are especially good for a healthy coat of fur, you know—and then, bang!, here it was Witchville, and the beach was filled with these spring-loaded traps. I mean, what's a princess to do?"

"Okay." Simon knelt down to get a better look at the trap. "I'll see if I can help."

"Oh," the princess added as an afterthought. "And watch out for the other traps."

Clank!

Something snapped beneath his Acme Kitchen Wonder. He turned the flashlight beam on the thick metal jaws that had snapped shut inches from his fingers.

"Thanks for telling me," he replied drily.

"Wait a moment!" Sneed called. He ran off into the darkness. He returned a minute later, now carrying a large dead branch, which he proceeded to poke into the beach around the princess.

There was a chorus of clanking, which subsided finally with more than a dozen of the nasty little traps hanging from the branch. Sneed poked around the area a few more times, but there were no further clanks; the only noise was the lapping of the waves and the gentle bell-like tones the traps made as they knocked against each other.

Sneed threw the trap-laden branch farther up the beach. They heard another half-dozen clanks as it hit.

"There," Sneed said efficiently. "I think it's safe now."

"All right." Simon knelt by the furry princess's foot. "Let's see what we can do."

He directed the flashlight beam so that it illuminated the silvery metal trap where it gripped the princess's webbed foot. Trickling lines of blood descended from the half-dozen points where the trap's sharp teeth had punctured her skin. Simon felt along the bottom of the trap, looking for some sort of release lever that would pull back the spring. There was nothing there. The trap was so primitive he would have to pull apart the jaws with his fingers.

"Excuse me," Sneed interrupted as he watched Simon try to get a grip on the two halves of the trap, "but there might be a better way."

Simon looked up at his indecisive friend, now mostly lost in shadow.

"There might be?"

"Well, yes," Sneed replied a touch uncertainly. "You see, there is a button on the side of the Acme Kitchen Wonder."

Simon looked at the gadget which he had gripped between his knees to give a steady beam. He saw a small green button off to one side. He let go of the trap and let his thumb hover over it.

"This one?" he asked.

"I'm afraid not," Sneed replied. "It's the pink button, two below that one."

Oh, yes. Simon saw it now. There was a whole row of buttons, even smaller than the green one he had first noticed. He moved his thumb so that it rested over the pink button, then looked up at Sneed.

"What am I doing?" he asked.

"You are about to activate the Acme Kitchen Wonder Trap Neutralizer," Sneed replied. "I was given an Acme Kitchen Wonder during my stint as a postman as well."

"Oh!" Simon exclaimed, a bit surprised. "So you really know how to use this thing?"

"Only a couple of its functions, I'm afraid." Sneed shook his head sadly. "I was captured very quickly. Anyway, hold the Wonder about three inches away from the trap, with the light pointing between the jaws. Fine. Now press the button."

Simon did as he was instructed. A small, carved knife

flashed from the Kitchen Wonder, inserting itself between the two halves of the trap. The trap sprung open, and the hooked blade jerked back and then upwards, pulling the trap away from the foot, then tossing it into the air.

Clank!

The trap clamped shut again as soon as it was free of the blade.

"That would have been your fingers, had you tried to open the trap by hand," Sneed remarked.

"Thanks for telling me," Simon whispered, a bit startled by the course of events. His hands were his livelihood. He had almost gotten them sliced open, or worse, by that pair of metal jaws. He would have to be more careful.

The trap landed farther down the beach. A couple other traps clanked against it.

"Oh, thank you!" the princess cooed. She flexed her newly freed foot. It sported five small puncture wounds, but seemed otherwise undamaged. "You have freed a princess. I don't know how I can repay you!"

"Well, for starters," Simon replied, for he felt he needed some explanation, "you might give us some information. Like, exactly what kind of a creature are you?"

The princess sniffed haughtily at the postman's remark. "Must I always deal with peasants?" She stuck her duckbill in the air, but relented almost instantly. "Ah, I should not be so hard on you. You did save my life, after all. I, kind sirs, am a platypus."

"Oh, I see," Simon responded. "That explains everything."

"So happy to be of help," the platypus princess beamed. "I do wish I could give you some reward, like a magic whistle to receive my father's aid in times of crisis. Unfortunately, the royal stockroom is completely out of them. They've been back-ordered for months!"

Tasmania flapped her beaver tail on the beach in annoyance. "But what am I saying? You have an Acme

Kitchen Wonder! Simply blow the magic whistle attach-ment—it's there, right underneath the can opener," she pointed with her beak, "—and the might of King Anatinus will be yours! What more could be asked for?"

"What more, indeed?" Simon replied, for he felt that sort of reply was expected.

"So I thank you both a final time," the princess con-tinued. "And I ask one final boon."

"Which is?" Simon asked.

"Might you lift me up and toss me into the water, so that I don't get caught in the traps?" she responded.

Simon knelt and, with a grunt, lifted her aloft. She was about the same size and weight as a medium-sized dog. He asked Sneed to pick up the flashlight and show him the ocean.

Sneed shone the light into the flapping waves. The shoreline was only a half-dozen feet away. Simon lifted the princess higher still, ready to give her a good, hearty heave, but paused when he saw her big, brown eyes star-ing into his.

"You know," she said softly, "for a human, you're kind of cute."

"Oh. Thanks a lot," Simon replied, still not quite sure what to say. *"Bon voyage."*

He tossed her into the sea. She landed with a consid-erable splash, but bobbed to the surface a moment later.

The princess called a final goodbye, then swam away.

Sneed stepped forward, his flashlight beam following the retreating princess.

"You did a noble thing," he suggested.

"I guess so," Simon admitted. "With her attitude, I wasn't even sure I wanted to save her."

"Being a hero is not a pretty job," Sneed agreed. "But we had best get about our business."

That's when they heard other voices in the distance.

"Oh, no," Sneed moaned. "Not them. Anything but them."

CHAPTER
EIGHTEEN

"NOT WHO—" SImon began, but Sneed waved him to silence. The postman heard chanting in the distance.

> "The Boot Patrol is full of starch,
> Witchville's finest on the march!
> Sound off! One, two!
> Sound off! Three, four!
> Sound off! One, two, three, four!
> Three-four!"

"We've waited too long!" Sneed whispered hysterically. "The Boot Patrol is coming!"

"The Boot Patrol?" Simon asked. "What's the Boot Patrol?"

The chanting started again, a bit closer than the last time:

> "The Boot Patrol is such a rush,
> For all free will we soon shall crush!
> Sound off! One, two!
> Sound off! Three, four!

Sound off! One, two, three, four!
Three-four!"

"The Boot Patrol is The Evil One's enforcement unit,"
Sneed explained. "And they're the nastiest group of en-
forcers you're ever likely to meet!"

The Boot Patrol chorus chanted again. Simon realized they had to be moving at a goodly clip, for their
voices were much louder and clearer than before.

"The Boot Patrol's the place for me,
Let's all hear it for tyranny!
Sound off! One, two!
Sound off! Three, four!
Sound off! One, two, three, four!
Three-four!"

"We have to get away!" Sneed wailed. Oddly enough,
his voice seemed softer than before, more distant. "We'll
be trapped! It may already be too late!"

"Calm down," Simon said as he turned toward his
friend. But Sneed was no longer standing next to him.
Where could the rumpled fellow have gotten to?

"The Boot Patrol is really neat,
If you meet us, you're in defeat!
Sound off! One, two!
Sound off! Three, four!
Sound off! One, two, three, four!
Three-four!"

They sounded awfully close by now, perhaps just
around the bend in the road. Simon thought he saw a faint
light through the trees: a flickering light, like that thrown
by torches. What should they do?

"Sneed?" he called.

"Quick!" Sneed replied, but his voice sounded as if

he was calling from a distant hillside. "We have to get out of here! The Boot Patrol caught me, and turned me over to The Evil One. We can't let that happen to you!"

The rumpled man's voice was getting fainter with every word. Sneed was fading out on him! And Simon could hear the distinct rhythm of marching feet, only a little bit up the road.

"Sneed!" Simon called. "Don't leave me now! What should I do?"

Sneed's voice carried faintly, as if brought by a breeze from far, far away:

" . . . chance," it whispered. " . . . torture . . . certain death . . . unless . . ."

The breeze was gone. Simon could hear no more.

There was a rush of static. The radio came to life. Somebody was singing, half in German, half in English:

"Danke shane, darling, danke shane—"

"Flash!" the announcer's voice broke in: "Time for a WTCH late-breaking news flash! According to unconfirmed reports, Simon the Postman is about to be captured by the Boot Patrol, an action that will almost certainly result in the termination of his quest and even more certainly the termination of Simon the—"

He turned the radio off. He didn't need a voice shouting in his ear, telling him what he already knew. But Simon wasn't ready to despair. There had to be a way out of almost anything. Didn't there?

A dozen men goosestepped into view, three lines of them, four men across. They wore uniforms that made them look like state troopers, complete with the highly polished riding boots and striped jodhpurs, leather jackets, policemen's caps and—even in the darkness—those kinds of highly-reflective sunglasses that you can't see the eyes behind. Only the jackets were not standard trooper issue—they sported far too many chains. The four men at the corners all held torches to light their way.

All twelve men smiled when they saw Simon.

"The Boot Patrol can always lick them!
See! We've found another victim!
Sound off! One, two!
Sound off! Three, four!
Sound off! One, two, three, four!
Three-four!"

They marched straight for the postman.

"DON'T TURN US OFF!" the radio shouted from his pocket. "THE BOOT PATROL IS COMING! YOU'VE GOT TO GET AWAY!"

He had to get away. It was easy enough for the disembodied announcer to say. But how was Simon going to do it? They had him cornered on the beach. If he backed up in any of three directions more than a couple feet, the traps would get him. That meant, if he was going to escape, he had to rush straight for the Boot Patrol. He had no idea how the patrol would react to a maneuver like that, but, whatever their response, he didn't expect it to be pleasant. He wished he knew more about these guys, and the surrounding countryside, for that matter. He doubly wished that Sneed had had the fortitude to stick around a little longer before disappearing so he could have answered at least one or the other of these pressing questions. Now, he was all alone, with no one to help him.

Unless—

Simon still held the Acme Kitchen Wonder in his hand. What had the platypus princess promised him? All he had to do was blow the whistle attachment, and he would be aided by her father, king of the platypuses. That was more or less the gist of it.

The Boot Patrol had goosestepped itself across River Road. Twelve pairs of hands reached for Simon's collar. They chanted gratuitously:

"The Boot Patrol has passed the test,
For you are now under arrest!

Sound off! One, two!
Sound off! Three—"

"DO SOMETHING!" the radio screamed. "YOU
CAN'T LET THEM CATCH YOU! DO I HAVE TO
SAVE YOU FROM—"

Simon raised the appropriate portion of the Acme
Kitchen Wonder to his lips and blew the whistle.

And everything changed.

A great musical cry descended from the heavens, like
some angelic choir, except that these voices had a slight
animalistic edge to them—a bit of a growl here, a bit of a
chirp there. If his saviors were angels, Simon realized,
they were platypus angels. He felt himself being pulled
aloft, as if lifted by a hundred invisible hands, or perhaps
a hundred invisible webbed feet.

He was flying. He heard the angry cries of the Boot
Patrol, far below. And then their voices were lost in the
wind, as he sped out across the ocean, heading for a distant light. As he approached that illumination, he saw that
it was a shining palace, somehow glowing a dozen pastel
shades. But before he could determine the source, or even
the exact nature, of the illumination, he found himself
falling, swept in through a huge gateway at the palace's
center, and deposited, ever so gently, in the middle of a
huge, polished floor.

"It's him, Father!" cried a familiar voice. "Oh, it's him!"

Simon blinked, trying to get his bearings. He was in
some sort of huge ballroom, the distant walls festooned
with rich tapestries, each of them seeming to tell a story—
here, a platypus capturing a unicorn; there, a platypus in
full armor slaying a dragon.

"Are you sure he's the same one?" a commanding male
voice asked. "Humans look so much alike. And this one
seems none too bright."

"Father!" the platypus princess chided. "Have you no

feelings? He saved me from the trap! He is so bright, at least for a human!"

Simon pulled his gaze down from the wall hangings to look in the direction of the voices. There, seated upon a pair of plush raised chairs—Simon guessed you could call them thrones—were Princess Tasmania, now dressed in a robe of palest pink, and another platypus, with a great deal of gray in its fur, wearing a robe of regal purple.

"Simon," the princess announced. "So nice of you to drop in. I'd like to introduce you to my father, King Anatinus."

He was being introduced to the king. What did one do when introduced to royalty, especially platypus royalty? Simon executed a clumsy bow.

Apparently it met with approval, for the king chose to address him:

"We understand that you have rescued the royal daughter," the king announced. "We are greatly pleased with your efforts."

Simon smiled agreeably. What was that "we" stuff, anyway? Did the king represent a committee or something?

"Oh, Father!" the princess exclaimed. "But he must be in trouble, for I told him, if he but needed your aid, he had naught to do but whistle."

"Really?" the king replied, a touch perplexed. He beckoned to Simon. "Human, you have our leave to approach the royal personage."

Simon guessed that meant he was supposed to come over there. As he walked the considerable distance, another pair of platypuses peeked out from behind the two thrones.

"Oh, yes," King Anatinus said to the two new faces. "He's quite safe. He saved our daughter."

Both of the newcomers walked out from their hiding places, descending the red-carpeted stairs to stand beneath either side of the king's throne.

"We would introduce you," the king said as Simon approached, "but we have ourselves not been introduced."

Simon apologized. "Simon the Postman," he added.

"We are pleased to make your acquaintance," the platypus king replied. "Any human who rescues our daughter from Witchville treachery is a friend of ours." He indicated the two platypuses below him. "Let us introduce you to our advisors." He waved to his left, at a platypus whose fur was almost completely white, an animal who seemed stooped with age within his heavy scholarly robes of deepest jet.

"This," the king continued, "is our chief advisor and soothsayer, the wise Glenfizzlewizzle. Glenfizzlewizzle, Simon the Postman."

The aged platypus inclined his head. "Simon," he said deferentially.

"Glen—uh—fizzlewizzle," Simon stumbled in reply.

The aged platypus shrugged. "What can you do? It is the family name."

"And on our right," the king continued, waving his other hand at a far younger platypus, dressed in a green doublet and shining breastplate, "is the Honorable Roger, Chief Defender of the Realm."

The breastplated young platypus bowed rather stiffly. "Simon." He pronounced the syllables slowly, as if they were separate words.

"Roger," Simon replied, returning the bow. He decided it would be impolite to ask what the chief defender of the realm was doing hiding behind the throne.

"The Honorable Roger, if you please," the platypus replied haughtily. "I do not condone overfamiliarity."

"The Honorable Roger," Simon corrected himself, snapping the heels of his running shoes together. The gesture seemed to please the Honorable Roger no end.

"Very good." The king beamed at all assembled. "Now that we are all introduced in proper courtly fashion, let's get on to business." He looked sternly at Simon. "Being king of all platypuskind is a busy job, and we must budget our time. Our daughter has informed us that you are visiting to request our royal aid. How, therefore, may we serve you?"

Simon quickly told King Anatinus and his retinue about being trapped by the Boot Patrol, and blowing the whistle as a last resort.

"Ah, and a fine resort it was," the king applauded. "Then we have already served you by rescuing you from the Boot Patrol? May I say that that greatly pleases the royal personage. The very best service is one we are not even aware of performing. Well, it has been very pleasant meeting you, Simon the Postman. And now, we must attend to other affairs."

That was it? Simon had flown all this way to be dismissed? But how was he going to find the Wishbringer stone? More to the point, how was he even going to get back to Witchville?

"Wait!" Simon shouted as King Anatinus began to turn away. The Honorable Roger sent Simon a withering look.

"I mean—I beg your pardon, your majesty, but I was wondering—um—" Simon realized he had to get this just right to cover up his social gaffe. "—Er—I am afraid that I must petition your majesty for further assistance."

"What?" King Anatinus demanded. "Well, why didn't you say so? And what can we do for you, oh savior of our daughter?"

Simon explained his problem. One way or another, he had to find the Wishbringer stone.

"Ah," the king replied. "So we can help you locate the stone. Well, that is possible, is it not, Glenfizzlewizzle?"

The aged scholar nodded his grizzled beak. "Indeed, possible, oh my king. It is a moderately complicated process, however. The preparations and conjurations should take no more than three or four hours. After that, we should know the location of the stone in a very short time, say, another hour or so."

Another hour or so? Simon did his best to smile.

"I appreciate your efforts, your majesty," he explained, "but if I do not locate the stone by midnight tonight, Festeron will turn into Witchville forever."

"Really?" King Anatinus remarked. "How unpleasant. Everything is so time-dependent these days. Well, we might as well have Glenfizzlewizzle start it. You never know, he might get lucky."

"As your majesty requires," Glenfizzlewizzle replied with a bow. He hurried from the room.

"Now, if you will excuse us—" the king began again.

"Oh, Father!" the princess interrupted. "Can't you see that we have to get Simon the Postman back to the mainland so that he may search for the stone himself? Glenfizzlewizzle's conjurations may be too late!"

"Yes, my child, you are right. We must make every effort to foil Witchville's continuation." The king stroked his furry cheek in thought. "At the very least, they are a nasty neighbor. And they bear no love for our Misty Isle. Who knows what evil they might resort to if allowed to continue? They might even organize platypus hunts!"

"Father!" the princess cried in horror. The Honorable Roger cowered where he stood.

"No," the king insisted. "We must face up to these possibilities, no matter how horrible. We must send Simon the Postman back to Witchville, so that he might have a chance to save us all."

The princess dabbed at her eyes with an edge of her fine pink robe. She waved slowly to Simon. "Goodbye, oh noble hero!"

The king laughed, a short, quacking sound. "We think she rather fancies you. Good luck, Simon the Postman, on your noble quest."

He pulled a silver whistle from his robe and blew a single clear high note. He was rewarded by the return of the angelic choir. Once again, a hundred invisible webbed paws lifted Simon from the ground, and flew him out of the palace of the platypuses.

Before he knew what happened, he was standing on the edge of River Road, his heels toward the beach. His invisible guardians were gone, having deposited him more or less where they had picked him up a few minutes before.

He stepped out on the road, careful to put some distance between himself and the traps behind him. The Boot Patrol was nowhere to be seen.

"Sneed?" he called. He listened for an answer, or even a breeze, but the Witchville night was dead silent once again. He wondered for an instant if the Boot Patrol had gotten his friend, but dismissed the thought almost as soon as it occurred. Sneed was probably somewhere else on the island, searching for the stone.

Which is what he should be doing, too. He gathered, from what the magic shop proprietor had told him, that it should be somewhere close to The Evil One. His task, then, was to find The Evil One without The Evil One finding him.

He had already covered the northwestern corner of the island, and had seen no sign of The Evil One. He imagined she might be headquartered in town. Or in the graveyard. Either way, it was time for Simon to travel south. He checked to make sure his radio and glasses were securely tucked away, flipped on the Kitchen Wonder's beam, and turned to begin his journey.

He heard a woman scream behind him.

It sounded like Gloria!

CHAPTER
NINETEEN

HE SCREAM HAD COME
from the direction of the Magnifico cottage. It had to be
Gloria. But what could have happened to her?

In Witchville, Simon realized, anything could happen.

He turned the flashlight beam on the road and raced
to her aid. It took perhaps a minute, and in that time she
did not scream again. Simon hoped he wasn't too late.

He saw the cottage at last. Someone had turned the
front porch light on, and it shone through the trees.

The radio turned on.

"HEY!" the announcer's voice screamed. "WAIT A
MIN—"

He turned the radio off. He knew he was running
into danger. And, as soon as he did, the radio would inform the danger, loud and clear, that Simon was there.
Maybe he should get rid of the little plastic box. It was
starting to get annoying.

He redoubled his speed and rushed into the clearing.

He heard a woman giggle. It sounded like Gloria.

"Oh, Brad!" she whooped. "You're such an animal!"

Gloria sat on the front porch swing, but she was not
alone. A man, dressed in a Boot Patrol uniform, held her

in a bear hug. The man turned to regard Simon through his dark glasses. Even with those glasses, Simon recognized the face behind them. It was Brad MacGuffin.

"Oops," Simon said. "I must have taken a wrong turn somewhere. Don't let me disturb you." He unobtrusively tucked his Kitchen Wonder into one of his pockets and began to whistle. Everybody stared at him. He turned and walked casually away.

"Oh, god!" Gloria exclaimed. "It's that creepy postman!"

Brad laughed. "Patrollers!" he yelled. "Front and center!"

Eleven other members of the Boot Patrol melted out from the woods. One of them, a bit more disheveled than the rest, had Shirley on his arm.

"See who came to visit!" Brad called to the others. The others laughed, an ugly sound.

Simon was surrounded.

"Bring out the boot!" Brad announced.

Their laughter was even harsher this time. And what was even worse, Gloria joined in.

A pair of the Boot Patrollers returned to the forest. A moment later they returned, carrying a six-foot-high boot.

"Very good," Brad commended the others. "Now strap him in!"

Simon found himself grabbed by more than a dozen hands and dumped, head first, into the boot. The hands strapped his arms and legs to the leather interior, then zipped the boot's side up to the top so that Simon was completely enclosed by the dark. He could, however, still hear the voices.

"Well, babe," Brad murmured. "I gotta go. Duty calls."

"Oh, Brad!" Gloria complained. "The Boot Patrol can be such a drag!"

"Hey, babe," Brad replied. "I don't want to hear you talk like that. A man's gotta do what a man's gotta do.

Besides, once it gets past midnight, this place will be Witchville forever!"

Somebody clapped her hands. "And I'll never have to be goody-goody Gloria again."

"Hey, babe. You can be as mean and nasty as you want."

Everybody laughed at that.

"Let's go, men!" Brad commanded. "The Boot Patrol never sleeps!"

Simon felt the boot get hoisted aloft. They were going to carry him away.

"Oh!" Gloria called after them. "I'll see you at the movies when you get off work. Like we planned?" She giggled. "Let me know what you do to him. Any neat tortures, stuff like that."

"Don't worry!" Brad called back. "The Boot Patrol is going to give him a reception he'll never forget. That is, if he lives that long!"

Once the laughter died down, the Boot Patrol began to chant:

"We caught a guy in a suit!
Who was smoking an old cheroot!
He tried to run,
But we caught him for fun,
And then we gave him the Boot!
The Boot! The Boot! The Boot!"

The chanting was bad enough, but they seemed to be swinging the boot in time with their chant. Simon was glad he hadn't eaten anything since breakfast.

"We caught a girl with a flute!
On which she was tempted to toot!
Take music, she said,
But we took her instead!

And then we gave her the Boot!
The Boot! The Boot! The Boot!"

Simon counted twenty-eight verses of that thing before they reached the station. He heard the Boot Patrol march from dirt road to pavement, then across the brick and concrete, up the station house steps, bouncing the upside-down postman every step of the way. They stopped smartly, depositing the boot with a thud.

Simon saw light. Someone was unzipping his prison. Hands roughly pulled him from the restraining straps and dragged him from the boot, placing him on his own unsteady feet.

"Sergeant!" the Boot Patrol cried in unison. "The prisoner is ready for inspection!"

Simon tried to focus on the room around him. It was the same jail lobby he had been in before, although it now looked as though it was in need of a good cleaning. His head was spinning; it was difficult to look at any particular location for any length of time. If not for two members of the Boot Patrol holding up his arms, Simon was sure he would have fallen down long ago.

The sergeant's door slammed open. MacGuffin strode into the room, wearing a variation of the Boot Patrol uniform sporting chains not only on the jacket, but on pants, boots, and cap as well.

MacGuffin smiled when he saw Simon.

"Eczema!" MacGuffin began. "Halitosis! Cellulite!" He took a deep breath, attempting to regain control. Simon blinked. The dizziness was overwhelming.

"YOU WILL LOOK AT ME WHEN I'M TALKING TO YOU!" MacGuffin barked in his ear. A member of the Boot Patrol grabbed Simon's chin and jerked his head up so that he looked straight into the sergeant's steel-gray eyes.

"Much better," MacGuffin remarked. "I will forgive you for dropping off during the name-calling. After all, what use have I for name-calling now, when I can do whatever I want with you?"

The sergeant paused while the Boot Patrol enjoyed a hearty laugh. MacGuffin's face blurred in Simon's vision. The postman decided that he felt definitely unwell.

"Ah, yes," the sergeant continued merrily. "The Boot Patrol is going to have some fun with you."

The Boot Patrol cheered exuberantly.

"And when we're done with you," MacGuffin sneered, "we get to hand you over to Mr. Crisp."

Whistles and catcalls came from the Boot Patrol this time.

The sergeant leaned even closer. "And when he's done with you, he gives you to The Evil One."

The Boot Patrol was silent.

MacGuffin grabbed Simon's collar. "What have you got to say to that?"

Simon couldn't hold it in any longer. He promptly threw up on MacGuffin's shoes.

The sergeant screamed. "Filth! Tooth decay! Bladder blockage! You've soiled my boots! No one soils the boots of the Boot Patrol! You're in for it now! All our good humor is gone! From now on, all your torture is strictly business!" He waved to the Boot Patrollers. "Take him to the cell!"

"The cell, Sergeant?" the Boot Patrol asked in unison.

"Yes, you know the one I mean! The one in the subbasement, underneath the dungeons. The one we reserve for very special guests!" He began to turn away, but paused to add an afterthought. "Oh, and feed him, too. We don't want him losing his strength *too* soon."

Sergeant MacGuffin stomped back into his office, slamming the door behind him. Simon was dragged from the room by the myriad hands of the Boot Patrol. They dragged him through a hallway, past two rows of cells far grimier and more decrepit than anything Simon had seen during his last stay within these walls. Then they dragged him down the stairs.

There was a barred window on the first landing, through which he heard the moans of the hopeless. They dragged him down further still. There was a barred window on the second landing, through which he heard the screams of the damned. The Boot Patrol didn't stop there either, but took the steps down again.

They stopped at the third landing, and one of their number stepped forward, holding a large ring of keys. After a moment's search, he found the right key for the ancient iron door. The aged mechanism unlocked with a clank of protest, and the Boot Patroller grabbed the handle and yanked the door toward him. The hinges shrieked like a soul in agony. Even in his semi-delirious state, Simon wondered how long it had been since they had used this place.

There was no light on the other side of the door. The Boot Patrol relit a couple of their torches. With one torch leading the way and another behind, they dragged Simon through the door and into a corridor that seemed to have been hewn out of solid rock. The leading torchbearer waved his brand before him, clearing away spiderwebs and other obstacles, while the torch carrier in the rear held his torch high overhead to light the way. The tunnel was damp, and the moss that covered the walls and ceiling glowed an odd blue-green in the torchlight. The patrol's goose-stepping boots echoed down the corridor with drumlike precision, but there were other noises down here, too; scurrying sounds and high feral cries, noises made by whatever lived down here all the time.

The Boot Patrol stopped, and Simon once again heard the clank of keys and the complaint of hinges long unused. The patroller in the lead stepped out of the way, and Simon was thrown through the open doorway into a cell, if the tiny room into which he had been tossed could be so dignified.

There was no furniture here, not even a cot; nothing, in fact, save a bare earth floor strewn with something that might have been hay in a former life. The cell itself wasn't even square, but sloped down from the doorway so that the ceiling met the floor a half-dozen paces in, like some corner of a cave—which, Simon realized, was probably what this was, a cave they had made into a jail cell. The ceiling sloped rapidly, so that while he might be able to stand at the doorway, anywhere else he would have to stoop or kneel.

"Comfy?" one of the Boot Patrollers—he thought it might be Brad MacGuffin—said. "We've brought along a little something for you to eat, too. All the comforts of home."

A pair of hands produced a heaping bowl of something-or-other and placed it in the corner of the cell, next to a second dish that Simon guessed would contain water. Other hands set one of the torches in some sort of iron holder just outside the cell.

The person Simon thought could be Brad sneered. "We'll give you light to see what you're eating. We're not inhumane, after all. In an hour or so, of course, the torch will go out. Then you'll be in darkness—for hours or maybe days. You'll have plenty of time to catch up on your sleep, and even more time to think things over. And who knows? Maybe we'll feed you again, eventually."

The Boot Patrol laughed as they slammed and locked the cell's iron door. Simon looked up as their laughter and marching feet receded. The bowl was maybe ten feet away from where they had dropped him. He knew he wouldn't be able to walk over there, but maybe he could crawl.

He pushed himself up to hands and knees, but had to wait a moment for the vertigo to pass. He moved his right hand forward with exaggerated care, then his right leg. So far, so good. He did the same with his left arm and leg, then his right again. He had covered half the distance. He looked up at the food, small, white granules of some sort, rice perhaps. It was hard to tell more in the flickering torchlight.

He took a deep breath, and resumed his movement. He realized he was thirsty. How long had it been since he'd had a drink of water? He angled himself so that he would reach the water bowl first.

He stopped before he took a drink. There was a dark green pattern on the surface of the water, a scum of some sort, like something was growing there. Simon didn't feel so thirsty anymore. Maybe, he thought, I can eat a couple bites and come back and clean it off.

He turned to the food. This close, he noticed something that he had missed before.

Part of the food was still moving.

Simon backed away from the wriggling whiteness. The dizziness came over him again. He could no longer keep his balance. He fell over on his side, still looking at the wriggling bowl. But the bowl was getting hazy, the torchlight dimming.

Simon passed out.

CHAPTER TWENTY

SERGEANT MACGUFFIN stared at the row of medals. This time, he thought, he could have it all. And who deserved it more than him? Certainly not that pantywaist of a postman, rotting down there in the underdungeon. Not even The Evil One's allies, Mr. Crisp and Miss Voss, a couple of lily-livered pantywaists if he'd ever seen them. Oh, perhaps The Evil One herself deserved it; it was she, after all, who'd set this whole thing up. But, also after all, she was an old lady. She wasn't going to live forever. And who was going to take over Witchville after she was gone?

Sergeant MacGuffin had some definite ideas about that. And about Witchville, too. Here, at last, was a place where a man could be a man.

There was a knock on the door. MacGuffin looked up from the display case.

"Enter!" the sergeant barked.

His pantywaist of a son, Brad, waltzed into the room.

"I have a report, sir!" Brad barked, trying to sound militarily correct. It was a wasted effort.

'Let's have it, patroller," MacGuffin said anyway.

"The prisoner has been escorted to his cell and fed, sir, as per your order, sir!" Brad replied.

"Very good, patroller," MacGuffin answered, although he didn't think it was very good at all. That weakling of a son of his had no style, no delivery. There was no edge to his shout, no sense of danger. He was out of place in this new man's world.

Brad clicked his heels and saluted not at all smartly.

"Dismissed," MacGuffin remarked.

But Brad hesitated. "Uh—sir?"

MacGuffin allowed his eyebrows to rise a fraction of an inch. "Yes, patroller?"

"I was wondering, sir, if you needed me to go see Mr. Crisp." Brad looked up at his father's frown. "It's just that I knew you were supposed to tell Crisp when you captured the postman, and I'd have a problem delivering that message later tonight, because I'm expecting to have a heavy date, you see, and—"

The pantywaist's voice died in his throat.

"You dare bring that up with me now, patroller?" MacGuffin shouted, barely containing the full force of his rage. "I know Crisp has asked to be informed, and he will be informed, in due time, with due process!"

"Oh—uh—certainly sir—" Brad began.

"Silence!" MacGuffin demanded.

"Well—uh—I just wanted—" Brad babbled on.

"I told you you were dismissed!" the sergeant roared. "So dismiss yourself!"

The patroller saluted and fled. MacGuffin sighed. What a pantywaist. Unless he shaped up soon, there'd be no place for him in the new man's world of Witchville. He must have gotten it from his mother. What a total wimp she had been, complaining about MacGuffin's target practice sessions at three in the morning, and even denying his occasional requests for dinners of raw meat. Imagine!

Today, though, MacGuffin was in charge. It was Witchville, and he could do whatever he wanted, whatever was needed for a man's place in the world today.

Anybody who disagreed with him, he just took every second one, stood them up against the wall, and had them shot. It was a simple solution, and very effective at keeping the townspeople in line. It had worked with the Boot Patrollers, too, and, frankly, now that it was all over, the sergeant thought that twelve made a more efficient unit. Twenty-four had just been too ungainly. They had had too much time off, too much leisure in which to think. Funny how things often worked out for the best like that in Witchville. His only regret, occasionally, was that Brad had not been one of the twelve chosen to go up against the wall.

But he had no time to dwell on past triumphs. He had to plan tonight's battles; struggles that pantywaists like his son would never understand. That's why he omitted certain things from his conversations with Brad, like the fact that he had decided not to give the postman to Crisp after all. Why take chances by handing over the problem to a couple of parasites like that librarian and the postmaster, always clutching each other every minute this place was Witchville. That Simon slime could probably walk right by them and they'd be too busy looking into each other's eyes!

He snorted with disgust. MacGuffin wished sometimes that The Evil One would let him whip some of the other minions into line. And he'd start with Voss and Crisp. Many were the times he'd dreamed of lining one of the two of them up against the wall and having that one shot. It would certainly help the survivor see reason. They'd see then that it was a man's world! And more than that! A man's solar system—galaxy—even universe!

MacGuffin picked up the riding crop from his desk and whipped it a few times against the nose of the moose head that dominated one wall. Yes, by Witchville! It was time for some action. The moment had come for him to deal with that Simon scum, once and for all, and show that pantywaist postman there was no place for him in this man's world. That's why he wouldn't give the postman to anyone else. If you want to see the job done right, MacGuffin had often said, then you should kill the job yourself. Which was exactly what he intended to do.

He opened the office door. He hadn't given much thought to precisely how he was going to kill the postman. Now, if there had been two postmen, he could have put Simon up against the wall and had him shot. There was a certain symmetry in that sort of death that appealed to MacGuffin. Unfortunately, that symmetry did not work anywhere at all as well with a solo victim.

The sergeant sighed. He'd come up with something. He could think the whole time he was descending all those stairs. But he knew one thing for sure: Whatever method of death he devised, he would make sure that it would show Simon that it was a man's cosmos after all.

"Danke shane, darling, danke shane—"

Simon awoke, totally disoriented. He was in complete blackness; he couldn't see a thing. But there was music playing somewhere.

The radio!

"That's right!" the announcer's voice cut in, "this is WTCH, making sure you are awake and alert!"

Simon remembered now. He had been captured by the Boot Patrol, who had dragged him down into this underdungeon, but for some reason hadn't bothered to search him. That meant that he was still carrying not only the radio, but the Acme Kitchen Wonder and the magic truth glasses besides!

He sat up. Maybe there was a way out of here after all.

"And why, you may ask," the announcer continued, "has WTCH turned itself on again, when you repeatedly turn us off, even though we are only broadcasting for your own good? Well, we live in hope that you'll start listening to our warnings for a change and go out there and find the Wishbringer stone!"

The radio sounded upset. Simon supposed it had some justification. He had turned it off, after all, when it was trying to warn him that he was running into the middle of the Boot Patrol.

"So what do you have to say for yourself?" the radio demanded.

Then again, Simon thought, if it was going to badger him, he had half a mind to turn it off again.

He apologized instead. The radio had already saved his life at least once. He'd be foolish to completely disregard such a valuable tool.

"Apology accepted," the announcer replied. "And now it's time for a WTCH news flash!"

"Thanks, Stan," another voice took over. "This just in: Sergeant MacGuffin has started down the stairs to the underdungeon of the Witchville Jail."

"Sergeant MacGuffin?" Simon asked. "Coming here?"

"Let me read the rest of it, please," the second announcer replied drily. "Where was I? Oh, yes. Informed sources have let us know that he intends to kill Simon the Postman!"

"Thank you," the first announcer's voice took over. "We now resume our regularly scheduled programming."

"Danke shane," the singer's voice began again. "Darling, danke shane—"

"Wait a moment!" Simon shouted. "I'm trapped in a cell, and you tell me someone's coming down to kill me? What am I suppose to do?"

The song stopped.

"Oh," the announcer's voice broke in, "now you want our help."

"I'd appreciate it," Simon replied.

"I don't know," the announcer said doubtfully, "with that cavalier attitude you had before. Do you *really* want our help?"

"Of course I do!" Simon could feel his good manners slipping away. He struggled to control himself. "I said I was sorry! What else do you want me to do?"

"Okay," the announcer murmured. "Maybe we're being a little hard on the guy. Is it time for a WTCH news flash?"

"I think I could rustle one up," the second announcer replied.

"Don't touch that dial!" the first announcer stated more assertively. "It's time for a WTCH news bulletin."

"Thanks, Stan," the second announcer replied. Now that he was listening carefully, Simon thought he heard a rat-a-tat-tat noise behind the second announcer, like a teletype machine or something. "This just in: An escape route has been discovered in Simon the Postman's jail cell!"

"An escape route!" Simon demanded. "Where?"

"Patience," the second announcer chided him. "You've made me lose my place again. Ah, here we are: Yes, the escape route was found directly behind the carcass of the dead rat in the cell's southwest corner!"

Dead rat? Well, with the condition of this cell, Simon wasn't at all surprised. The rodent probably passed away trying to eat the food.

He fished in his pockets for the Acme Kitchen Wonder. He had no idea what part of the cell constituted southwest, but he hoped the rat carcass would show him the way. Unless his luck wasn't with him, and there were a great many rat carcasses in here.

His fingers closed around the familiar plastic and metal tube. He pulled it free of his pants pocket, where he now remembered hastily stuffing it when he was confronted by the Boot Patrol. He cradled the Wonder in both hands, searching carefully for the flashlight's on-off switch. The gadget buzzed when he hit one button, and chimed when he hit another. Once again, he promised himself he would look at the instruction booklet, as soon as he had the time.

The third switch turned on the flashlight. The beam illuminated the food and water dishes in front of him. Oddly enough, the food bowl was now empty. Simon figured that his dinner must have crawled away.

Still, he reflected, despite the fact that he hadn't eaten since morning and had been running around ever since, he felt remarkably clear-headed. It was remarkable what a short catnap, combined with the adrenalin-pumping fear of imminent death, could do to revive one's spirits.

He moved the flashlight's beam quickly through the interior of the cell. He was lucky—there was only one rat's carcass, pushed up into the far corner. The rest of the cell, besides the food bowls and a few miscellaneous things crawling here and there on the floor, was surprisingly empty. He moved quickly to the southwest corner, using the Kitchen Wonder to flick the carcass, which was quite petrified, out of the way.

"Further reports indicate," the second announcer's voice resumed, "that there is a loose stone in that corner of the cell, which, when pushed properly, opens the secret escape route."

Simon shone the light on the wall. The announcer had been correct; this particular wall was built of close-packed chunks of granite, perhaps fifteen to twenty of them. Simon decided he'd better start pushing.

He pressed the first stone in the corner. Nothing happened.

"Flash!" the first announcer's voice broke in. "We interrupt this WTCH News Bulletin to give you an even more important WTCH News Bulletin!"

Simon pressed the second stone. Still nothing.

"That's right, Stan," the second announcer's voice replied crisply. "We've learned that Sergeant MacGuffin has reached the landing outside the underdungeon, and is at this moment searching for the proper key!"

Simon pressed the third stone, then the forth. Zilcho.

"We suggest," the second announcer continued, "as a

WTCH public service, that our listening audience give some serious thought to getting his rear in gear!"

Simon thought he heard some sort of clattering down at the end of the corridor. Could it have been the sound of a key, turning in the lock?

He couldn't panic. Could he? He resisted the urge to start pushing every stone he could get his hands on. The radio had said to press a stone behind the dead rat. What if that stone wasn't in the wall? What if it was in the floor? He stomped down hard on the corner of his cell. Still noth—

He managed to grab both the radio and the Kitchen Wonder as the floor dropped out beneath him.

CHAPTER
TWENTY-ONE

"DANKE SHANE, DAR-
ling, danke shane—"

Simon once again thought fondly of losing the radio.
He was sliding down a long, smooth chute; then the chute
ended, and he seemed to be falling through open air.
Maybe this particular escape hadn't been such a good idea.
He felt his muscles tense, waiting for that killing impact
as, any second now, his body was dashed against the rocks.

He hit something soft instead.

"Oof!" Simon exclaimed as he heard metal springs
complain beneath him. Whatever he had landed on quivered for a moment, then was still. Simon felt around himself cautiously. He seemed to have landed on a pair of
cushions, supported by a heavily padded backboard of
some sort. Apparently, his life had been saved by landing
on an overstuffed couch.

"Oh, my," remarked a voice, which somehow managed to be deeply gruffed and distinctly feminine at the
same time, "someone has dropped in."

"Thank you for seeing me—" The radio's music cut
off abruptly. "FLASH!" the announcer screamed. "THIS
IS AN EXTRA-SPECIAL, SUPER-IMPORTANT WICH
NEWS BULLETIN!"

Simon turned the radio off. It was rude to visit someone and have that sort of nonsense blaring in your ear.

"You were saying?" he asked the voice.

"Simply making idle conversation," the gruff voice replied. "Are you sure you don't want to listen to the radio?"

"Why?" Simon asked, suddenly concerned that perhaps he had done the wrong thing. The radio was probably trying to warn him about something or other. Could it be warning him about the owner of this voice?

"Allow me to introduce myself," the voice's owner continued. "I am a Grue."

"Very pleased to meet you. My name is Simon, and I'm the postman."

"I see," the Grue replied. "I take it that you're not from around here?"

"I'm afraid not," Simon answered. "How could you tell?"

"Well, for one thing, you didn't shriek and cower, or try and run blindly away from me when I introduced myself. You see, Grues have a reputation—"

"FLASH!" the radio interrupted. "SCIENTIFIC EVIDENCE STRONGLY SUGGESTS THAT NO ONE HAS EVER SEEN A GRUE—AND LIVED TO TELL ABOUT IT—"

Simon turned down the radio. "Is that your reputation?"

"It certainly is," the Grue replied.

"Well," Simon remarked reasonably. "I could see where you might be upset by that kind of misrepresentation—"

"Oh, no," the Grue interrupted. "It is a reputation based on fact, pure and simple. No human being has ever seen a Grue and lived. We in Gruedom are quite proud of that tradition."

"Does that mean," Simon said, forcing the words out, "that you are going to have to kill me?"

"Is that what it sounds like?" The Grue chuckled. From the power projected by that voice, Simon imagined this particular Grue might be quite formidable. "But you haven't seen me, have you?"

No, Simon had to admit, he hadn't.

"Then," the Grue explained, "as long as no one turns on any lights, you are perfectly safe. So relax a little. It's so seldom that I get a chance to talk."

Something screamed behind Simon, an intense noise, rather like a freight train in heat.

"Excuse me a moment," the Grue remarked. "I have to tend to the baby."

"You have a child?" Simon asked. "Does that mean there is a Mister Grue?"

"Well, after a fashion. You wouldn't know about Grue mating rituals, would you? They only happen every seven years." The creature sighed. "One night of passion, and seven years to pay."

The baby screamed again, even louder than before. Simon felt the floor shake beneath the sofa.

"There, there now," the momma Grue cooed. "Is it-tumbittums hungry?"

The Grue child screamed its reply. Dirt dislodged from the ceiling and fell on Simon.

"Simon the postman?" the adult Grue called. "I would appreciate it if you closed your eyes very tightly."

"LISTEN TO HER—" the radio screamed. Simon turned it off and tucked it in his pocket. While he was thinking of it, he put the Kitchen Wonder away as well.

"Uh—certainly," Simon replied, doing what he was told. "Might I ask why?"

"Because otherwise I would have to kill you," the Grue replied cheerily. "No cheating now! You could say that we Grues have eyes in the back of our heads. And in a number of other places besides."

Simon heard what sounded like a refrigerator door opening, followed by the clank of bottles. A moment later,

Craig Shaw Gardner

the baby's cries were interrupted by a heavy-duty sucking sound.

"There," momma Grue spoke up. "You can open your eyes now. It would have been such a shame had you inadvertently seen something by the light of that little refrigerator bulb. You seem like such a nice young postman. I'd hate for you to have an accident."

Simon thanked her.

"It's the least I can do," she assured him. "But I haven't properly introduced myself. My name is Amy Sue."

"Amy Sue Grue?" Simon replied.

"I know, but what are you going to do?" Amy Sue replied. "My parents thought it was cute."

"I see," Simon replied, not knowing what else to say. The shock of his arrival here was starting to wear off. He wondered if there was some way he could get out of here—alive.

"But enough of this small talk," Amy Sue continued. "I have questions about the outside world. Being a single mother and all, it's very hard to get out and do things. I mean, finding a sitter is simply impossible! So, what's been happening out in Festeron?"

"It's Witchville, now," Simon answered.

"Again?" The Grue whistled. "That Evil One just doesn't know when to give up, does she? But wait a minute! If this is Witchville, and you're the postman, doesn't that mean you have a job to do?"

Simon told her it certainly did. He tried to sketch out the situation as briefly as possible.

"Then what are you doing down here, jawing with little old me?" the Grue demanded. "Not that I don't appreciate it. Still, it seems to me you have a country to save."

"I do," Simon agreed. "If only I could find the Wishbringer stone!"

"Oh, is that all?" Amy Sue asked. "Well, I know just the place to start. Give me a second here to wipe my hands on my apron." Simon felt something hard and scaly encircle his hand. The scaly thing pulled. "Come with me."

The Grue had passed within a few inches of him, her breath hot on his cheek. Simon wrinkled his nose; the exhalation had smelled of rotting meat.

"Here we are." Simon felt himself lifted aloft with the ease of a mother lifting an infant. "The tunnel starts right above your head."

Simon raised his hands and waved them about until he hit one of them against the corner of something. He ran his hand down and found what must be the floor of the passageway.

"Got it?" the Grue asked.

Simon told her he did.

"Good. I'll give you a push."

"Um, pardon me?" Simon asked as he was lifted farther aloft.

The Grue hesitated. "Yes?"

"Could you tell me where I'm going?"

"Oh," Amy Sue replied. "Silly of me. I got a bit too enthusiastic there. This tunnel leads up to the movie theater."

The movie theater? Wasn't that where Gloria was going? Maybe, Simon thought, he could save her yet. And defeat The Evil One in the process!

"You see," the Grue continued, "when this place has been turned into Witchville, The Evil One always shows short subjects filmed at her current headquarters. She tends to change her place of operations every time she starts up Witchville, incidentally. Sound pretty paranoid if you ask me. Anyway, get yourself into the movie theater, and you'll be able to tell right when the shorts come on exactly where The Evil One is located. And, according to what Gail told you at the Magick Shoppe, wherever The Evil One is, the Wishbringer stone must be nearby. There. Is that enough of an explanation?"

Simon replied that it was a great explanation. If he had been getting explanations like that since he had come to Witchville, he went on to say, he might actually understand what was going on.

"Explaining is one of those skills you can hone if you live alone and talk to yourself a lot," the Grue said modestly. "But don't feel sorry for me. Only five and a half years to go, and I expect to have a night of passion even better than the last one!"

She lifted him again, depositing him on the gently rising floor of the tunnel.

Something clattered on the floor below. The baby Grue returned to screaming.

"What a monster!" Amy Sue muttered. "Drop back anytime. But make sure I've turned out the light first!"

Simon thanked her and began to crawl.

CHAPTER
TWENTY-TWO

SIMON WAS AT LAST truly thankful for the long sleeves on his postal jacket. While the slope of the tunnel was gradual enough to make the climb reasonably comfortable, the tunnel itself seemed to have been somehow hewn from solid rock, with enough sharp shards of granite littered across the floor to cut him to pieces, had he not been wearing the heavy-issue postman's uniform.

He saw a light up ahead; faint, but a light nonetheless. He redoubled his crawl, and reached the tunnel's end in less than a minute.

He poked his head out and saw that he was surrounded by bushes. He pulled himself completely out of the hole and peeked over the bush tops.

He was on the edge of Festeron Circle; or at least what had once been Festeron Circle. Simon guessed it must be Witchville Circle now. The statue above the fountain had been changed. Instead of Phineas T. Fester, it was an elderly woman in a granny dress, holding both her fists aloft in triumph. Simon stared. Could this be a representation of The Evil One? Even the fountain below seemed to have changed. It was still working, but it no longer seemed to be spewing water. Pouring from the spigots instead was a darker, heavier liquid, like industrial sludge.

But the light he had seen in the tunnel was still behind him. Simon turned around to see what else he could discover from his hiding place, and saw that he was only a half dozen feet from the movie theater, now called (of course) "The Witchville".

He frowned up at the marquee:

BEYOND THE VALLEY OF THE ULTRA-NIGHTMARE
ON FRIDAY THE 13TH
with
EMMANUELLE MEETS GODZILLA
Delightfully Air Conditioned!

Simon whistled softly. The movie fare had certainly changed since the last time he had been here. But this was where Amy Sue Grue had told him to go. He wondered if he could just go up and buy a ticket. But then he remembered he had no money. The last coins he'd owned had been scattered by the ogre when Simon first tried to cross the toll bridge. Well, maybe there was some way he could sneak in. He wasn't called Simon the thief for nothing. He walked four feet to his right, still keeping the bush in front of him, so that he might get a better view of the ticket taker's window and entranceway beyond.

His breath caught in his throat. Miss Voss was seated in the ticket taker's window. Miss Voss hadn't liked him even back in Festeron—he hated to think what she would want to do to him now.

"Psst!" somebody hissed very loudly.

Simon looked around, but didn't immediately see anybody. Could it be Sneed?

"Oh, bother," a deep female voice remarked.

Simon felt something grab his ankle. He looked down to see his shin enclosed by an incredibly large, gray, and scaly hand. An eye opened on the hand's middle knuckle and blinked at him.

"You went the wrong way," remarked the voice, which by now Simon realized belonged to Amy Sue Grue. The hand pulled Simon's ankle, along with the rest of the postman, back into the tunnel.

When Simon opened his eyes, he was once again in total darkness. Something hard and scaly knocked both of his ears.

"Ow!" Simon remarked.

"You looked down at my hand," the Grue explained.

"But you grabbed my ankle!" Simon protested. "How was I to know—"

"I'm sorry," Amy Sue replied dourly, "but we have very strict rules about Grue sightings. You see a Grue hand, you get your ears boxed. Lucky for you that you didn't see my arm up to my elbow. That's when the retribution gets serious."

Simon didn't want to know. "What did you drag me back down here for?"

"Because you went the wrong way." The Grue sighed. "Of course, now I realize that I didn't tell you that the tunnel branched off in two directions. That's one of the occupational hazards of spending seven years at a time doing nothing but talking to oneself: no matter what you're going to discuss, you already know about it. When I saw you going the wrong way, I knew I had to climb up and pull you back to the tunnel branch where you should have turned right in the first place. So you go this way."

She pushed Simon to his right and slightly upward. He crawled into another dark tunnel.

"Now get moving!" Amy Sue chided. "You've only got a couple hours to find the stone. But do feel free to come back. Just let me know that you're coming."

Simon thanked her and crawled away again.

This time, after a moment's progress, he saw a red light overhead. As he got closer to the opening above, he heard voices. He paused, afraid of discovery, straining his ears to make out the words:

"But darling," said a man's voice, distraught. "What do you see in that big lizard?"

"I'm sorry, Michael," a woman's voice breathed sensuously. "But that 'big lizard', as you put it, is the only one for me."

It was only when the dramatic music welled up that Simon realized he was listening to the movie. This tunnel hole must lead inside the theater! He climbed the rest of the way as quickly and quietly as he could, hoping that the soundtrack would mask his movements.

The tunnel ended in a little alcove, cut off by a curtain from the rest of the theater. A small, red "Exit" sign shone overhead. Simon stood in the alcove and brushed the granite dust from his uniform, then peeked through the curtains. There didn't seem to be anyone seated in this corner of the movie theater. It was too dark to see any farther; he'd have to look for Gloria later. He walked quietly from the alcove and took the nearest seat.

There was a woman on the screen, young, blond, and lovely, wearing the sort of short black lingerie that seemed to reveal more than it covered. She sobbed into a small, black handkerchief.

The camera moved in to a close-up of her face.

"Goodbye, Godzilla," she breathed rapturously. "Who knew that I would have to meet a monster in order to experience—" she paused significantly, "—a real man." She waved through the window.

The camera cut to Godzilla. Godzilla waved back.

"Wwwoonnnnkkk!" the giant reptile replied, then turned and trudged into the ocean depths.

Across the screen, blue letters against the red sunset, came the words "The End—Or Is It?"

The lights came up in the theater for a moment. Simon looked cautiously around, his heart quickening when he realized that Gloria might be only a few feet away.

The room was completely still. He sighed. There was no-body here but him.

The lights went back down almost immediately. A cheerful voice announced through the loudspeakers:

"And now it's time for another visit with The Evil One, in 3-D with wraparound sound!"

"Thanks, Stan," an old woman's voice chortled glee-fully. "And I'm so glad to be back among you once again."

Simon turned back to the screen. This was what the Grue had told him about; his chance to discover The Evil One's secret headquarters.

Something was wrong. The movie was blurry and out of focus, full of double images. Simon realized he wouldn't be able to recognize anything on this screen. What had the announcer said? 3-D with wraparound sound? Didn't you need glasses to watch 3-D? But they probably had all the 3-D glasses out in the lobby, right there where Miss Voss could recognize him and give him back to the Boot Patrol and The Evil One. So there was no way he could watch this film, and no way he could discover The Evil One's secret headquarters.

Unless—

Simon pulled the magic plastic glasses out of his in-side breast pocket and carefully slid them over his ears and nose.

The 3-D image came into sharp focus.

"Ah, there you are," The Evil One said. "We've been looking for you for ever so long." What was she talking about? Simon looked at her surroundings. Three quarters of the room she stood in seemed to be dominated by ad-vanced scientific equipment, large, gleaming machines full of multicolored lights. In the room's remaining corner, Simon saw what appeared to be rows and rows of long wooden benches that had been pushed out of the way.

It only took Simon a moment to place them. He'd seen benches like that just once in Festeron, in the First Church of Festeronian Science!

"Now be a good postman," The Evil One continued, "and don't move until my minions arrive, so that we may greet you properly." She cackled evilly.

Postman? Simon started. That meant she knew where he was! He had to get out of here. He stood up, ripping off the glasses and stuffing them back in his pocket.

"What?" The Evil One's voice thundered over the loudspeakers. "Where have you gone? You can't escape me. No one can escape me! My followers will find you, wherever you hide!"

So he had become invisible to her? Perhaps, Simon mused, she could only see him in the theater when he was wearing the glasses to see her. It made as much sense as anything else that had happened so far.

But how was he going to get out of here? He didn't really want to go back into the tunnel and revisit the Grue. What if, for example, he dropped in on her when her refrigerator door was ajar? Simon shivered at the thought. Besides, the church that had become The Evil One's headquarters was just on the other side of Witchville Circle. If he left from one of the side exits of the theater, he could be there in a minute or less.

That was his decision, then. He would find the most likely fire exit and hope that the door wasn't connected to an alarm. Then he would get over to the church as quickly and quietly as possible.

"Oh, we're in luck!" a woman's voice called from the other end of the theater.

Simon whirled around. Were his pursuers here already?

"The feature hasn't started yet," the woman called to others who still stood in the entranceway. But this woman was no pursuer.

This woman was Gloria.

Simon somehow found himself running up the aisle toward her.

"Gloria!" he called.

"Eek!" she screamed. "It's that drag of a postman! Somebody call the Boot Patrol!"

"That won't be necessary," a man's voice called from behind Simon. "We have the situation well in hand."

Simon felt his wrists caught from behind, then something metallically cold slid over both of them. He knew that feeling. He had been handcuffed.

A man in a dark blue uniform with gold braid at the shoulders walked forward into Simon's field of vision. It was Mr. Crisp.

"Ah," the postmaster smirked. "You have returned to us at last."

A woman walked up, wearing a red, frilly, tight-fitting dress that emphasized her ample cleavage. It was only when Simon looked up into her stern, no-nonsense face that he realized it was Miss Voss.

She smiled grimly at him with her full, red lips, adding, "And we know just what to do with him."

CHAPTER
TWENTY-THREE

THEY PAUSED FOR A MOment as they led their victim from the movie theater. Violet looked to her beloved, and saw within his eyes the same excitement that coursed through her veins.

"Dearest," he whispered, his voice ragged, as if he had torn that single word from deep within his soul.

"Darling," she replied, running her tongue slowly across her lower lip. He looked at her with an intensity that made her entire being ache with longing.

"Corkie," she added with a tantalizing half-smile.

"You vixen!" her lover cried, roughly grabbing the sleeves of her red taffeta gown, the fabric clinging just so, showing off her best attributes to magnificent advantage. "You know what that does to me!"

She pouted up into the manly postmaster's face. "Oh, I know I shouldn't be cruel. It's simply that I want you so—" She paused. "But where's the postman?"

They both looked around, and saw that Simon had edged a dozen feet away during their conversation, and looked as if he was about to make an escape attempt.

"Oh, no, you don't!" Crisp cried in that direct way that she found so endearing. He bounded across the sidewalk, grabbing the postman before he had a chance to run. He brought the miserable young man back over to her. It was the first time she had taken a really good look at him. Actually, if you cleaned him up and gave him a new postal uniform, he might be rather handsome. She found herself particularly attracted to his hands, which looked both dexterous and powerful, trapped as they were in Crisp's handcuffs. Were the situation different—but no, she was sworn now to the bold postmaster, and would forswear all others. She looked away from the handcuffs, into her beloved Crisp's ruggedly handsome face.

"The handcuffs," she whispered huskily. It had been a stroke of luck that the postmaster had brought that particular piece of equipment with him, although she knew that he had originally had a different, more intimate reason for carrying them. But that intimacy would have to wait. They had a postman to dispense with, so that Witchville might be theirs forever.

He gave her a knowing smile in return. "We can no longer tarry. We must take this fellow some place where we can deal with him."

Her heart quickened. What a grand adventure this was! There was, of course, but one fitting place for this to end.

She spoke the words, her lips trembling ever so slightly

"The library."

"Of course," her lover replied, as if it would have been foolish to mention anyplace else. "The library."

But a new voice called out as they turned to go. A woman's voice.

"Wait a minute!"

All three of them looked up to see the newcomer as she raced from the movie theater. She was a young woman, dressed in that determinedly casual way that the teenagers had, with tight-fitting pants and a white blouse, the top three buttons oh-so-carelessly undone, covered by a man's leather jacket, which only served to increase one's awareness of her femininity. She had a triangular face, pretty and open, complemented by masses of long, ash-blond hair pushed back by the night wind, the very picture of adolescence on the verge of adulthood. Violet was envious for a moment, for she, too, remembered that special time, when she had also been trembling on the edge of budding womanhood.

"What can we do for you, young lady?" Crisp called. Violet looked doubtfully into her lover's eyes. Did she see something there beyond mere helpfulness?

"Gloria!" Simon the postman shouted, shifting out of his slouch so that he came to full attention. Violet noticed that his expression had changed as well. Was that hope she saw in the young man's gaze?

The young woman—Gloria?—frowned. "I wish I could stop this creep from shouting at me all the time. In fact, that's one of the reasons I stopped you."

Violet walked over and took the postmaster's arm, just so the young woman would know the proper order of things around here. She gave young Gloria her best motherly smile.

"I wouldn't worry," Violet said. "Once we are done with him, this particular postman will never bother anyone again."

"I know that, too," Gloria insisted. "But I have a favor to ask of you."

"Anything, my dear," Crisp replied, much too quickly for Violet's liking.

The young woman smiled tentatively. Crisp smiled back. Violet didn't believe he bought so easily into her little-girl-lost act.

"You know I was the one to spot the postman," she began.

"Yes?" the postmaster encouraged.

"And I know that now you are going to take him off to some secret place—"

Crisp nodded agreeably.

"To torture him, no doubt," she continued, "until, when he can no longer feel the pain, you will dispense with him entirely."

"All this and more," Violet interjected. "Does it offend your young sensibility that we will treat this man in this way? Did you come here to plead for mercy, that we might spare him?"

"Heck, no," Gloria replied enthusiastically. "I want to watch!"

"Why, of course," Crisp responded before Violet could think of an excuse to turn her down. He placed his free hand on Violet's other shoulder, and looked deep into her eyes. "We must be teachers, my dear," he said, speaking in that most manly of whispers. "We cannot keep this to ourselves. It would be unfair to future generations."

He gently pulled her hand from his arm, but then slipped that arm around her waist and holding her tightly as he further twisted about to grab the postman's shoulder with his free hand.

"Come along, now," he called to the girl, who followed all too eagerly, Violet thought.

And then they began to walk, back to the library, and their destiny.

CHAPTER
TWENTY-FOUR

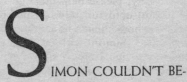S IMON COULDN'T BE-
lieve this!

That he'd been taken prisoner by Mr. Crisp and Miss
Voss was bad enough. But that the arrest had been made
possible by Gloria squealing on him was virtually beyond
belief. Now he was being led away to the library with a
very short future in store, made up mostly of torture and
death. And Gloria had asked if she could watch! Simon
didn't want to think about it.

Crisp had led them all in a brisk march, so that they
made it to the library in a matter of minutes. It looked, if
anything, more ivy-covered than before, with thick, red-
dish-green growth covering everything but the great
wooden double door. Simon looked more closely at the
weed-like fronds as Miss Voss unlocked the entranceway;
he had never seen ivy before that also sported thorns.

Miss Voss pushed open the door.

"Help!" an all-too-familiar voice cried from somewhere within. "Help me, please!"

Miss Voss smiled wickedly. "Looks like one of my
little traps has snared a visitor."

Mr. Crisp pulled the librarian to him, and looked

deep within her eyes. "I never doubted that they would for an instant."

"Corkie!" Miss Voss replied passionately.

"My darling!" was Crisp's sincere reply.

The two of them seemed to forget about everything else, absorbed completely in each other's gaze. Simon had almost escaped the last time this had happened. If Crisp would let go of his shoulder, he was ready to try it again.

"Help me!" the whiningly high voice shrieked again. "Somebody, please help me!"

That, unfortunately, seemed to break the spell. Crisp and Voss both spent a moment clearing their throats, Crisp turning to Simon with a no-nonsense, don't-you-even-think-of-trying-anything stare, while Miss Voss led the way into the library. She flicked on the lights.

"Help me!" The voice, surprisingly, came from up near the ceiling. Simon looked up to see Princess Tasmania hanging upside down, one webbed foot caught in a thick rope noose. The platypus saw him as well.

"Oh, brave postman!" she called. "I came here looking for a book, and see what happened? You can't imagine how boring it gets on the Misty Isle without something to read! Can you save me again?"

Both Crisp and Voss cackled evilly at that, Crisp twirling Simon about so that the princess could see the handcuffs.

"He is our prisoner, too," Miss Voss sneered. "It's so nice that the two of you know each other. It'll make it so much cozier when you die together!"

This time, Gloria's laughter joined with the others.

Crisp walked over to the wall. He turned to Gloria. "Young lady?" he asked.

"Gloria," she introduced herself.

"Yes, Gloria. If you'd like to help, we could use someone to stand under this beast and catch her."

"This beast!" Princess Tasmania erupted. "Do you have any idea who you're dealing with?"

Nobody paid any attention to her. Gloria walked over beneath the platypus, holding out her arms. Crisp threw the switch.

"I am a royal—oof—" the princess spoke and gasped as she plummeted into Gloria's arms. For an instant, Simon wished that Gloria might hold him that way someday, but then he remembered what she had become. Now, he realized, he not only had to rescue her, he had to somehow bring her back to her senses.

"Oh, Corkie," Miss Voss breathed. "You are so talented at throwing switches."

"Because they are your switches," Crisp replied nobly. "I am throwing them for you."

"You've always had such talented hands," the librarian replied throatily.

"So you've told me before," the postmaster murmured.

"Corkie!"

"My darling!"

"Ouch!" Gloria interrupted. "This creature tried to bite me!"

"Because you were holding me all wrong!" the princess retorted. "Don't you know anything about platypus anatomy?"

Both Mr. Crisp and Miss Voss spent a busy minute clearing their throats.

"On with the torture!" Crisp declared.

"Oh, you're so manly," Voss replied with a little shiver. "How shall we begin?"

The postmaster considered for a moment. "This is your library. You should decide what happens to them."

Miss Voss sighed. "Oh, Corkie. You are always so considerate." She paused, smiling to herself. "Eenie, meenie, minie, mo. What shall we do with them! Oh, I know!" She clapped her hands gleefully. "Take them to the automatic stamper."

"The stamper?" Gloria asked eagerly. "Pardon me, but what's the stamper?"

"Normally," Miss Voss replied excitedly, "just a machine we use in the library that automatically stamps due dates in the books."

"In indelible ink," Crisp further explained.

"We have made a few little adjustments in it, however," Voss added. "Now the stamper can work on humans—" She paused to gaze fondly at the platypus. "Or on anything else."

Crisp chuckled. "It will be the last due date they ever see!"

"Indelibly," Miss Voss added. "So if we can simply move our victims behind the counter?"

"You can't do this to me!" the princess screamed as Gloria carried her behind the Returns desk.

"Don't listen to her, dear," Miss Voss counseled. "Victims always go on like that."

"But I am a privileged platypus!" Tasmania continued.

"Soon," Miss Voss added easily, "to be a flattened platypus."

"But I am a member of the royal family," the princess pleaded.

Miss Voss looked about the room, considering. "This is a library. We must have recipes for platypus around here somewhere."

"Pardon me," a voice said in Simon's ear. "But I knew we'd find each other eventually."

It was Sneed! Or at least Sneed's voice. Simon wondered if he could casually look around the room without drawing too much attention. Yes! There he was, directly behind Crisp, only semi-transparent! Simon could see a firm outline of his coat, pants, and hat, even part of his face!

Maybe, the postman hoped, Sneed was on the road to recovery and visibility. He wondered if he could risk saying something to his friend. He glanced over at Crisp, but the postmaster was absorbed in watching the struggling platypus.

Simon nodded at the semi-invisible man.

"I think I've located the stone!" Sneed called excitedly. Simon glanced nervously at his captors.

"Oh, don't worry about the others," his wispy friend reassured him. "They're too busy setting up their dire torture devices to notice anything else."

"Ow!" Gloria screamed. "This thing bit me again!"

"Besides," Sneed continued, "I think you have a special gift for seeing me. It's another reason I feel you might be the ideal postman of Festeron."

The Ideal Postman of Festeron? Simon shivered at the thought.

"A royal platypus always goes down fighting!" Princess Tasmania announced.

"Well, she asked for it," Miss Voss replied. "Let's close her beak for good."

"I regret that I have but one life to give for Misty Island!" the princess remarked.

"What do you suggest?" Mr. Crisp asked as he looked around the Returns area. "That we somehow clamp that beak shut?"

"But I have other regrets," Tasmania continued, a tear falling from her large brown eye. "Father, if I had known I was not coming back, I would have cleaned the bathroom. Honestly!" She drew a ragged breath. "Think fondly of me."

"Clamp it shut!" Voss replied. "And quickly!" She pointed at her desk. "Open the top drawer!"

Crisp strode over to her desk.

"Do you think there's some way you could get me out of this?" Simon whispered to Sneed. Sneed had been right. Nobody else seemed to notice.

"Do you still have the Acme Kitchen Wonder?" Sneed inquired.

"In my pocket," Simon whispered back.

"You're almost out of here already," Sneed replied.

Crisp opened the drawer.

"There's nothing in here but rubber bands!" he declared.

"Exactly," Miss Voss replied. "One of the basic tools of the library trade. And what better way to silence our annoying guest?"

"Of course!" Crisp exclaimed, at last catching her drift. "We wrap her in rubber!" His eyes wandered to Miss Voss.

"Rubber," she replied, running her tongue slowly between her teeth. "Oh, Corkie!"

"My darling!" the Postmaster replied as he grabbed a fistful of rubber bands and lifted them to his heart.

"And I regret never learning a foreign language," the princess continued. "And how about a musical instrument? I've always greatly admired the oboe, with its deeply resonant to—"

Crisp firmly grasped the platypus's beak, encircling it with more than a dozen of the multicolored rubber loops. He looked a final time at Miss Voss. They cleared their throats together.

"Let's set up the stamper and get this over with," Voss said impatiently. "Then we can get on to—other things."

"Other things," Crisp whispered. He hurriedly wheeled a large machine away from the wall, all gleaming metal save for a hole in its middle large enough to insert, say, a platypus, or a human head.

"Time to stamp!" Miss Voss whispered as she walked up to the machine. She brushed the cool metal with her hand.

"Trrffmmm!" the platypus replied.

"Time to stamp!" Crisp agreed happily, joining his beloved at the machine. They spoke in low tones, adjusting dials together on the stamper's side.

"Time to stamp?" Gloria looked a little uncertainly at the bundle of fur she held in her hands.

"Time to get you out of here!" Sneed called to Simon. He frowned, and the postman could see the worry lines around his eyes. Yes, Sneed was definitely becoming more substantial.

"I just—" Sneed grunted with the effort, "—have to become—solid enough to grab—the Kitchen Wonder—" He took a deep breath. "And the directions." His hand reached out to Simon's pocket. At first, Sneed's fingers didn't seem to be making any contact with the metal and plastic device, but then Simon felt it move against his shirt.

"There!" Sneed cried triumphantly. "Almost . . . got it!" The substantially-more-together man smiled at the postman, the Kitchen Wonder in his hands.

"Now," Sneed asked. "Where are the directions?"

The directions? It took Simon a moment to remember where he had left them.

"Still in the box," the postman replied. "In the opposite pocket."

Crisp looked at Simon. "Talking to yourself? It won't do you any good. Once we get this stamper working, the platypus will be gone in only a second. Then you're next."

"Got the directions!" Sneed enthused. "Pardon me for a moment while I look up 'unlocking handcuffs'." He ruffled through the pages. "Ah, here we are!"

STAMP!

The noise startled Simon, and caused Sneed to drop the directions. They had the stamper working.

"Pretty powerful," Crisp commented.

"But not powerful enough," Voss insisted. "I think we can double the pounds-per-square-inch. I want to stamp them right out of Witchville!"

Gloria was beginning to look uncomfortable. Perhaps, Simon hoped, her basic goodness would surface yet.

Sneed retrieved the directions and moved behind Simon to work on the cuffs. "With you in a jiffy!" he promised.

STAMP!

"Closer," Crisp commented.

"Oh," Voss replied petulantly. "But I so want it to be perfect!"

The postmaster smiled reassuringly. "Then, for you, darling, we will make it perfect."

"Excuse me?" Gloria asked in an uncertain voice. Yes! Simon thought. She can take no more of this wanton cruelty. Deep in her heart, she was still the Gloria he knew and loved.

"Oh, my," Crisp replied solicitously. "You're looking a little green around the edges."

"What did I tell you?" the librarian interjected. "This younger generation just can't take it. The minute you get ready to torture a young man, and they get second thoughts."

"Oh, I don't care what you do the postman!" Gloria insisted. "But inflicting that kind of pain onto a poor dumb animal like this—I mean, even in Witchville, you have to draw the line someplace."

"There!" Sneed called triumphantly.

Simon heard a faint click, and felt the handcuffs fall from his hands.

"Now let's get out of here," Sneed encouraged.

"Not yet," Simon replied quietly. "We have to rescue the platypus."

"Oh, how could I have thought otherwise?" Sneed replied. "How noble!"

"Very well," Crisp said to Gloria. "If you feel that way about it, we'll stamp the postman first. Then you may be excused."

Gloria smiled, obviously relieved. "Thank you for your consideration."

But Miss Voss grabbed Mr. Crisp's hand. "Aren't you being a little *too* considerate?"

Crisp looked instantly concerned. "Why, darling, what do you mean?"

"I see the way you look at that little tramp!" she replied angrily.

"Why, dearest," he replied, genuinely stricken. "I do believe you are jealous."

"Of that piece of trash?" She laughed harshly. "Never!"

Crisp's frowned deepened. "Now, dearest, we must be careful how we speak of the younger generations. We have a responsibility—"

"See?" she demanded, waving her hands about in an agitated fashion. "You constantly defend her, placing her above me—"

Crisp caught both her wrists. "How can you say that? I would never place anyone above you, ever!"

Miss Voss hesitated, staring at her lover's stern gaze. Her voice trembled when she spoke again:

"Do you mean that, Corkie?"

"With all my heart." The postmaster allowed himself the slightest of smiles. "With one exception." He raised his eyebrows meaningfully. "There are certain—" he cleared his throat, "—situations where I might be—above you, for just a bit."

"Oh, Corkie!" Her hands clasped his wrists in turn. "Do you mean it?"

He pulled her closer. "You know exactly what I mean. And there are—certain situations where you would be above me, as well."

"Oh, yes, yes!" Miss Voss breathed heavily. "Why do you tantalize me so?"

The postmaster released her wrists so that he could grip her shoulders. "Only so you know that I am true to you—"

"Yes, Corkie?" Miss Voss prompted.

"Forever!" he concluded, his gaze locked with hers.

"Corkie," she whispered.

"My darling Violet," he replied.

"Corkie."

"My darling."

"This would be a good time to leave," Sneed suggested.

Simon realized his friend was right. Crisp and Voss were further gone than he had ever seen them before.

"There's one last thing I have to do." Massaging his wrists where the cuffs had dug into his flesh, he strode quickly over to Gloria.

"Corkie," Miss Voss moaned. "Oh, my Corkie."

"My . . . darling," Crisp groaned in response.

Simon faced Gloria. "Give me the platypus, now."

"Oh," the young woman replied, somewhat startled. "How did you get out of—"

"Now," Simon repeated.

Gloria looked at him strangely. "Uh, sure. Anything you say." She held out Princess Tasmania. Simon lifted the platypus gently from her arms.

"Corkie, Corkie, Corkie!" Miss Voss's breathing was getting rather heavy.

"Oh!" The postmaster drew her to him. "My darling, darling, darling!"

Simon stared at Gloria for another instant. He had to make a decision, now.

But what did he have to lose?

"You're coming with me, too," he said.

"But I'm supposed to be helping—" Gloria began.

"Now," Simon replied.

"Oh, uh." Gloria stared up at him, an oddly interested smile on her face. "Okay." She took his arm. "I didn't know you could be so forceful."

"Good." She was touching his arm! Still, Simon realized, if he lost it now, he would lose everything. He had to stay cool, no matter what. He jerked his head toward the door. "Let's go."

They moved quickly around the clenched librarian and postmaster.

"Cork—"

"My darl—"

The two kissed at last as Simon opened the library door and ushered the others out.

"What now?" he asked Sneed.

"Like I told you, I have found the—"

"SHOW ME THE WAY TO GO—" a drunken snatch of song interrupted Sneed's quiet speech, "—TIRED AND I WANNA—"

Gloria's father staggered around the corner of the library. He stopped when he saw Simon and the others. Gloria let go of Simon's arm and took a step away.

"Excuse me," he said with exaggerated care. "I am looking for my daughters."

"Oh, Witchville," Gloria muttered. "This is so embarrassing!"

"Wait a minute!" Her father peered over the top of his glasses. "*This* is one of my daughters!" He staggered forward. "Oh, daughter, I've missed you so!"

"Oh, gross!" Gloria backed away even further.

Simon stepped between them. "Mr. Magnifico—"

"Oops," Gloria's father replied as he lost his balance. He fell heavily against Simon, pushing both of them to the ground.

"Brrrf!" Princess Tasmania voiced a muffled protest as she was knocked out of Simon's arms. She rolled gently against a nearby tree.

"Simon!" Sneed hissed. "You've lost everything from your pockets!"

"Drat!" Professor Magnifico remarked. "Didn't see that pothole. But I've lost my glasses." He felt around on the ground. "Oh, no, here—"

He stopped talking and gasped.

"Oh, my," he said in a much more sober tone of voice.

Simon looked up at him, and realized Gloria's father had put on the magic plastic glasses by mistake.

"What's happening here?" the professor asked. "Are we in Witchville?"

"Don't you remember?" Simon asked.

"Not a thing," Magnifico confessed. "One minute I was down in the basement, tinkering with my small appliances. Then—nothing."

"Good heavens, Simon!" Sneed interjected. "Do you realize what this means?"

The professor blinked up at Sneed. "Oh, hello there. Didn't you used to be a postman, too?"

"When he put the glasses on," Sneed explained, "the professor broke the hold Witchville had over him. He's back to his Festeronian self!"

"Is that what happened?" the professor replied. "How interesting! Just think of the implications!"

"Maybe," Sneed continued, "if we use these glasses on everybody, we can turn Witchville around!"

Simon stared at the little man, who now looked as solid as he had ever seen him. But Sneed was right; the professor was once again his philosophically tinkering self. And, even more important, since Sneed was right, it meant they could use the glasses on Gloria!

"A noble experiment," the professor concurred. "Here, let me give you these."

He pulled the glasses from his face, then blinked, befuddled. "Now where was I—Oh, yeah—HAD A LITTLE DRINK ABOUT—"

Simon snatched the glasses from his hand as the professor fell face first into the grass.

"Apparently," Sneed remarked, "the glasses only work when they're physically on somebody."

Simon's radio turned on.

"Danke shane . . . Darling, danke shane—"

That meant something was about to happen. He had to get Gloria over on his side, fast.

Gloria backed away further still. "What are you looking at me for? I should have never followed you outside.

You were so forceful in there, I just lost my head for a moment. I should go back through that door and tell those two to capture you again." She glanced at the hand she had used to hold Simon's arm, a look of extreme distaste crossing her face—a look that said at the very least that the hand was in severe need of washing, and that perhaps it would be better still if she simply chopped it off at the wrist. "I knew you were a creep from the first! Keep those glasses away from me!"

"That's telling them, my dear," another woman's voice said. "I never realized how much potential you had."

Simon spun to face the newcomer: another old lady, this one dressed in a flannel shirt, rumpled jeans, and work boots.

"Allow me to introduce myself." The old woman nodded to Simon. "I am The Evil One."

CHAPTER
TWENTY-FIVE

"**S**HE MOST CERTAIN-
ly is," Sneed whispered in terror.

"Ptuui!" Princess Tasmania interjected. "Free at last!
Some hero you are, not even taking the rubber bands off
my beak!"

Simon didn't mention that he had left them there on
purpose, to better their chances for a clean escape. He
had other things to worry about now, anyway. He stuffed
the glasses back in his pocket, then picked up the radio
and the Kitchen Wonder.

The Evil One held out her hand to Gloria. "Come to
me, my dear. I will make sure you are properly protected."

Gloria circled Simon and the others at a safe distance.
She stopped behind The Evil One.

"Much better," the old woman cooed. "But this time,
everything will be much better." She smiled at Simon and
Sneed and Tasmania. "I am so glad we had this chance to
talk, before your untimely demise."

"That's what you think, sister!" the platypus princess
exclaimed. She waddled quickly over to Sneed and Simon.
"Postmen! Toss me the Kitchen Wonder! And grab my
paws!"

The two men did as she asked, while the princess

deftly caught the Wonder in her beak. She blew a single, clear, high note on the Wonder's whistle.

"Curses!" The Evil One screamed as everyone once again heard the angelic platypus choir.

Simon blinked, and he once again stood in the platypus palace. The princess was next to him, and Sneed was on her other side.

"How did we get here so fast?" Simon asked.

"Practice," Tasmania assured him. "It's all in how you wiggle your tongue when you blow."

"What is it now?" King Anatinus called from his throne. His two advisors peeked meekly out from behind either armrest.

"I have saved the postmen, Father," the princess replied. "It was only fair, after all the times they have saved me."

"Oh, so it's Simon again!" The king waved jovially, then glanced behind his throne. "It is quite safe." The advisors sheepishly emerged and descended the steps, Glenfizzlewizzle on the left, the Honorable Roger on the right. The king looked back to the postmen. "And we welcome the other fellow, too. We're sorry, but we've forgotten your name."

"Think nothing of it. Happens all the time." Sneed introduced himself.

"Oh, that's correct!" the king replied, snapping his webbed fingers. "You were the one who saved the princess from the trap in the church tower!"

"Alas, no," Sneed corrected. "That was my predecessor. Or perhaps it was the fellow who came after me. No, I saved your daughter from the trap in the open grave."

"We remember now!" The king nodded his head happily. "It was during one of those periods in which she insisted upon taking solitary walks."

"It gets so boring on the Misty Isle," the princess replied. She looked up at Simon. "Or at least it had been, until now."

"If you say so, dear," her father condescended. "But the postmen will be happy to hear that Glenfizzlewizzle has been making progress!"

Glenfizzlewizzle nodded his gray and ancient head. "I have located the general vicinity of the stone. It is definitely somewhere on the island of Greater Witchville—that is, if it is not hiding somewhere in North Festeron—but I should be able to eliminate that secondary location from our search in a matter of minutes!"

"Excellent!" King Anatinus applauded. "And, as an extra surprise, we can tell you that the Honorable Roger has been working as well."

"Indeed I have," the Honorable Roger agreed. "I have called out the Platypus Guard."

"The Platypus Guard?" Simon asked.

"An elite fighting unit, skilled in murder and mayhem, their battle instincts honed to razor sharpness," Roger explained. "Of course, they're not here quite yet. It takes them a few hours to get together. Platypuses, unfortunately, are not all that fast on their feet."

"And that fighting unit will be on direct orders to assist you in any way that you desire!" King Anatinus announced proudly. "That is, as soon as they all get here."

Simon thanked them. Unfortunately, he added, he didn't think they had enough time to stick around.

"Spoken like a true fighting man!" the Honorable Roger replied. "If the Platypus Guard ever manages to assemble, it will be an honor to fight by your side!"

"Well, perhaps it would be best if we used our magic to send them back," the king announced. "Any final thoughts before we do so?"

"Father!" the princess called. "I ask a boon!"

"A boon?" her father asked, pausing in the grand gesture he was about to make.

"Yes," Tasmania replied quickly, as if, should she hesitate, she would surely lose her nerve. "Before Simon the postman leaves, I should like to give him a farewell kiss."

"Ah," the king chuckled. "This is a boon we most easily grant."

"And remember the prophecy!" Glenfizzlewizzle added shakily. "*If* he is the proper young man!"

"He is certainly a hero," Tasmania sighed.

"And you are a princess," her father added. "So proceed."

Prophecy? Princess? Hero? This sounded to Simon like more than an ordinary kiss. He knelt so that Tasmania could reach his lips with her bill.

Nothing else happened. Tasmania decided to try it again. Simon decided that it felt like kissing a spatula. Nothing else happened the second time either.

Everyone let out a groan of disappointment.

"What," Simon said, turning to the king, "was she supposed to turn into an enchanted princess?"

Anatinus shook his head sadly. "We were more hoping that you would turn into an enchanted platypus. But no matter. I imagine that you'd like to get back to the mainland and your search for the stone."

"I'm afraid we must," Simon replied.

"How noble," Sneed agreed.

"Very well." The king drew a whistle from the pocket of his robe, and blew.

Simon opened his eyes. They were in a forest. And this part of Witchville didn't seem as silent as the others.

"Where are we?" he asked.

"Wait a second," Sneed replied. They listened quietly for a moment. There was a sound out here that Simon didn't recognize, a clacking of some sort.

"As I suspected," Sneed said at last. "We are in the northeast woods."

"How can you tell?" Simon asked.

"Can't you hear them? That clacking—it is the sound of the wild mailboxes."

He paused again. The clacking seemed to be getting closer.

"For the most part they are easily domesticated," Sneed continued a moment later, "especially if you have some mail. But we must get back to town. It was hard for me to stay quiet on the Misty Isle, for I have found The Evil One's headquarters!"

"Which is?" Simon asked helpfully, although he was already pretty sure of the answer.

"The First Church of Witchville Science!" Sneed announced proudly.

"Really!" Simon replied in his best astonished voice. "How clever of The Evil One. I never would have thought of it."

"So," Sneed asked eagerly, "do we go and get it?"

"I think so." Simon turned on his flashlight beam, and noticed that the platypus king had handily set them down upon a dirt road. It might have been his imagination, but the clacking seemed to get even louder with the light. He considered shining the beam out into the woods, but thought better of it.

"Besides," he added softly, "I'd just as soon get out of here. It's a little spooky."

"The woods up here can be a little wild, yes," Sneed agreed. "But it's better than a lot of places in Witchville."

"It is?" Simon replied as Sneed walked through the flashlight beam, casting solid shadows behind him.

"Oh, sure." Sneed smiled knowingly as he waved for Simon to follow him. "Pray we never have to visit the graveyard."

Simon prayed. The clacking sound receded behind them, but for some reason, it was a long, long time before it vanished completely.

CHAPTER
TWENTY-SIX

THEY CAME INTO TOWN
from the north road, as quietly as they could. Once they
had left the wild mailboxes behind, the eerie quiet of the
Witchville night settled around them once again, so that
their every footstep sounded like a gunshot, and every
whisper sounded like a shout.

Luckily for them, there was no one else about. There
was not another sound beyond their footsteps, their
breathing, and their occasional whispered exchange, even
as they approached The Evil One's statue in Witchville
Circle.

Sneed placed a very solid hand on Simon's shoulder.
"We're here." He pointed to the church on the right-hand
side of the road. Simon never would have recognized it.
The outline of the building was more or less the same,
but the church itself seemed to have fallen to ruins since
this afternoon. Half the windows were smashed, and the
double front doors appeared to be falling from their hinges.

It also looked utterly deserted. There was not a trace
of light, and a fine layer of dust seemed to have settled
upon the church's steps. Simon resisted the urge to ask
Sneed if he was sure about this. After all, hadn't Simon
seen the interior of this church in that 3-D Featurette?

"The Evil One is very good at disguising her head-quarters," Sneed whispered as they climbed the steps. "Sometimes too good." He grabbed the doorknob and pulled it toward him. It pulled away from the decaying wood with a groan.

"Look at this rot," Sneed remarked as he tossed the doorknob aside. "It's her specialty."

As if to confirm Sneed's speculation, the radio turned itself on.

"Danke shane . . . Darling, danke shane—"

Simon turned the radio off. He already knew they were moving toward danger. Besides, he had no desire to let the screaming radio announce their presence.

Sneed grabbed the door and pushed it out of the way, hinges screaming as they turned.

"Sounds like an alarm system to me," Simon remarked.

"You may be right. But there's less than an hour 'til twelve. I'm afraid we don't have time for subterfuge." Sneed boldly led the way inside.

The taller Simon brushed a fistful of cobwebs aside as he followed. He shone the flashlight beam around the alcove they had entered. At the end of the passageway was a second set of doors, much more solid-looking than the rotted wood one they had just passed. Sneed strode forward and tried the knobs. They were locked. The man in the rumpled coat turned back to Simon.

"Might I borrow the Kitchen Wonder?"

Simon passed the flashlight-and-apparently-anything-else-you-might-want to Sneed, who had just fished out a wad of paper from his crumpled raincoat.

"I kept the directions," he explained apologetically as he rapidly flipped through the pages in his hands. "Ah, here it is. Unlocking doors." He brought the Kitchen Wonder to within an inch of his nose. "Handy little gadget. Now where's the mauve button?" He frowned for a moment, then nodded. "Got it."

"THIS IS THE NEGLECTED WTCH!" the radio blared. "AND WE MIGHT HAVE A BULLETIN!"

Simon turned the radio off again, wondering if the volume could have hurt his eardrums. There seemed to be a problem with this magic warning system. If whoever was inside the church hadn't known about them before, they did now.

"Here I go," Sneed whispered. He carefully placed the Kitchen Wonder against the key hole. "Stand back now," he warned.

Simon was astonished by the change that had come over his rumpled friend. He had become direct, decisive, and was now taking charge. Simon was glad that he hadn't let on that he already knew Sneed's secret, for the rumpled man's discovery of The Evil One's hideout had given him a purpose and made him a changed man.

Sneed pressed the button, and the Kitchen Wonder made a high-pitched whirring sound. A look of alarm spread across the rumpled man's face as he started to vibrate. He shouted as he released the button, and both he and the Wonder were thrown to the floor.

Simon knelt by his friend. "Are you all right?"

Sneed took a deep breath. "Oh, dear, yes."

Simon looked up at the keyhole. "What's the matter? Was the door booby-trapped?" He wondered for an instant if that was what the radio was going to warn them about.

"Oh, dear," Sneed remarked as he rose shakily from the floor. "I'm afraid I hit the lavender button by mistake. I think that's the one that turns on the blender. It's so hard to tell them apart in the dark."

Simon stood again, too. His friend's newfound confidence seemed to be evaporating as rapidly as it had arrived. Simon wondered if there was some way he might be able to bring it back.

"Well, why don't you try again?" he asked Sneed matter-of-factly.

"Should I? Oh, you're right, I should." Sneed sighed. "It's having to cope with all this insubstantiality, I'm afraid. One little setback and I fall to pieces."

He put the Kitchen Wonder up to the keyhole again. "Stand back, now, please," he said with somewhat less authority than before.

He pressed another button. This time the Kitchen Wonder whirred softly. And the door unlocked with a solid click.

"Shall we?" Sneed whispered.

"They haven't gone after us yet," Simon replied. "Who knows? Maybe The Evil One is out somewhere? Maybe we can get the stone and get out of here before she comes back?"

"THIS IS WTCH, TRYING FOR ONE FINAL TIME!" the radio screamed. "ARE YOU GOING TO LISTEN TO US, OR ARE YOU GOING TO GET YOURSELF KILLED?"

This time, Simon only turned the radio down. Even though the midnight curfew loomed, it wouldn't hurt to hear the announcer's warning. The radio, after all, had saved him before.

"There," the radio replied when it realized it wasn't being turned off. "That's better. Sometimes I wonder why I bother with this thankless job, anyway. But here's Phil with another bulletin."

"Thanks, Stan, and this is an important one. Whatever you do—"

The radio paused as the church doors swung inwards. Gloria stood on the other side, smiling at them.

"Too late!" Phil announced. The radio shut itself off.

"Maybe there's somebody here after all," Gloria remarked. "And maybe you're just dead meat. Oh, Evil One! They're here!"

"Already?" the old woman's voice called from somewhere far away. "And I'm so busy now. Could you be a dear, and make sure our visitors are captured and killed?"

211

"Certainly!" Gloria turned to her left. "Oh, Brad! It's your turn!"

Brad? Simon thought. Brad MacGuffin? But that meant they had run into—

> "The Boot Patrol is so sublime!
> They'll beat you up at any time!
> Sound off! One, two!
> Sound off! Three, four!
> Sound off! One, two, three, four!
> Three-four!"

The sound of boots echoed through the wooden church. The patrol was right around the corner. If they didn't do something soon, they'd be captured. But what?

Sneed grabbed the lapels of Simon's post office jacket.

"Run!" the rumpled man screamed.

Simon decided it was as good an idea as any.

The radio turned itself back on.

"I'VE GOT ANOTHER BULLETIN!" Phil screamed.

"Yeah?" Simon replied.

"THERE'S MORE OF THEM OUTSIDE!"

And there were, half a dozen smiling men in uniform, standing in a semicircle a few paces from the church steps.

"RIGHT! GO RIGHT!" the radio directed. "INTO THE BUSHES!"

Simon pulled Sneed into the shrubbery as the rest of the Boot Patrollers emerged from the church. They greeted each other with a chant:

> "The Boot Patrol makes people gulp,
> Before it grinds them into pulp!
> Sound off! One, two!
> Sound off! Three, four!
> Sound off! One, two, three, four!
> Three-four!"

"NOW GET YOURSELF ONTO RIVER ROAD! HURRY!"

Simon and Sneed emerged from the bushes, and saw that they were headed west. They heard the Boot Patrol clomping toward them down the sidewalk.

They ran.

CHAPTER
TWENTY-SEVEN

ND THEY KEPT ON
running. But no matter how they ran, their pursuers were
never far behind.

"The Boot Patrol will never lack,
For we shoot people in the back!
Sound off! One, two!
Sound off! Three, four!
Sound off! One, two, three, four!
Three-four!"

"Okay," the radio announced somewhat more softly,
for Simon had finally turned it down. "Here's another bulletin. Reliable sources say that Simon the Postman and his
friend Sneed have almost reached River Road. Experts
suggest that the best course the two could take is to turn
right on River Road, then climb the hill to the old tree
stump."

"Old tree stump?" Simon asked.

"They're leading us to the underground passageways,"
Sneed explained. "The island is riddled with them."

"Thank you," the radio replied, and went back to
playing soothing music.

"Wait a moment!" the other announcer's voice broke in. "I have a brand-new bulletin!"

"Can't it wait, Stan?" the first announcer asked. "We've almost managed to elude their pursuers."

"I'm afraid not, Phil," Stan replied. "This situation could be potentially serious. But for more on this, we need a traffic update. Glen?"

"Okay, Stan, Phil," a third announcer's voice broke in. "We have a real bottleneck up ahead. Going north on River Road—"

What was the radio talking about? They had almost made it to River Road already; Simon could hear the ocean crashing against the pebble beach. And when their pursuit started chanting again, they sounded closer than ever.

> "The Boot Patrol is so sublime
> For we can catch you any time!
> Sound off! One—"

"That's right," Glen continued on the radio. "There's trouble ahead, caused by a stalled Sergeant MacGuffin."

"Sergeant MacGuffin?" Sneed and Simon yelled as one.

"He's waiting for you, hiding in the trees. And he brought an arsenal with him." The announcer cleared his throat. "WTCH suggests you turn left on River Road and take the alternate route."

"But Glen!" Stan's voice broke in. "That's the road to the graveyard!"

"There are no other routes available," Glen replied with finality. "It's less than forty minutes to midnight, after all."

The flashlight beam showed a pebble beach with crashing waves just beyond. The two postmen skidded to a halt. Simon looked behind, and saw a definite flicker of torchlight around a bend in the road.

"What do we do?" he asked Sneed.

"What can we do?" the rumpled man replied despairingly. "We turn left!"

Simon thought he heard faint screams in the distance, like someone calling out names, as they turned toward the graveyard.

"Flash!" Phil's voice came from the radio. "It's time for yet another WTCH Late-Breaking Bulletin!"

"What is it *this* time?" Simon wailed. He was running out of breath.

"Well, if that's going to be your attitude," Phil replied, "maybe I won't read it to you after all."

Simon barely restrained his urge to smash the radio in the road.

"Hey!" he yelled at the plastic box. "We're under a little pressure here!"

"Oh, yeah," the radio replied a bit more humbly. "Well, I'll stop editorializing now. And I will remind you that WTCH recognizes its responsibility to air opposing points of view."

"So what's the bulletin?" Simon demanded.

"Oh, that. Let me find it—"

"I have it here, Phil," Stan's voice broke in. "And an important WTCH Late-Breaking Bulletin it is, too!" Simon could once again hear the teletype machines in the background. "It appears that the southern portion of River Road has its obstacles as well. Recent calls to the station have let us know that a certain postmaster and his librarian consort have set up a trip wire across the road. Informed sources say that, once this trip wire has been activated, a giant net will descend, trapping any beneath it."

"Have you got anything to add to that from the traffic point of view, Glen?" Phil asked.

"Only that it's likely to happen in the next minute or two, Phil," the traffic reporter replied.

Sneed and Simon had slowed down to a walk.

"What should we do?" Simon asked.

"Have no fear," Sneed replied. "Take the Kitchen

Wonder." He flipped quickly through the directions. "Ah. Here it is. Detecting trip wires. You simply have to hold down the yellow switch on the bottom."

Simon held the light in front of him as he walked briskly forward. They heard chanting in the distance:

> "The Boot Patrol is your best bet
> 'Cause you haven't lost us yet!
> Sound off! One, two!
> Sound off! Three, four!
> Sound off! One, two, three, four!
> Three-four!"

Despite their boast, they sounded a bit farther away than before. It must have taken them a minute to determine which way Simon and Sneed had turned. Now that they were on the right trail, though, Simon had no doubt they would catch up quickly. Especially since the postmen had to somehow avoid the trap up ahead.

The Kitchen Wonder began to beep.

"The trap!" Sneed whispered. "It's just ahead!"

"What's that noise, dearest?" a man's voice called from one side of the road.

"What noise, Corkie-workie?" a woman's voice replied from the other side. "That beeping? I believe it's an alarm of some kind."

"Oh!" the postmaster shouted. "When you call me Corkie-workie, it drives me even wilder! But what kind of alarm, lover? Is someone in the trap?"

"Well, The Evil One didn't tell me there was an alarm. Perhaps we should check."

"Very well, dearest. I shall go."

"No, darling Corkie. We shall both go. And we will meet in the middle."

"They do go on!" Sneed whispered. All Simon could do was nod, as he listened to the approach of the Boot Patrol, already alarmingly nearer than they were before.

"The Boot Patrol—no ifs or buts,
Is coming to rip out your guts!
Sound off! One, two!
Sound—"

Simon's attention was drawn back to the trap in front of them as Mr. Crisp descended a tree and Miss Voss crawled out from behind a rock.

"I don't see anything, darling," Crisp whispered.

Miss Voss nodded, her bosom heaving with the strain of her recent exercise.

"Still, Corkie, I think it wise to check."

"Shall we?" he whispered. And they ran together with exquisite slowness, somehow paying more attention to each other than to the potentially damaged trap.

"Oh, darling!" Crisp moaned.

"Corkie!" Voss replied.

Simon was not at all surprised when he heard the sharp twang of the trip wire. The postmaster and librarian squealed together as the net lifted around them and pulled them from the ground.

"Corkie! Look!" She pointed at Simon. "It is the postman."

"Yes, my darling," the postmaster replied bravely. "But he is beyond us now."

"Then we are trapped here together?" For some reason, Miss Voss seemed to be breathing even faster.

"There is nothing we can do!" Crisp shifted around so they faced each other in the net.

She took his hand.

"Oh, dearest!" the postmaster whispered.

Their fingers intertwined.

"Corkie!" the librarian replied.

Their heads grew closer.

"My darling!"

They gazed deep into each other's eyes.

"Corkie-workie!"

They both breathed heavily.

Simon nudged Sneed forward. They quickly circled The Evil One's imprisoned minions and were none-too-soon out of hearing range.

They could still hear the Boot Patrol, however.

"The Boot Patrol is on the way—
There is no hope. You'd better pray!
Sound off! One, two!
Sound off! Three, four!
Sound off! One, two, three, four!
Three-four!"

"The gate to the cemetery isn't far now," Sneed called to Simon.

"So you know your way around in there?" Simon asked.

"As much as anyone knows the cemetery. Maybe we'll be lucky, and the gate will be locked."

"Maybe we'll be lucky?" Simon glanced behind him. That torchlight looked awfully close. "But then the Boot Patrol will get us!"

"Compared to the cemetery, that might be lucky." Sneed lifted the light so that it shone farther ahead. "Oh, no. I think I see the gate. And I think it's unlocked."

The radio started to play in Simon's pocket.

"Danke shane, darling, danke shane . . ."

"Flash!" Stan's voice came on. "We have a WTCH Late-Breaking News Flash! Simon and Sneed have been seen approaching the Witchville Cemetery. Unconfirmed reports have attributed many deaths to this same cemetery—"

"FLASH!" Phil's voice overwhelmed Stan. "HERE'S AN EVEN-LATER-BREAKING WTCH NEWS BULLE-TIN! ACCORDING TO INFORMED SOURCES, THE BOOT PATROL HAS BEEN PICKING UP SPEED, AND WILL CAPTURE THEIR PREY IN UNDER A MINUTE!"

"FLASH!" Glen the traffic reporter's voice cut in, somehow even louder. *"THIS REPORTER HAS JUST LEARNED THAT A WILDLY CAREENING SERGEANT MACGUFFIN IS RUNNING OUT OF CONTROL ON RIVER ROAD, AND IS DUE TO PASS THE BOOT PATROL AT ANY SECOND! ALTERNATE ROUTES ARE ADVISED!"*

"But the cemetery is certain death—" Stan pleaded.

"BUT WHEN THE BOOT PATROL CATCHES THEM," Phil advised, "THEY'LL BE QUICKER ABOUT IT!"

"SERGEANT MACGUFFIN WILL BE QUICKEST OF ALL!" Glen screamed. *"HE'S GOT A ROCKET LAUNCHER!"*

"But if they—"

"THERE'S NO WAY THEY COULD—"

"THEY CAN'T DO THAT BECAUSE—"

There was a burst of static, replaced a moment later by a low-pitched whine.

"This is a test," another announcer's voice began. "This is only a test. Were this a real emergency, you would be instructed to turn to—"

Simon turned it off. Their situation had finally gotten too perilous even for a magic radio.

"Come on!" Sneed yelled, grabbing Simon's lapel and pulling him through the open gate. "We're going inside!"

CHAPTER
TWENTY-EIGHT

T HINGS LOOKED DIF-
ferent in the graveyard.

For one thing, there was a fine mist that hung over everything—the trees and paths, the crypts and headstones. For another thing, that mist seemed to glow faintly.

"Spirit wraiths!" Sneed explained. "Watch out. They're tricky!"

Simon stuck close to his friend's side, trying to get used to the unnatural light. For the past few minutes, they had done nothing but escape. And time was running out. Simon imagined it had to be awfully close to midnight. Somehow, they had to get things back under control.

"What will The Evil One try to do next?" he asked.

Sneed frowned at him. "What do you mean?"

"Who will she have waiting for us in the graveyard?"

Sneed sighed. "I think you're missing a basic concept here. No one would be stupid enough to wait for us in the graveyard. Not even The Evil One." He looked up at the floating mists. "That is, at least, nothing still alive."

Simon didn't care for this line of argument. "Then what are we doing here?"

"We're trying to get out!" Sneed started to run. "Now follow me!"

Simon ran after the very solid Sneed. At the moment, actually, Simon was the one who was feeling a little transparent. Sneed was the one making decisions now, but that only made sense. Sneed, after all, knew the territory. Simon wondered if he could still be a hero if he never got to initiate any action.

Simon noticed uneasily that the mist was following them.

"It's the wraiths!" Sneed gasped, redoubling his speed. "They're after us!"

"Where are we going?" Simon called back.

"We've got to find an open grave!" Sneed replied.

Simon wondered if he should stop asking questions. Lately, the answers only made him feel worse.

He felt something pulling at his clothing. Was it the wraiths?

"Isn't there something we can do?" he asked, shrugging his shoulders in a vain attempt to shake them off. He felt something cold slide beneath his collar and ooze down his back.

"Nothing that I know about!" Sneed replied, brushing at his sleeves as he ran. "At least, nothing that anybody has ever lived to talk about!"

Well, Simon thought, he had been asking questions again, when by now he should know better. The coldness was creeping up his pants leg now, and seemed to be seeping into his socks. There had to be some way out of this! He hadn't come all this way to be swallowed by clammy wraiths! But there was no place to turn.

Unless—

What about the radio? It had been dispensing advice since this place had turned into Witchville, and even saved his life once or twice. And here it was, still in his pocket. Simon reached over to turn it on.

"Come on, WTCH," he murmured. "I need a bulletin now."

The radio came on with a burst of static.

"—only a test. Were this a real emergency, you would be instructed—"

Simon turned the radio off. It looked as if their situation might have short-circuited it for good. The coldness climbed over his shoulders to his chest, and had found a way into his shirtsleeves, rising from his wrists to his elbows. Simon almost asked what would happen when the wraiths totally covered them, but decided he wouldn't like that answer any better than the ones he had gotten before.

That's when they heard the chant behind them:

"The Boot Patrol's by far the best;
We'll smash your skull and leave the rest!
Sound off! One, two!
Sound off! Three, four!
Sound off! One, two, three, four!
Three-four!"

Sneed stopped and looked behind them, open-mouthed. "They shouldn't be in here. The Boot Patrol never comes into the graveyard!"

Simon hesitated too. But shouldn't they keep running? Weren't they easier targets for the wraiths if they were standing still?

But then he realized the wraiths had left them. Sneed and he were standing in the dark.

"Where did they go?" Simon asked.

"The wraiths? I imagine they went after fresh meat." Sneed shook his raincoat. "Despite appearances, I'm not as solid as I might be. The spirits had a tough time getting a grip on me. And, no offense, but compared to the Boot Patrol, you're pretty tired and puny yourself. If I was a wraith looking for a satisfying meal, I'd leave you in an instant to go after the goose-steppers. All in all, they are a much hardier group of souls."

Sneed turned and started to walk. "But we have to find that open grave."

"Still?" Simon protested. "But the wraiths are gone, and they'll take care of the Boot Patrol. Won't they?"

Sneed shook his head. "There's too many of them. The wraiths will pick off three, maybe four, but the rest of them will keep on marching in our direction." He stopped abruptly. "Here we are. I knew this thing was around here someplace. Jump in."

Simon saw he was pointing into an open grave.

"Why?" he asked.

"Because it leads to a secret passageway, one of the secret underground tunnels that criss-cross the island! Now jump! You never know when the wraiths might have second thoughts!"

Another tunnel? Simon wondered, as he jumped, if this one also led to the Grue. Sneed jumped down next to him, grabbed the Kitchen Wonder, and flashed the Wonder's light around.

"There!" he said, pointing the beam at something shiny on the grave's right-hand wall. On closer inspection, Simon realized it was a doorknob.

> "The Boot Patrol will take a slice,
> What we can't cut, we then will dice!
> Sound off! One, two!
> Sound off! Three, four!
> Sound off! One, two, three, four!
> Three-four!"

They sounded awfully close. Apparently, the wraiths had hardly slowed them down at all.

"Open the door!" Sneed exclaimed. "The Boot Patrol has already overstepped its limits by coming into the graveyard. They'll never follow us into an open grave. Once we're in the tunnels, we'll be safe!"

Simon opened the door, which groaned even more loudly than the one at the church. Sneed led the way, shining the flashlight beam before him. Simon followed, making sure the door was shut firmly behind them.

"This island is positively riddled with tunnels. Now, if I can remember the way, I can have us back outside The Evil One's headquarters in a matter of minutes!"

They came to a place where the tunnel split into two branches. "Let's see," Sneed mused. "This way, I think. We have to observe a little caution down here. These tunnels can be tricky, and some of them lead to places where you'd rather not go. We could wind up climbing into the jail, or even worse."

"The Grue?" Simon asked.

"How did you know about that?"

"I've met her."

"But that's impossible! No man has ever seen the Grue and lived!"

"Oh, I've never seen her. But we did talk for a while in the dark."

"Really? Yes, I suppose that would be all right. There are no legends about anything happening to people who've listened to the Grue."

They came to another branching of the tunnel. "Right," Sneed remarked, walking into the left-hand corridor. "The Grue is quite civil, then? Perhaps you can introduce me sometime when we're not racing to save Festeron?" The rumpled man sighed. "At least we've eluded our pursuers."

Simon heard a noise behind them, a definite, groaning creak of an opening door. A moment later, the door slammed shut.

> "The Boot Patrol will take a shot,
> When we get done you'll leak a lot!
> Sound off! One, two!
> Sound off! Three, four!
> Sound off! One, two, three, four!
> Three-four!"

Sneed looked over his shoulder. "What are they doing down here? They never come down here!"

Simon put a reassuring hand on his friend's rumpled sleeve. "I have the feeling that The Evil One wants us a lot—so much so that they're willing to break a few rules."

"Well, we have to get out of here!" Sneed's voice had suddenly taken on a nervous edge that Simon hadn't heard in quite some time. They came to another fork in the tunnel. "This way, I think. No, maybe this way! Oh, who cares!"

They ran down the right-hand branch.

The radio turned on.

"Danke shane, darling, danke shane—"

"WTCH is back on the air!" Stan's voice trumpeted. "And have we got a news bulletin for you!"

"Wait a second!" Simon demanded. "I thought you guys were gone for good. What happened to you in the cemetery?"

"Sorry about that," Stan replied. "We just don't work in graveyards. Everybody has their limits."

"But now it's time," Phil broke in, "for a WTCH traffic update. Glen?"

"Thanks, Phil. Thanks, Stan," Glen replied. "A couple problems on the underground arteries. For one thing, the Boot Patrol has entered the area with a march that far exceeds the speed limit."

As if in response, the Boot Patrol chanted:

> "The Boot Patrol will take a stab,
> And rid you of unsightly flab!
> Sound off! One, two!
> Sound—"

"That Boot Patrol has never been a group to obey the law," Phil chuckled. "What a bunch of wild and crazy guys. But you said there were a couple of problems, Glen."

"That's right, and the second one is potentially more

serious. A couple of other travelers down there have taken a wrong turn, and are about to enter a Grue's nest!"

"What?" Sneed screamed, almost beside himself. "I must have taken the wrong corridor!"

> "The Boot Patrol has got a hunch;
> We're going to make you lose your lunch!
> Sound off! One, two!
> Sound off! Three—"

"Calm down!" Simon commanded his friend, even though the Boot Patrol did sound awfully close. He looked back up the tunnel, and saw what looked like the first glimmers of flicking torchlight. "There's a way out of this yet!"

> "The Boot Patrol will make you gulp,
> Then beat you to a bloody pulp!
> Sound off!—"

Simon grabbed his friend's arm and began to run. "Into the Grue's nest!"

"Into the what?" Sneed replied hysterically.

"You heard me!" He turned to call down the corridor.

"Yoo-hoo! Amy Sue! You have visitors!"

CHAPTER
TWENTY-NINE

IMON GRABBED
Sneed's hand and turned off the flashlight. They kept on running.

> "The Boot Patrol will stomp and tear,
> And rip and shred and crush; so there!
> Sound off! One, two!
> Sound off! Three, four!
> Sound off! One, two, three—"

"I have visitors," a gravelly female voice said close to Simon's ear.

"Yes, sorry to drop in so unexpectedly," Simon replied. He waved in the general direction of where he hoped his rumpled friend was. "This is Sneed."

"So happy not to see you," Amy Sue replied. "I presume Simon has told you the rules?"

Meekly, Sneed assured the Grue that Simon had.

"Good," Amy Sue replied. "The more the merrier. So, what brings you to my part of the tunnel?"

Simon explained that he had brought her a midnight snack.

As if on cue, the Boot Patrol chanted:

Wishbringer

"The Boot Patrol has quite a sting,
And we can handle anything!
Sound off! One, two!
Sound off! Three, four!
Sound off! One, two, three, four!
Three-four!"

"I think I see the faintest glimmer of reflected torch-light," the Grue replied jovially. "I think it's time for my two visitors to get a close and personal tour of one of my closets."

Simon felt strong fingers pick him up by his uniform collar. The knuckles that brushed the back of his neck were as hard as stone. Sneed gasped as the Grue did the same to him. They moved quickly through the Grue's apartment. Then Amy Sue released her grip, and Simon fell into something soft. He heard Sneed start to breathe at his side, then felt the air on his face as a door slammed shut. There was another sound, a firm click, as if somebody had just closed a padlock, followed by the heavy footsteps of Amy Sue retreating across the room.

The Boot Patrol's chant was very, very close:

"The Boot Patrol is on a spree,
So watch out now 'cause we're—aaieee!"

There was a great deal of crashing and screaming for a few seconds, then silence. They heard the sound of a key in a lock. The door swung open.

Amy Sue burped.

"Excuse me," she remarked. "I shouldn't eat so fast. But it's so seldom I get a treat like that these days. Flame broiled, too."

Sneed made a muffled gagging sound.

"So," Amy Sue asked, "can you folks stay and chat, or are you still running your errands?"

Simon explained that they had to leave. If they didn't

rescue the stone in the next few minutes, Festeron would become Witchville forever.

The Grue sighed. "I understand. It's a busy, busy world out there. Well, stop back again sometime after you've saved the day." Simon felt Amy Sue's rough fingers on his collar. "I'll direct you to one of the tunnels up. Feel free to drop in again, especially if you're going to bring lunch."

Simon waited for her to push him in the hole, then started climbing. He could hear Sneed huffing close behind him.

They came out beneath the bushes next to the movie theater.

Sneed gasped in great lungfuls of air

"I can't believe we're still alive."

Simon nodded. "Hopefully, neither will The Evil One. This time, maybe we can take her by surprise."

"What nobility!" Sneed sighed. He handed Simon the Kitchen Wonder. "Lead on. You're the hero now."

"Danke shane . . . Darling, danke shane—"

"Time for another WTCH Bulletin!" Stan announced.

"What is it this time?" Simon asked.

"Only seventeen minutes until Festeron becomes Witchville forever!" the radio replied.

"Thank you," Simon said.

"Thought you'd like to know," Stan offered.

"Good," Simon replied. "Now keep quiet."

He turned the radio off and waved for Sneed to follow him. The two of them moved quickly over to the church.

"There's got to be another way into this place!" Simon whispered.

"I'm sure there is," Sneed replied. "But The Evil One is awfully good at disguising it."

And they had hardly any time left! Simon didn't want to use up precious minutes looking for a hidden entrance. But there was nothing else they could do if they wanted to avoid walking in through the front door.

Unless—

Simon pulled the magic plastic glasses from his inner pocket. If anything could see through The Evil One's duplicity, these could. He placed the plastic nose over his own, and blinked.

The church looked whole and new again, as it had in Festeron. And he could see lights on in all the windows.

He waved to Sneed again. "Follow me!"

The two of them walked around to the back of the church. Simon couldn't believe his luck. There was a door back here, wide open!

"Where are you going?" Sneed asked a touch hysterically.

"In through here." Simon looked over the top of his glasses, and found himself staring at a brick wall protected by a barbed-wire fence. "This isn't really here." He moved his hand forward, still expecting to be cut by one of the barbs. Nothing happened. "See? It's an illusion."

Simon grabbed Sneed's arm and led him into the church. They found themselves in a quiet hallway, with closed doors at either end.

"Now," Simon whispered, "we simply have to figure out where The Evil One keeps her headquarters."

"Look for stairs," Sneed suggested. "The Evil One prefers higher elevations. You know, inaccessible towers, places like that."

The door to their left started to open.

"What should we do?" Sneed whispered. "Run?"

"Yeah," Simon replied, running as he spoke. "Right toward that opening door. We don't have time for subterfuge. We have to grab whoever's there and make them tell us where The Evil One is hiding."

They made it to the door as Gloria stepped through. She had changed clothes; now she was wearing a military-looking khaki coat with tight-fitting pants and high-heeled boots, sort of the female equivalent of the Boot Patrol uniform. Simon had to admit that on her it looked good.

He grabbed her arm as she walked into the hall.

"Gloria?"

She looked at him with a mixture of surprise and disgust. "You're back again? Wait until I tell The Evil—"

Sneed grabbed her from behind, his hand firmly over her mouth. She struggled against the rumpled man's relentless hold, her eyes full of anger.

Simon stared at their beautiful captive. How could he make her talk? There was no way he could hurt Gloria. But the minute they let her go, she'd raise an alarm. And they couldn't just hold her here; there was hardly any time left. Simon felt trapped. There was nothing they could do.

Unless—

He quickly took the magic glasses off and placed them on the struggling Gloria. She stopped struggling and blinked. Simon told Sneed to let her go.

"What?" Gloria blinked again, then smiled tentatively. "Why, Simon, what a pleasant surprise. Where are we? What are we doing here?"

"Oh, no," Simon replied. "Don't you remember anything?" It hadn't occurred to him that, if her attitude returned to its Festeronian beginnings, her memories would return there as well.

"Remember what?" Gloria frowned. "I seem to have been dreaming."

Simon quickly sketched out what had happened since Witchville had taken over. Gloria's frown deepened.

"I—I remember now," she replied hesitantly. "And I thought they had been nightmares. That was me doing all those things? What an awful person!"

Simon told her she shouldn't worry about it. It hadn't been her making those decisions, it had been Witchville.

"No." She shook her head defiantly. "I shall never forget those things. I shall have to learn to live with them."

Simon looked down at the firm set of Gloria's lips, and the defiance in her eyes. Here, at last, was the woman he had wanted so much for so long. There was an ache in his chest that would not go away. He couldn't help himself. He had to ask her.

"Gloria," he began, and this time it was he who was hesitant, "it's—so wonderful to see you back as your old self." He swallowed. "I was wondering. Might I kiss you?"

Gloria appeared a bit shocked by the suggestion. "Should I? I don't know if a proper girl would—" She looked deep within Simon's eyes. "Still, you did rescue me from The Evil One's spell." She smiled ever so slightly. "I suppose a hero deserves just a little kiss."

At last! Simon took her in his arms, and she fell, limp, in his embrace. Her head tilted back, her eyes closed, lips parted. And the magic glasses fell off her face.

Gloria's eyes snapped open. "What are you trying to do to me, you piece of slime! Wait 'til I tell The Evil—"

Sneed quickly retrieved the glasses and put them back on her face.

Gloria's large eyes looked innocently up at Simon. "So, are you going to kiss me, or not?"

Simon leaned forward, lips at the ready. Gloria relaxed. The glasses started to fall.

"What? You creep! How dare—"

Sneed grabbed the glasses while they were still half on her face, trying to replace them as she shook her head.

"Oh, Simon. I'm wait— . . . So, you piece of filth, not going to let me . . . oh, Simon, dearest, I feel so fun— . . . I'll show you, you dweeb— . . . I'm frightened, hold me . . . Evil One! Come here! Your victims . . ."

Simon decided that this was perhaps not the best time to kiss her after all. He stood up straight, making sure that Gloria could stand as well, the magic plastic glasses firmly planted on her nose.

"This will have to wait," he told her solemnly. "We have to find the stone before midnight."

"Of course!" she agreed all too readily. "This is no time to be thinking of ourselves. We must save Festeron! But where would the stone be?" Her pretty brow furrowed deeply, as if she was trying to remember a dream. "I know! Anything of value, she keeps in her laboratory. I'll show you the way."

"Danke shane . . . Darling, danke shane—"

Simon immediately turned the radio down. "What is it this time?"

"Only twelve minutes left to find the stone," Stan replied.

"Thanks. I don't need to be reminded." He turned the radio off. "Let's go."

Gloria led the way through the door she had so recently opened. They went down a short corridor, then up two flights of stairs, to a sign marked "Broom Closet, Keep Out."

Simon put a restraining hand on each of his companions' shoulders. He heard something, a voice calling from up above, at the end of a third flight of steps. He could make out the voice, faint but clear.

"Help me!" the voice cried. "Somebody please help me!"

"Not again," Simon muttered, taking the final set of steps as quickly and quietly as possible.

"How noble!" Sneed murmured behind him.

The stairs led up to the bell tower. And there, tied within an immense amount of rope, was Princess Tasmania.

"Trapped again?" he asked, doing his best to free her hands and feet.

"Alas, yes," she replied. "I could not stay away. The view is so much better here than on the Misty Isle."

"I'm sure it is." He finished untying the final knot around her wrists. "You'll have to do the rest of this yourself. I have an island to rescue."

"Oh, thank you, my hero!" the princess called after him as Simon ran down the steps. "It really is too bad you're not an enchanted platypus."

"I'm back," Simon said softly as he spotted the others.

"Through here," Gloria said, opening the door to lead the way. Simon and Sneed walked as silently as they could behind her.

So this, Simon thought, was The Evil One's laboratory. He didn't know what he had expected, but it wasn't quite this. One side of the room was dominated by gleaming scientific equipment; test tubes, petri dishes, bunsen burners, and something that looked an awful lot like a mainframe computer. On the far side of the room were three bubbling cauldrons, surrounded by piles of what looked like dried herbs, as well as some dried other things, which Simon hoped he was only identifying because of an overactive imagination. Between these two areas was a small corner painted a cheerful yellow, containing a stove, refrigerator, and a small table. It reminded Simon of nothing so much as a breakfast nook. His grandparents had always had breakfast nooks. Apparently, The Evil One did too.

The stone was here, somewhere in this room, but they had less than twelve minutes to find it. And, as he recalled, it was invisible as well, unless you were wearing the magic glasses. Which Gloria had on this very minute. So could she see the stone?

"Gloria," he asked her softly. "Look around the room. Do you see anything glowing?"

"Danke shane—" the radio began. Simon turned it off. He didn't want to know how little time they had left.

Gloria frowned as she glanced about. "Why, yes I do." She pointed toward the kitchen, but stopped when she heard the door open behind her.

"Answer the boy," an old woman's voice commanded. "I'm just as interested as he is."

It was The Evil One, now dressed in flowing robes of the deepest black.

She waved her sleeves at the three others in the room. "Since I'm about to begin my world conquest, I thought I should dress in the proper fashion. You know by now, of course, that this time I will let nothing stand in my way." She paused to smile at Simon. "Besides, black is such an appropriate color for your soon-to-be-forthcoming deaths."

CHAPTER
THIRTY

"NOW, MY DEAR," The Evil One chortled. "Where is the stone?"

"I'll never tell you!" Gloria declared, crossing her hands over her heart.

"Oh, give me those glasses, you silly girl." The Evil One ripped the magic plastic frames from Gloria's nose.

"What?" Gloria sneered. "Oh, Witchville, what that slime wanted me to do! The stone is over there, in one of those open canisters!"

"Really?" The Evil One peered through the plastic glasses for an instant. "Ah. I see the glow coming out of the middle one. Most helpful." She threw the glasses to the floor, grinding them into the linoleum with her foot. "We won't need these, anymore."

Simon looked at Sneed. He felt the way the rumpled man looked.

"What are we going to do?" Simon whispered.

"We have one last chance!" Sneed murmured back. "I still have the Kitchen Wonder directions. Give me a minute while I look up 'subduing witches'."

"Oh, no, you don't!" The Evil One crossed the room with alarming swiftness, plucking the Wonder from Simon's hand. "There will be no Acme gadgets used in my laboratory. This is what I do with Kitchen Wonders." She strode over to her nearest cauldron and dumped the metal and plastic contraption inside. It sizzled when it hit the fluid.

"DANKE SHANE, DARLING—FLASH! YOU GUYS ARE IN REALLY SERIOUS—"

"And this, too," The Evil One ripped the radio from Simon's pocket and smashed it to the floor. "Nothing can stop me now!"

There was an explosion behind her.

"We think not," two elderly voices said as one. Simon's mouth opened involuntarily. It was the magic shop owner and the woman who had given him the Kitchen Wonder!

"Gail! Hortense! What are you doing here?" The Evil One demanded. "That's not in the rules!"

"Rules?" Gail the magic shop owner replied. "It seems to us that somebody else has broken all too many rules already!"

"What do you mean?" The Evil One laughed nervously. "Surely you can't—"

"Violation number one!" declared Hortense, the former owner of the Kitchen Wonder. "The Boot Patrol is not allowed to enter the Witchville Cemetery!"

"Is that breaking the rules?" The Evil One replied meekly. "I thought I was only slightly bending them."

"Hah!" Gail replied. "Then how do you explain violation number two? The Boot Patrol is never supposed to use the underground passageways."

The Evil One shrugged. "So they got a little overenthusiastic. Boys will be boys, you know."

"I suppose," Hortense continued, "if it was all you had done, we might have forgiven violation number three—destruction of the plastic glasses. I always thought those things were a little silly myself. But then you compounded it with numbers four and five—smashing the magic radio, then melting the Kitchen Wonder! It was then that we could take it no longer. This time, you have gone too far. We have come to stop you, now!"

"So you say," The Evil One snapped, "but I don't agree. This time, I have decided that I must go as far as I have to go to win. And nothing can stop me—not my bungling assistants, not these meddling postmen, not even you, dear sisters."

"We'll see about that, Gladys!" Gail waved her hands in the air. A light appeared above her head, then coalesced into a magnificent golden eagle.

"Ooh!" Simon, Sneed, and Gloria said as one.

"I'm in this fight, too!" Hortense flapped her hands about as well, and a pale blue light grew above her, changing into a perfectly formed miniature horse with dark blue wings.

"Ah!" the spectators remarked.

"We'll see about that!" The Evil One did some gesturing of her own. Her light was a sickly green, and resolved itself into a creature that was somehow half-scorpion, half-spider.

"Ick!" the audience replied.

The creatures of light approached each other, the eagle and horse flying, the spider thing walking across the air. They met in an explosion of light. Simon had to shield his eyes. When he looked up a second later, all three were gone.

Gail smiled. "You see, Gladys? We are too strong for you. Any magic you might try, we can defeat."

The Evil One stared at her sisters. She looked as if she was about to cry. "You always did like to gang up on me!"

"Now, Gladys—" Hortense began with a frown.

"It's not fair!" The Evil One replied petulantly. "I'm going to hold my breath until I turn blue!"

Gail looked uncertainly at her good sister. "Well, Hortense. Maybe we are being a little hard on her." She turned back to The Evil One. "All right, Gladys, what would you like us to do?"

"Oh," she began uncertainly. "I don't know, sisters. Perhaps you could—" Gladys snapped her fingers, "—stand right there while I take you prisoner!" Huge snakes appeared out of nowhere, wrapping themselves around the other two sisters so that their arms were pinned to their bodies.

The Evil One laughed. "My sisters always were such saps!" She looked over at Simon and Sneed. "Now, who shall I kill first?"

But her concentration was disturbed by one of the strangest sounds Simon had ever heard, a great and virtually indescribable commotion on the other side of the door, like a hundred feet waddling all at once.

The door slammed open with surprising force.

"Oh no, you don't!" a high, squeaky voice announced. "It's the Platypus Guard!"

The Honorable Roger waved a webbed paw in Simon's direction.

"One good rescue deserves another!"

"Quick!" Simon shouted back. "Save the old ladies!"

"The ones with the snakes?" The Honorable Roger either made a face or he didn't. Simon found it hard to tell with platypuses. "Ick!"

Still, he waved his fellows forward with a short, curved sword.

"Platypus Guard to the rescue! And remember," Roger paused dramatically, "our furry legs have poisoned spurs!"

The Platypus Guard waddled forward, fifty strong. It was a slow but awesome sight. The Evil One began two or three half-hearted conjurations, but was obviously too astonished to complete any of them. The Guard lifted Hortense and Gail upon their amassed furry forms, and ushered them from the room.

"Flash!" the smashed radio parts buzzed from the floor "Only—two minutes—" The radio sputtered and died.

"I'll win yet!" Gladys cried, running toward the canisters.

But Simon had gotten there ahead of her, sneaking stealthily toward the kitchenette during the mass platypus action. He rushed the final few feet, flipping all three canisters so that their tops were against the table surface.

He looked up at The Evil One.

"If you want the stone, you're going to have to find it first." Then, without lifting them from the table's surface, he switched the positions of two of the canisters.

The Evil One laughed derisively. "You think to fool me with your stupid parlor game. You should have left it behind on the Festeron Fun Pier! I have worked all my life to be ten times stronger and ten times smarter than anybody else. You can see it in the way I beat my sisters. And it goes double for a stupid postman!"

"Really?" Simon replied as he switched the canisters again, then once again. "Are you sure you know where the stone is?"

The Evil One appeared on the other side of the table. "Of course I know!" she hissed.

He rapped on the canisters. "Well, I think you have exactly enough time to pick one of these before midnight."

"There!" The Evil One pointed to the canister on the left.

Simon lifted the cylinder from the table.

"Really? I don't see anything." He shook his head. "No, I don't think the stone could be there." He paused and grinned. "Unless, of course, it's invisible."

"Give it to me!" The Evil One swept her hand across the table top where the left-hand canister had been.

The bell in the church tower began to strike.

One. Two. Three.

"It's not there!" the old lady screamed. "You think you can keep it from me?"

The bell rang. Four. Five. Six.

"Well, no one can stop The Evil One!" She clapped her hands, and a ball of green fire leapt forth, pushing Simon against the wall.

Seven. Eight.

"I have it now!" She reached for the center canister.

Nine. Ten.

"It's not there? No!" She shot Simon a hate-filled glare. "You've fooled me!"

Eleven.

"But your days of treachery are over!" She lifted the final canister. "Witchville forev—where is it?"

Twelve.

And everything changed.

The laboratory disappeared. Advanced scientific equipment, bubbling cauldrons, and efficiency kitchenette all faded from view, replaced by a storeroom full of discolored choir robes and battered hymnals. The Evil One's black robes disappeared as well, replaced by a flower print granny dress.

Her two sisters, *sans* snakes, walked back into the room. Gladys pounded her fists on the bare floor.

"There, there, sister," Gail murmured reassuringly. "You knew, in your heart of hearts, that it would end this way."

"I hate this dress!" Gladys remarked bitterly.

"And we've asked Sergeant MacGuffin to come over," Hortense added. "He'll put you someplace nice and quiet, where you can rest. He will be a few minutes, though. Something to do with all his men disappearing."

Gladys pounded the floor again. "I despise this squeaky-clean community."

"Yes, dear," Gail replied. "And I think we've given you more than enough opportunity to vent your frustration. That's why we're going to put you away for a nice, long rest."

"And I especially hate my goody-goody sisters!" Gladys wailed as she redoubled her floor pounding.

The good sisters looked apologetically at Simon.

"She gets like this—" Hortense began.

"Nothing we can do—" Gail added.

"Best if she rests—" Hortense agreed.

"Yes," Gail amplified, "it must be frustrating for the poor dear."

The sisters' commiseration was interrupted by the

sound of myriad waddling feet. Princess Tasmania stood in the doorway, flanked by the Honorable Roger and the Platypus Guard.

"The time has come to leave you, Simon the hero," the princess intoned. "But I do not leave with a heavy heart, for I have spoken with the two witch sisters." She graciously waved a webbed paw at Hortense and Gail, then glanced at Simon for an instant before self-consciously turning her gaze to the floor.

"I've asked—" She hesitated, then summoned her courage to begin the sentence anew. "I've asked them if they might be able to turn you into an enchanted platypus."

Gail nodded. "We told her we'd work on it."

"So you see?" Tasmania bubbled. "The future is rife with possibilities! I don't know when I have been so excited!"

Simon, not knowing quite what to say, did his best to nod and smile.

"But, come, my bold soldiers," the princess proclaimed. " 'Tis time for us to return to the Misty Isle."

The entire Platypus Guard pulled out silver whistles and blew.

When the dust settled a moment later, only the humans remained.

"Oh, Simon!" Gloria cried. "I am so glad I am back to my senses!" She ran to him, her arms flung wide, but stopped herself two paces short of contact. "But no. That would not be proper. Come! I will shake your hand firmly to show you my gratitude."

Simon shook her cool and lovely hand. He could no longer doubt it. Festeron had returned to stay.

"So," Gail remarked. "We have only to repossess the Wishbringer stone, and everyone can relax." She turned over the three canisters. "Which one did you hide it in?"

"This one," Simon replied, and held up the stone he had so thoughtfully palmed.

EPILOGUE

Including another
false ending or two

CHAPTER
THIRTY-ONE

HINGS WERE BACK TO
normal in Festeron.

It was a beautiful morning, sun shining, birds singing,
a gentle breeze cooling the day. Simon had never seen
anyplace so peaceful, so cheerful. He just wished he could
experience it in something besides a mailman's uniform.

He shifted the strap farther up his shoulder. This was
the second load he'd taken out of the post office today,
and it seemed twice as heavy as the first.

At least Sneed was giving him a hand. Now that Festeron was back, the rumpled man seemed to have solidified for good, or at least for the time being. Between the
two of them, Simon thought, they might actually be able
to conquer the backlog of mail piled up at the post office,
in three weeks to a month. That was, as long as nothing
else happened to Festeron.

It was strange. Once the Witchville night was over,
everyone praised him as a hero. He had given the Wishbringer stone back to the two good sisters; it had become
visible with the return of Festeron, and actually looked
quite ordinary, little more than a smooth-sided overgrown
pebble. Besides that, Sneed had told him how lucky he
had been not to have to use it. Apparently, to make your

wishes work properly, you had to use all sorts of extra props and devices. Whatever the truth about the stone, Simon was glad to be rid of it.

Hortense and Gail had been overjoyed to have the stone in their possession once again. They promised to shower Simon with gifts, and give him anything he wanted within reason.

Unfortunately, quitting the post office was not within reason. It had been so long since they had been able to find a decent postal carrier, they just couldn't let him go. Besides, he had been made a postman by court order, and only the High Court of Festeron could change that. Which everyone assured him the court would address, just as soon as they got back from vacation.

"Vacation?" Simon had blurted, perhaps a bit thoughtlessly.

"Oh, yes," everyone assured him. The court always went on vacation whenever Witchville took over. After all, what good was a court where there was no justice?

It wasn't so bad, Sneed assured him after the others had left and Sneed had managed to calm Simon down. Being a postman wasn't such a bad job. Lots of fresh air. Good exercise. Meet interesting people. If Simon could just relax, he might actually enjoy it. And who knew? After a few months—half a year at most—well, perhaps a year at the outside, the High Court would see what a good job he had done and let him leave—or at least take a vacation. Oh, Sneed added, he might have to defeat The Evil One once or twice more during that time, but there were problems that came with every job, weren't there?

So Simon started delivering mail, resigned to his fate. The first package in this load went to Miss Voss, who was looking particularly tired and haggard this morning. At least, she spoke abruptly with him. Mr. Crisp, back up at the post office, hadn't managed a word. Simon imagined that night in Witchville had been particularly hard on them.

There was a sign on the door of the Festeron jail advertising for qualified police help. Having looked at Crisp and Voss, Simon could imagine what kind of a mood Sergeant MacGuffin was in. Simon left the jail's mail on the front step.

Good exercise, he told himself. Fresh air. Meet interesting people. He might get used to this job eventually.

"Oh, Simon!"

The postman paused. He recognized that voice. It was Gloria. She ran over to him, her long hair blowing in the wind.

"I'm so glad I caught you," she began with a smile. "I've been thinking about what you said last night."

Last night? Simon couldn't exactly remember what he had said last night, at least not after he had learned he might have to spend the rest of his life as a postman.

"It's true," Gloria continued helpfully. "I've been thinking about what you said about the differences in my behavior when Festeron turns to Witchville. Perhaps you are right, and were I not so prim and proper here and now, I wouldn't become so horrendous when The Evil One takes over. You told me I should try new things. And I think you're right."

"I am?" Simon replied. He vaguely remembered saying things like that. He had been a touch distraught, and could have said anything.

"Yes you are, Simon the Postman," Gloria replied. "It's time you asked me out."

Simon's mouth felt suddenly dry. Gloria Magnifico was going to go out with him? Well, she was if he asked her.

So he did.

She pondered it for a second. "Well, I guess we could. Of course, we'll have to have a chaperone. And I must be home by ten!" She impulsively grabbed Simon's hand. "Oh, this is so exciting. I've never done anything this daring! Tonight, then!"

She squeezed the postman's hand a final time, then danced away.

Meet interesting people. Fresh air. Good exercise. Maybe, Simon thought, this job wasn't so bad after all.

"Oh, Simon!" Somebody else was calling him now. A man's voice. Simon turned around to face the speaker.

It was Mr. Crisp. And he was smiling.

"You are doing an excellent job as a mailman," Crisp said as he approached. "Everybody tells me so. But now it's time to take that sack off for a little while."

"It is?" Simon replied.

"Most certainly. I have a special job for you. I've got it here somewhere."

He reached inside his uniform and pulled out a crumpled envelope.

Mr. Crisp's smile broadened.

"It's special delivery."

Simon looked at the envelope. It was addressed to the Magick Shoppe.

CRAIG SHAW GARDNER has written numerous short stories and novels. To his continuing amazement, a number of them have been published. His stories have appeared mostly in original anthologies like *Shadows, Dragons of Light,* and *The Year's Best Fantasy.* He is also the author of the ongoing Ebenezum series, the most recent volume of which is *An Excess of Enchantments.* Mr. Gardner lives in Cambridge, Massachusetts, with his wife, too many books and records, and Diva, the cat that rules the household.